THE FALSE PROPHET

RELICS OF GOD
BOOK 2

Matt James

Copyright © 2024 Matt James

No part of this publication may be reproduced, stored in a retrieval system, or transmitted, in any form or by any means without the prior written permission of the publisher, nor be otherwise circulated in any form of binding or cover other than that in which it is published and without similar condition being imposed on the subsequent purchaser.

The right of Matt James to be identified as the Author of the Work has been asserted by him in accordance with the Copyright, Designs and Patents Act, 1988.

All characters in this publication are fictitious and any resemblance to real persons, living or dead, is purely coincidental.

Cover design © Matt James used under

Creative Commons licenses

Also by Matt James

THE JACK REILLY ARCHAEOLOGIAL THRILLERS
The Forgotten Fortune
The Roosevelt Conspiracy
The Dorado Deception
The Undying Kingdom
The Venetian Pursuit
The Lost Legion

THE CHARLEE FLYNN ADVENTURES
The Cursed Thief
The Golden Tiger
The Jaguar Blade (2025)

RELICS OF GOD
The Blood King
The False Prophet

THE ZAHRA KANE THRILLERS with Nick Thacker
Empire Lost: A Prequel
The Anubis Plague
The Sixth Seal

THE UNSEEN
Origin
Desolation
Perseverance
Inferno
Nightmare: A Short Story
Petrified: A Short Story

STAND-ALONE NOVELS
Dark Island
Cradle of Death
Sub-Zero
The Dragon
Midnight Mass

THE DANE MADDOCK ADVENTURES with David Wood
Berserk
Skin and Bones
Venom
Lost City

THE HANK BOYD ADVENTURES
Blood and Sand
Mayan Darkness
Babel Found
Elixir of Life

OTHER STORIES
The Cursed Pharaoh
Broken Glass
Plague
Evolve

Praise for Matt James

"The words of a Matt James story flow like the best rivers. Smooth and subtle at times, interrupted by danger and thrills at every churn of whitewater. This guy is the real deal!"
—Ernest Dempsey, *USA Today* bestselling author of POSEIDON'S FURY

"Matt James is my go-to guy for heart-stopping adventure and bone-chilling suspense!"
—Greig Beck, international bestselling author of TO THE CENTER OF THE EARTH

"If you enjoy globetrotting adventures jampacked with over-the-top action, then you'll love Matt James' work!"
—Nick Thacker, *USA Today* bestselling author of THE ENIGMA STRAIN

"Matt James is a must-read! The thrilling action, unexpected turns, and rip-roaring chases across the globe are fantastic adventures every time! You won't be disappointed."
—Andrew Clawson, bestselling author of THE ARTHURIAN RELIC

"Matt James is the gold standard for archaeological thrillers!"
—Luke Richardson, international bestselling author of THE TITANIC DECEPTION

"If you're looking for a fast-moving tale with action to spare, give Matt James a try!"
—David Wood, *USA Today* bestselling author of SERPENT

"Searching for relentless action and harrowing adventure in dangerous locales? Look no further than Matt James!"
—Michael McBride, international bestselling author of CHIMERA

"Matt James writes thrillers that define the genre! Neck-breaking speed and hairpin plot twists. Top notch!"
—Craig A. Hart, bestselling author of SERENITY

"Matt James reminds devotees of Indiana Jones and Nathan Drake why their love for rock-solid action-adventure springs eternal!"
—Rick Chesler, international bestselling author of ATLANTIS GOLD

"Matt's novels need a pause button. They do not stop!"
—Lee Murray, *Bram Stoker Award* winning author of INTO THE MIST

"If you like thrills, chills, and nonstop action, then Matt James may just be your next favorite author!"
—John Sneeden, bestselling author of THE SIGNAL

"Matt James is the Michael Bay of thriller authors. He loves action, suspense, and making things go boom!"
—Richard F. Paddon, author of CASH IS KING

For everyone who has supported Jacob and Naomi's story.

Thank you.

THE
FALSE
PROPHET

RELICS OF GOD
BOOK 2

"Influence can be a powerful weapon."

Prologue

Saint Petersburg, Russia

It had been five weeks since Gideon had killed his former superior, Alpha. He'd taken another week to gather himself and take stock of his situation. He knew that Beta would send hit squads after him. Gideon had openly threatened the lives of the remaining Acolyte leadership, the Hexad, and had done so only seconds after killing Delta, the Prime Minister of England, Peter Hughes. But Gideon also knew that painting a target on his back would lead him to what he wanted: the identities of those he sought.

Since fleeing London in the dead of night, Gideon had resumed his hunt. It had led him here, to Saint Petersburg, the second-largest city in all of Russia with Moscow, the nation's capital, being the largest. He had tracked his target to an apartment penthouse overlooking the murky waters of the Moyka River. Gideon was honestly a little perplexed why someone of such high regard, in both the military and his own secret societal group, would choose to live here instead of

Moscow.

To stay out of the spotlight, Gideon decided. *Zeta prefers the shadows*. He smiled. *Like me.*

Zeta was just one of six regional heads of the Acolyte, an organization that, until recently, Gideon had happily served. Including Zeta, four were left breathing. He was here to make sure that the number became three. The Acolyte's uppermost boss, the recently deceased, Alpha, had betrayed Gideon. Therefore, all of the Hexad had also betrayed him.

Now, they must pay with their lives.

Seven years ago, Mossad operative Michael Mizrahi's wife had been murdered after her identity had been leaked by someone inside the Israeli counterintelligence agency. Back then, Mizrahi, callsign: Gideon, had been the best agent they had ever had. It was only after he learned that it had been Alpha, Director Elijah Hirsch, who had been the source of the intel leak, that Gideon had turned against his former masters. Not only had Hirsch lied about who had been responsible for Maya's murder, but then he had willingly brought an unsuspecting Michael into the fold of the Acolyte ranks.

Hirsch had used Michael twice—lied to him *twice*.

But now, there was no Michael. There was only Gideon, the Judge of Man.

And Zeta is next, he thought.

Gideon had been surprised how easy it was to identify the supposedly unidentifiable. The Hexad, the people manning the positions, were supposed to be impossible to name. For Gideon, all it took was a few calls, as well as a handful of threats. He had started with a low-ranking Russian agent, then worked his way up higher. These local operatives didn't need to be involved with the Middle Eastern branch of the Acolyte to know who Gideon was. Everyone feared him, especially his own comrades. They knew the stories surrounding his effectiveness. His methods too.

So, here stood Gideon, riding in an elevator up six stories to Zeta's penthouse apartment. The man was said to live lavishly. He preferred the company of young women, enjoyed top-shelf booze, and adored illicit narcotics. It sickened Gideon to find out that a slob-of-a-man, a drunken, strung-out slab of sweaty meat, had been one of the Acolyte leaders.

It made Gideon think. What other disreputables sat atop the organization?

No matter, he thought. *They'll all be dead soon.*

Gideon had come to an agreement with Jacob Fehr, now also formerly of the Mossad. If Jacob let Gideon live, he would personally hunt down the Hexad bosses. He'd been a little shocked when Jacob had agreed to it too, not that Gideon had planned on deceiving the man. Gideon had every intention to keep up his end of the deal. He may have been a ruthless killer, but Gideon still held honor in high esteem. If he did, indeed, go back on his and Jacob's agreement, could Gideon live with that? None of that mattered. He had wholeheartedly meant what he had said, hence him being in Russia now.

Gideon was not nervous. Taking lives had become a redundancy to him, similar to the way a chef might make a pizza or the way a father of three might grill a hotdog. But he couldn't escape the enormity of where he was and what he was about to do. Gideon's mission wasn't just to kill these handful of men, it was to burn down the Acolyte entirely from the inside. Without leadership, they would descend into chaos. Would they collapse overnight? Probably not. But Gideon did know that each of the six regions would battle for power and attempt to overthrow the other. And their civil war would result in headlines that the masses would devour. Once the world found out about the Acolyte's long history of death and manipulation, only then would they truly be dead and buried.

The Army of God had their own mission in all this, one Gideon had no real interest in. The Relics of God were something he had studied but were nothing he truly desired. His heart had also been in field work. He was an assassin, not a scholar.

The elevator slowed, then stopped. A soft chime announced that Gideon had arrived at his destination. He took a deep breath and refocused himself. He no longer thought about the bigger picture. All Gideon cared about, in this moment, was the next kill.

He drew his suppressed Glock 17. He could've brought a pistol possessing more punch, like a Heckler & Koch USP45, but found it mostly pointless. Larger, harder-hitting rounds weren't necessary in most gun-wielding professions. Gideon's *occupation* was one of them. Nobody wore ballistic helmets and rifle-rated plate carriers. Everyone he was about to kill, would easily fall to his nine-millimeter handgun.

Or his knife.

The doors slid open. As they did, Gideon presented his weapon and shot the first man he saw in the forehead. His intel told him that the only men that would be with Zeta would be his bodyguards and that the women wouldn't be any trouble. They were only there to provide pleasurable company to the man.

The guard's head snapped back, and he fell to the marble floor. Gideon didn't exit the elevator yet. He simply turned into cover and allowed the opening to be pummeled by return fire first. Debris peppered his back, but it was of no concern. Once the initial barrage stopped, he spun, lifted his Glock and gunned down the next two men. The first stepped into view on his left, and the other on the right. Each took a single shot to the skull.

Three bullets.

Three corpses.

Gideon doubted he'd have to reload before leaving. He still had fifteen rounds left. Gideon highly doubted there'd be that many people left to kill, not unless the young women got involved. He waited for more return fire, but it didn't come. Slowly, Gideon stepped up to the elevator's exit. He leaned out and gave the circular, private lobby a quick once-over. The only thing of interest to Gideon was the door directly across the space. It was undoubtably locked and trying to break it down would make too much noise.

I need a key, he thought.

Gideon kept his gun drawn and continually glanced up at the door while he searched the trio of bodies. The first one held nothing of interest except a pack of cigarettes and a lighter. Gideon removed a cigarette from the pack and placed it between his lips. Then he flicked the lighter's ignition wheel and held the small flame to the end of the cigarette. Gideon inhaled and slid over to the next body. He wasn't much of a smoker, but he did find a pleasantness to the nicotine as it entered his system, stymying the adrenaline spike that came with ending someone's life.

The second body turned up nothing as well. The third body, however, gave Gideon what he was looking for: the key to Zeta's apartment. It made sense for one of the guards to have a key on them. If something ever happened inside the general's apartment that needed intervening, they needed a way inside.

Gideon stood, then made his way across the lobby area. He nonchalantly flicked the cigarette away and unlocked the door.

Gideon quietly opened it, but didn't step inside. He waited to be noticed first. After twenty seconds of nothing, he edged in to find the entry hallway empty. Gun up, he moved like a wraith. He crept forward to find two girls passed out on top of each other in the middle of a large, horseshoe-shaped sofa. To Gideon, they both looked dead, possibly of overdose.

Or they could've simply been unconscious...

There were broken bottles on the floor in random places, as well as stains that could've been anything from dried booze to urine. Based on the odor, it smelled like both. There was also the distinct scent of BO too. This was truly a disgusting place.

Through a door to Gideon's left, a toilet flushed. He hurried over, spun to face the door, and leveled his suppressed pistol at it. When it opened, he shot the man in the head. Everyone inside of the apartment was killable, though Gideon didn't have eyes for the girls. He knew that most of them had been forced into this lifestyle.

To be safe, Gideon kicked the dead man's feet back inside the bathroom then shut the door.

"Who are you?" a feminine Russian voice asked.

Gideon casually slipped his gun back into the holster beneath his left armpit, hiding it from view under his jacket. He turned to find a mostly naked blonde standing before him. She would've been a looker, except for the needle scarring on the inside of both of her elbows. Her sunken, gaunt face and body were also a turnoff. She spoke to him in her native language, a language Gideon knew fluently. He'd spent some time in the country after "dying" on his last mission with the Mossad.

She caught him looking her up and down. "See something you like?"

"No," he replied, watching her examine his scarred face, "do you?"

The young woman shrugged. "That all depends on how much you are willing to pay."

"General Agafonov is expecting me," he said flatly, diverting anymore conversation regarding whatever service she was offering. "Take me to him."

The addict rolled her sleep-deprived eyes, yawned, and turned around. "Fine. Follow me." She led him deeper into the large living space, past the sofa containing the pair of unconscious girls. "By the way, have you seen Dmitri?"

"Dmitri?"

"We were just about to have a good time. Said he was going to the bathroom first." She glanced back at Gideon. "You haven't seen him?"

Dmitri must've been the man he'd just shot.

"No, I haven't," Gideon replied.

She shrugged. "His loss. Believe me. The man does not pack...if you know what I mean?" Gideon wasn't amused. She sighed and waved for him to follow her. "Come, the general is this way."

There was a second hallway in the back of the living area. She led him down it and past four doors. What was behind them was left to one's imagination. But there was "activity" behind two of them based on the sounds emanating from within. Gideon sneered. *This* was what Zeta was doing with his time instead of operating his arm of the Acolyte.

He's a disgrace, Gideon thought. Even if he wasn't here to kill the man, he'd do it now, just based on what he'd seen thus far.

The hallway dead-ended at a set of doors. Gideon's guide grabbed the one doorknob and opened it. She led him into another living space. This one was smaller, though even more extravagant than the first. Gideon had seen similar layouts in other upscale residences, where the master bedroom was really its own luxurious suite—its own separate home. Beyond the door was, yet another, vulgar display of living.

The coffee table was littered with liquor bottles, empty takeout boxes, and lines of cocaine. More girls were present as well. One was collapsed atop an oversized love seat. The other was sitting up against it with her chin resting against her chest. Gideon didn't have to get close to see that both had enjoyed the drugs. Their faces were covered in remnants of the white powder.

He stopped and stared at the pair. They couldn't have been more than a year or two out of their teens. "Where is he?" Gideon growled.

"Through there," the blonde said, pointing at a grandiose set of French doors.

Gideon stepped away. "Leave me."

"Excuse me, but you—"

He stopped, looked over his shoulder, and glared at her. He didn't say another word.

She shut her mouth and melted under his stare. She backed away from him until she was at the hallway door. When she stepped over the threshold, she closed it.

Gideon drew his pistol, faced the general's bedroom doors, and took a deep breath. Once again, he wasn't nervous about the upcoming kill. He needed to get himself under control because of what he'd seen so far. It enraged him. Now, more than ever, did he want to end Zeta's life, but he needed to be of clear mind when he did it. Despite his reputation, Gideon was always level-headed when he was on the job. It was only after he found out about Alpha's involvement with Maya's death that Gideon had felt himself begin to come unhinged. Even after killing the man with his bare hands, Gideon could still feel himself occasionally slip away into a rage-induced madness.

He opened the French doors to find a slightly comical scene. There was only a single person inside, and he was lying naked, spread eagle atop a plush bed. His wrists and ankles were tied to the bedposts, and his eyes were covered with a sleep mask.

"Hello?" the older man asked. "Vera, Alisa, is that you? I am ready for you, my dears."

Gideon thought back to the two women passed out in the room behind him. Apparently, they were supposed to be in here, pleasuring the general and not filling their system with more drugs and alcohol.

From what Gideon knew about this man, besides his personal interests, was that Fedor Agafonov was a balding, thickly built man in his early sixties. He'd been a successful boxer in his youth, and had won several competitions within the Russian armed forces. But all Gideon saw was a sweaty, glutinous, hippo with too much time on his hands.

Gideon stepped around the foot of the king-sized bed, making a point of not hiding his approach. He doubted any of the girls, specifically Vera and Alisa, moved with the stalking gait or the weight that Gideon did. The excited jovialness of Zeta's exposed face, and his body language, changed as Gideon drew nearer.

"Who's there?" he asked, yanking at his bonds. "I demand to know!"

Gideon didn't say a word. He wanted to see the look on Zeta's face when he removed the sleep mask from his face. Gideon wanted to see the startled look in the man's eyes quickly transform into fear. Everyone in the Acolyte knew Gideon, the bosses even more so.

Gideon lifted his pistol, keeping the end of the suppressor two inches from Zeta's nose. He used his free hand to rip the sleep mask off. Then, he enjoyed the show.

The Russian was about to berate whoever was ruining his fun, but didn't get the chance. The gun in his face kept him quiet. His eyes crossed while looking at it, then they shifted away from the weapon and up to its owner.

"Hello, Zeta."

"You!"

Gideon smiled. "Yes, me. I am Gideon, the Judge of Man." His eyes narrowed. "But I am also man's executioner. You and the other filth sitting atop the Acolyte have been found guilty." He compressed the trigger of his Glock, fully intent on shooting the man here and now.

"No! Wait! That... That was Alpha, not us!" Zeta barked, leaning away from the pistol. "He was an arrogant fool. But I can give you anything you want. I can also protect you from the other heads."

Gideon lowered the weapon and made his way around to the foot of the bed. "See, general, that was your first mistake," he stopped and aimed his pistol at the man's head, "thinking that I need protection from anyone."

But there was something Gideon did want from him.

"I require information."

"Name it," the general quickly replied.

"Epsilon. Who is he, and where is he?"

Zeta glanced away, understandably nervous. "I don't know where he is, but his name is Yao Xiaowen. Last I heard, he was hanging around the Huangpu area."

"Shanghai?" Gideon asked.

"Yes."

Gideon cocked his head to the side a little and grinned. "Thank you."

He lowered his aim, but still pulled the trigger, sending a round sizzling between the Russian's bare legs. Then he pulled the trigger nine more times, watching as the suppressor began to heat up. It wasn't an immense heat, but it would be enough. Then, without a word, Gideon leaned forward and pressed the searing suppressor against the Russian's exposed privates.

The general reacted as Gideon figured he would. He wailed.

After five seconds, Gideon removed the device of Zeta's torture, taking pleasure in the man's whimpering.

"Stop… Please, stop," he begged, blubbering like a baby. "I'll give you anything. Just please, stop…"

Gideon stared at Zeta, leveled the pistol at his face, and pulled the trigger, ending the wretched man's life in an instant.

"You can't give me what I want," Gideon said, lowering his gun. "No one can."

He spun to find the blonde from earlier standing within the open bedroom doors. But her eyes weren't on Gideon. They were on the deceased general. Gideon stepped up next to the stunned woman and stopped. Typically, he removed all witnesses from the field before leaving, but not now. He didn't care who knew about what he had done. If anything, he wanted others to find out. He wanted word to get back to the Acolyte that he had succeeded here.

To Gideon, the look on the woman's face was a bit off. She wasn't sad or even terrified, for that matter. To him, she looked relieved. It confirmed his earlier supposition. Most of these girls, if not all of them, weren't here willingly.

He sighed. "Leave." The blonde turned her head and looked up at him. "Save as many of your friends as you can and leave."

She opened her mouth to say something. "I've already killed all the guards on this level. There is nothing from stopping you other than yourself."

She closed her mouth, then nodded. "Thank you." He stomped away. "Wait!"

Gideon stopped and faced her. "What?"

"I don't even know your name."

He turned again and moved across the private living space. "It's better that *you* don't. It's also best that you aren't here when his people show up." Again, he stopped and looked back at her. "You could be seen as a liability." That made her stand straight. She understood him, loud and clear.

Gideon exited the general's quarters and continued into the common area. The girls on the first sofa were just coming to, it seemed. Gideon didn't pay them any attention as he made his way to the exit. When he opened the front door, the elevator dinged, and it opened. Four men stepped out, in shock over the state of the lobby area.

"Hello," Gideon said, shutting the front door behind him. "My name is Gideon, the Judge of Man." He lifted his non-gun hand and pointed at the group. "And you have been found guilty."

The foursome each reached beneath their sports coats, but Gideon was still gripping his Glock hard in his right hand. It didn't matter that he only had four more rounds in his pistol's magazine.

Four bullets for four enemies.

He brought up his weapon. *That's all I need.*

1

Silicon Valley, California, USA
1 Week Later

Liam Bailey's own news network was vividly covering the assassination. He picked up his glass of Eagle Rare 17 Year bourbon and sipped it, absorbing what was being said. With Zeta dead, there was no reason to hide the way the man had lived. As far as Liam was concerned, the matter—the man—was dead and over. General Fedor Agafonov had lived wildly and had abused young women, yes. But Zeta would never be linked to anything other than his own misdeeds and the Russian military.

As the Beta of the Acolyte, Liam was now in charge of the secret cabal. Alpha's daughter wanted his rightful place as leader of the Hexad. The Hirsch family line had led the group dating back to when the Acolyte had been born, nearly 2,000 years ago.

But Liam had no such wish to give up control. He didn't need to, either. With, yet another, member of the Hexad dead, he had seized emergency control, and would only relinquish power once Gideon was captured or killed. Even after that, Liam had no plans to step aside. He'd kill the Alpha-in-waiting, as well as his family, before he'd let it happen.

Eight of the general's guards had been gunned down as well. Each had only taken a single round too. Liam knew of Gideon's expertise. It was clear to Liam that Gideon was putting on a show for him, one that was supposed to ignite an inferno of fear within him and the other Hexad leaders.

It was working too.

Liam didn't fear for his life, but the others did. He'd just gotten off a call with them before turning on the eighty-eight-inch, 8K, smart TV mounted on the wall across from him. Despite his wealth and status, Liam's office at Prophecy Global Inc. was modest in size and design. The only expensive items he had in it were functional; TV, chairs, couch, desk, ceiling fan, area rug. Each piece, on their own, cost more than what ninety-nine percent of the country's population could afford, but they were constantly in use. People watched the TV, sat on the chairs and couch, and scuffed the luxurious rug with their dirty shoe bottoms. Based on what was present here, no one would ever know about Liam's deep, passionate knowledge of the occult and everything surrounding it. There were few in the United States that knew more about Biblical artifacts and their *real* history more than him.

The best thing about running a clandestine operation, like the Acolyte, was the anonymity it provided him. The murder of a prominent Russian general resulted in no phone calls to him, other than the remaining Hexad members. They took their identities very seriously. They, and only they, knew who each other were. But there was always a loose thread in this sort of business. People like Gideon could start asking questions and investigating. If someone started sniffing around for too long, he or she would inevitably stumble upon another agent with a loose tongue. Liam figured that's what had happened with Zeta. His identity had been given up by one of his own men.

Liam had no idea why Alpha had gone to Scotland. There was a lot Elijah Hirsch had done that Liam didn't agree with, like keeping a monster like Michael Mizrahi in the fold after causing his spouse's death. It had been a kind of sick joke to Liam. Did Alpha enjoy torturing the assassin that much?

"Fool," Liam muttered, staring through the TV. "Amateur."

Liam's father had held the Beta title before him, and there was one thing he did, that Hirsch had not. Christopher Bailey never kept his enemies close, like Alpha had done with Gideon. Christopher had them swiftly eliminated so similar uprisings could never take place. Liam, like his father before him, didn't care how capable of a killer someone was. There were always more killers to hire. No, what Liam cared about more was staying in power. And to do that, he needed to remove his opposition from the battlefield *before* they had a chance to rebel, even if it meant killing his own people to do so.

Liam's eyes flicked down to his desk. He wasn't a sentimental man when it came to his personal life, but the one thing he did hold on to was family. There was a single framed photo sitting atop the desk. The photo wasn't of a significant other. Liam didn't have time for "love." Nor did the photo showcase his mother, father, or even grandfather. The formally dressed man was Liam's great-grandfather, who, during World War II, had been part of the greatest archaeological discovery ever.

Not that anyone outside of a select few knew about it.

Felix Neumann had been the Acolyte's Beta during the war, but he had also been a faithful follower of Heinrich Himmler. Dr. Neumann, and his other cohorts within the academic arm of the *Schutzstaffel*, the *Ahnenerbe*, had discovered what most considered humanity's greatest treasure: the Ark of the Covenant. The priceless artifact had been secretly removed from its hiding place, and the Ethiopian villagers that had been steadfastly watching over it, butchered and buried. The Ark was then covertly spirited out of Africa and into Germany to a place currently occupied by Acolyte scientists and researchers.

After the war had ended, Felix Neumann had come to America as part of Operation Paperclip. It was then that he began setting up an Acolyte command post here in the U.S. Had they had one there at the time, the war would've turned out quite differently…

To stay out of the press, and with the help of the American government, Felix Neumann had become Franklin Bailey. Liam adored his great-grandfather's story—his accomplishments. Did he agree with the man's antisemitic beliefs and disdain for Jews? No, of course not. But that didn't take away from the man's accomplishments. Regardless, Felix Neumann had always been held in high esteem within the family.

Then, he returned to Germany for a 'vacation' and died a week later.

Even after Neumann's death, his collected wealth led to some profitable investments. That fortune had been handed down and increased over the decades. When Liam had finally taken over the family trust, he had used a large sum of his inheritance to start his own social media giant, Delphi. And since its launch, Delphi's algorithm had been built for three purposes: to advance the Acolyte narrative, to discover future, worthwhile members, and to watch for Army of God movement.

The same could be said for Liam's most daunting venture, Prophecy Global News. As it stood today, PGN was the nation's number one news source, bigger than even CNN, MSNBC, or Fox News. It only hired likeable, attractive anchors that the mindless drones watching would adore, and more importantly, believe. The fact that most of the stories on PGN were entirely fabricated, or at best, marginally accurate, yet they still soaked in viewers, had always amused Liam. *Like moths to a flame*, he thought. Even their fluff pieces were mostly fictitious. He did have to hand it to the other news outlets, though. They, at least, attempted to weave their biases into *real* stories.

Most of the time... Liam found it quicker and cheaper just to make shit up. *And, yet, we are still number one.*

He grinned, then activated the television's picture-in-picture feature. CNN was currently covering the long-delayed funeral of Peter Hughes, the recently deceased Prime Minister of England. To everyone in the Acolyte, he'd been known as Delta. Because of the circumstances of the politician's demise, the English government had postponed the ceremony. Gideon had nearly removed the man's head from his body when he had slit his throat.

"Three down," Liam mumbled, "three to go."

All that was left was Epsilon over in China, Gamma in Colombia, and Liam himself. Even now, Delta and Zeta's heirs had already contacted Liam through trusted sources. He didn't care whether they took control of their predecessor's title or not. The only seat that could screw things up for Liam was the Alpha position. It had always been the traditional leader of all the Acolyte forces.

He stood. If Liam wanted to continue his tightening stranglehold on his own organization, he needed to act against them. A thought entered his mind, one that, if done properly, could end with him reigning over the entirety of the Acolyte until his time on Earth came. Not only would he truly become the most powerful man in media, but he would also become the most powerful man in every industry around the world. Then, and only then, could the Acolyte vision truly be implemented.

But he also needed the missing Relics of God.

Liam needed the Holy Grail and the Staff of God.

Acolyte researchers have long argued over the viability of the Grail if the Fisher King, Daniel Laird, should ever be slain. Some of the men that had survived the raid on Laird's Torridon estate had overheard that the man had been killed after being run-through by Gideon. At the time Gideon possessed the only weapon capable of mortally injuring Laird, the Spear of Destiny. Shortly after the failed operation, the Acolyte historians had nearly collapsed upon hearing of Larid's demise, but without a body to confirm his death, Bailey wasn't convinced. He still wasn't. The Hexad believed that Laird still lived until they were proven otherwise. Plus, with Liam's lineage dating back to Moses' family tree, he was confident that the supernatural power within the Holy artifacts would still work as they should, even though his scholars weren't so convinced.

"Tell me again what your fear is," Liam had said.

The nervous researcher stepped forward. "All our findings state that only a descendant of Christ can use the Grail, a descendant of Moses can wield the Staff, and the Ark..." He shook his head. "We just don't know what it wants. Nothing has worked. Then, there is also the possibility that none of it is accurate. Much of our research was destroyed during the Middle Ages. We've pieced much of it together since then, but there's still a lot we aren't sure of unless you want to rely on *faith*."

Liam sat forward. "But doesn't our research also say that there will be one who can wield them all?"

The researcher nodded apprehensively "Yes, but..."

"But?"

"But," he swallowed, "we haven't come across any physical proof of such claim. For now, we believe it only as a myth," he quickly added, "for now! We're still working it all out."

Liam believed that he was the one to wield them all. His father and grandfather before him believed that their line had birthed the chosen one.

Me.

Liam wanted them for himself, not for the Acolyte as a whole. *He* wanted to enter the gates of Eden. *He* wanted to experience the beginning—the dawn of creation—where Adam and Eve had once resided.

He also wanted what was said to still lurk within the garden.

The Relics of God would make him immortal.

The spiritual force contained within the garden would make him all-powerful.

Liam lifted his glass of bourbon again and drained it. When he set it down, he smiled wide.

2

Stromness, Orkney, Scotland

It had been a long time since Joseph had been homeless. The bombardment set upon him and the others on his Scottish estate had caused just that. Joseph was without a home now. Two of his closest allies, Isla and Ian MacDonald, were watching over the cleanup and rebuild of his beloved residence as he sat here and contemplated his next move.

It had also been a long time since he'd been involved in a war, and that was precisely what the Acolyte had done when they came after him. They had declared war. The Army of God was small, but what they may have lacked in numbers, they more than made up for with stealth, knowledge, and most importantly, belief. They were also an incredibly determined group, as well as a bit of a ragtag bunch.

Joseph was none other than the mysterious confidant of Jesus Christ, Joseph of Arimathea, a man that Gabriel had described as a "Biblical-era mob boss with a heart of gold." Joseph had been granted the *blessing* of immortality due to his godly lineage and the pure blood of Christ. It had secretly rewritten his DNA after he'd been coated in Jesus' blood during the Crucifixion. It had been the horror show of all horror shows and an event that Joseph had tried to forget for centuries, not that he ever could forget such a travesty.

Jesus had been his friend, not just his Lord.

He closed his eyes and smiled. *You still are*, he thought, breathing deeply. *I'll see you again soon.*

They had fled north, to Stromness, a town that William *Strom*, Joseph's head of security, had founded in the 16th century. Not only was William immortal, but he had also inspired the legend of King Arthur because of his leadership and fierceness. The Army of God's subterranean sanctuary, the Citadel, had been Camelot. Even Excalibur was real, though it had gone by a different name when Joseph had wielded it, long before William had been born, *Stonebreaker*. Once Joseph had taken in the young man, he had seen the person he would become and had given him the otherworldly blade.

Now, Joseph and William sat in front of a roaring fire, discussing what was next for the group. William's property had never been linked to his real identity. Whatever the Acolyte discovered about it wouldn't lead them to the Army of God. It would only lead to more questions that few knew the answers to.

They were safe...for now. But Joseph was under no illusion that there would come a time when their presence would be found out. When that time came, he hoped they wouldn't be here. So, for now, they rested and recovered, both physically and mentally. Joseph readjusted his recline, feeling a twinge of discomfort in his side. Though the wound had already healed, the sensation of being impaled lived on. The Spear of Destiny, the Holy Lance, had done its job. Because it had once pierced the side of Christ, it was the only thing on Earth that could remove his eternal gift.

Now, Joseph was mortal.

He picked up his coffee and sipped it, relishing in the warmth and flavor. William didn't skimp, even here while in hiding. The fridge and pantries were fully stocked, though mostly with nonperishable items. Fresh meals came nightly, but they didn't dare overbuy, just in case they needed to leave quickly, all of a sudden.

Footfalls echoed behind him in the otherwise silent great room. The center communal space of William's estate was two stories tall and consisted of a second-floor balcony that ringed the majority of the space in a horseshoe pattern. The only place that possessed no balcony was directly above the front door, behind Joseph. By now, he could identify the owner of the footsteps based on their gait and footspeed. These were quick and light. They obviously belonged to Naomi, a woman who *never* moved slowly.

"Any word from my brother?" she asked, stepping into view as she spoke. She didn't sit. She just looked back and forth from Joseph to William while waiting for one of them to answer.

"No," William replied plainly. As always, he didn't beat around the bush or mince his words. His answers and explanations were always blunt and borderline unemotive.

Joseph cleared his throat. "No, he hasn't. Jacob has been troubled, as we all have. He, more than most, is not accustomed to sitting idle for so long." Naomi opened her mouth to say something else, but Joseph beat her to it. "Leave him be, Naomi. I understand your worry, believe me, I do. But I also trust Jacob not to get himself into trouble. He's made a living at doing precisely just that."

"He's right," another voice said from above. Everyone looked up and to the left to find Gabriel Abrams leaning on the western banister. "Despite what the Mossad believes, Michael Mizrahi was not their best operative ever. Maybe for a time he was, but not for me. It's always been your dear brother." He scratched his head and glanced away. "Not that I'd be caught dead admitting that with him in the room."

"But this isn't anything like what he did in the Mossad," Naomi countered, returning her attention to Joseph and William.

"It absolutely is," Gabriel countered back. She gazed back up at him. He stood upright and folded his arms across his chest. "This is nothing for people like us." He opened his arms wide and grinned. "What we have here. This is the life."

Joseph didn't completely agree with Gabriel's sentiment, but he'd also been in much worse situations during his long life. Being stuck inside William's Stromness estate was one of the more pleasant, if he were honest. He'd been in Europe during the Black Plague outbreak. He'd also been in other parts of the world during widespread droughts and nation-wide famine. If this was what being on the run from the Acolyte was like in the 21st century, then yes, perhaps this was "the life," as Gabriel had put it.

For people like us, Joseph thought. That was also something Gabriel had said.

Joseph stood and placed a reassuring hand on Naomi's shoulder. "Relax. Jacob will be fine." He smiled. "Trust in him."

Gabriel left the banister and descended a set of switchbacking stairs leading down to the first floor. There was another set just like them on the opposite side of the room. He joined Joseph,

William, and Naomi below, plopping into a chair nearest the fire.

"Pretty remarkable what's coming out of Russia, huh?"

Joseph nodded. "Yes. It seems that Mizrahi is keeping up with his end of the bargain."

"But what happens when they're all dead?" Naomi asked. "Is he friend or foe to us?"

"Maybe he's neither," William replied. "He's no longer an Acolyte assassin. He no longer has any quarrel with us."

"Not true," Gabriel quickly said. "We know who he is and what he's been up to. We're a liability."

"I'm afraid that Gabriel is right," Joseph agreed, sitting, and leaning forward on his knees. "And until the time comes, if and when we see him again, we need to continue to view him as a viable threat."

3

The thing that Jacob had enjoyed about Orkney the most was the fact that it never got hot. In fact, it never got warm, period. Not unless you were sitting inside in front of a roaring fire. Since they'd been in Stromness, the hottest it had been was barely above fifty degrees Fahrenheit. The cool temperatures kept Jacob on his toes and mentally alert.

The last few weeks had been the first operation he'd been part of outside the Middle East in years. Regardless of who he was fighting, and why he was fighting them, Jacob had to admit that he was enjoying the change in scenery. Scotland was full of beauty. That was undeniable. The countries of the Middle East were too, but tasted of an entirely different flavor. A desert sunrise or sunset was always a majestic thing to witness, no matter how many times you've seen one. But then Jacob had watched the sun rise and set on either side of Orkney. It had been breathtaking.

The town's shopping district sat just south of the marina, along the western edge of a sheltered bay called Hamnavoe. Their hideout was in the northern end of Stromness, tucked into an endless sea of green. The property wasn't as vast as Joseph's back in Torridon, but it was still an impressive plot, one that Jacob couldn't even imagine the value of. It was, quite literally, two roads back to the estate.

He climbed out of one of William's five automobiles, a newer Vauxhall Astra Sports Tourer. The blue, four-door vehicle was essentially a sporty station wagon. None of the cars in William's garage were over-the-top or fit for a collector. They were normal, average cars that blended in with the others on the roads of Orkney. They had been purchased with strategy in mind. The one flaw in William's selections was horsepower. None of the cars had been built for speed.

Let's hope we won't need something that zooms, Jacob thought.

Two hundred feet from his curbside parking spot was the front to the corner store. So far, anything they had needed had simply been ordered and dropped off outside the estate's front gate. But Jacob had needed to get out. He had needed to get away from the others and clear his head. In actuality, there was nothing Jacob needed from town. William had made sure that their stay at his estate was comfortable.

The front desk to the corner store was off to Jacob's left, as was the business' operator, and presumably its owner. He was an older man, perhaps in his late-sixties, maybe even a tick older than that. He lifted his eyes away from a paperback novel and gave Jacob a polite smile and a nod. Jacob returned his welcoming with a small wave, then the other man returned his attention to the book. Jacob caught a quick glimpse of the front cover and saw the title: *Cash is King*.

"Any good?" Jacob asked, figuring a little small talk couldn't hurt.

The storekeeper looked up at him. "If you like crude

Aussieisms and bat-shit crazy action sequences, yes."

Jacob shrugged. "Who doesn't?" That made the old man laugh. "I'll let you get back to it."

The man nodded again. "Give me a shout if you need anything."

"Will do."

The store was stocked with your typical, quick-grab type items. A myriad of snacks, magazines, and a few novels, both used and new, including the one the owner was currently reading. There were also refrigerated drinks and a door with bags of ice behind it. Again, Jacob didn't need anything, but he wasn't about to window shop and not purchase anything.

A smirk formed on his face. Jacob reached out and snagged a copy of the local's read. He had plenty of downtime recently, why not grab something to eat away at the time spent sitting around doing nothing? Jacob also plucked a bottle of an orange-colored drink he'd never heard of before called *Irn-Bru*. This particular fridge had rows of the stuff.

Jacob held it up. "How's this?"

The shopkeeper looked up, squinting hard as he looked across the store. "The best in all of Scotland! Has a tangy, fruity taste."

Hence the orange coloring, Jacob thought, shrugging. He shut the fridge and made his way back to the front desk, dropping the plastic bottle of soda on the tabletop, along with the paperback.

"I'm going to take your advice and give it a try," Jacob said, tapping the cover of the book. He held up the Irn-Bru, "This too."

The local grinned. "You won't be disappointed. But if you are, you can bring 'em both back and pick out something else."

Jacob smiled. "I appreciate that. Thank you."

"Where you from, if you don't mind me asking?"

"The U.S.," Jacob quickly replied, "though my parents are from Israel."

The other man nodded as he rang up the items. "I figured as much." He stopped. "No offence meant."

Jacob grinned. "What gave it away, the beard, hair, and complexion?"

The shopkeeper laughed heartedly. "I guess you could say a little of everything." He bagged the items. "What are you in Stromness for?"

"Real-estate. Thinking of buying a vacation home here. I love this part of Scotland."

"Happy to hear that. We Stromnessians are very proud of our home. All Orcadians are."

Jacob nodded. "You should be. Beautiful area, though I believe you all get forgotten too easily."

The local smiled. "We prefer it that way," he quickly added, "but we do enjoy the company of outsiders from time to time too."

Jacob gave him a wink. "Thanks."

The TV behind the counter blared with a "breaking news" alarm. It caught both men's attention. They paused their cheery conversation and took in the report. The channel was tuned to PGN Scotland. The network's owner was a person of interest to the Army of God. Liam Bailey was either a member of the Hexad, or at least, a higher-up within the Acolyte. His companies, based on what Joseph and William had said, were essentially an extension of the Acolyte and their propaganda.

"*We have reports of a terrorist cell hiding deep in the north of Scotland someplace and authorities are in need of the public's help in identifying them,*" the bombshell, female anchor said. "*We've been given the names and images of three of people in question; a Gabriel Abrams, a Naomi Fehr, and a Jacob Fehr."*

Jacob's eyes opened wide as their images came up on screen. He grabbed his items and slinked through the front door. He tried to keep his eyes down, but ended up glancing through the front window of the shop. The older man was already on the phone, and eyeing Jacob as he spoke.

As soon as Jacob was out of the man's line of sight, he took off at a sprint and made it to his car in seconds. Stromness was small. That meant the police would be here in no time. Jacob needed to get out of town quickly and do so without being followed back to William's estate. He could've just as easily jammed his foot down on the pedal, but Jacob's training had taught him to take it slow and blend in. He casually pulled out of his parking spot and left. Jacob was on high alert. The authorities would identify his vehicle *if* he didn't get out of the shopping district of Stromness now.

Jacob removed his cell phone from his pocket and called Joseph.

"*What's wrong, Jacob?*" Joseph asked. He knew that if Jacob was calling him that there must be an issue.

"We have a problem."

"*What kind of problem?*"

Jacob glanced into his rearview mirror as he answered. "Turn on the local PGN broadcast."

He could hear Joseph moving around and now walking. Five seconds later, Jacob heard the same broadcast he'd been watching turn on in the background of the call.

"*Oh, no.*"

Gabriel's response wasn't as reserved. Somewhere in the background, he shouted, "*What the hell is this?*"

"*Isn't it obvious, the Acolyte are trying to flush us out,*" Joseph explained. "*Hang on, I'm putting you on speaker... Now, the entire world will be looking for us, not just them.*"

"What do we do?" Jacob asked, making a right-hand turn.

"*Get back here as quickly as you can, Jacob,*" Joseph replied. "*We'll figure something out. Though I do find it interesting that neither William nor I are mentioned.*"

"Yeah, same. I figured that the Acolyte would go out of their way to ID you guys."

"*Must be a public record thing,*" Naomi said. "*With the news coming out of Torridon, I bet PGN didn't want to confound things by having Daniel Laird mentioned.*"

"What about William?" Jacob asked.

"*I doubt they have enough intel on him to even name him,*" Joseph replied. "*His existence is extremely shrouded. Laird was too involved in the Graal Foundation to hide. Either way, Jacob, you need to hurry.*"

"Copy that. I'm on my w—"

Jacob's voice was cut off by something he saw in his overhead mirror. Twin police cruisers came screaming up behind him. They were still a hundred yards off, but were coming up fast with their lights flashing.

"*Jacob?*" Naomi asked.

"It's...nothing. I'll be back soon." He ended the call and tossed his phone into the passenger seat beside him. He sighed. "I hope..." Jacob glanced into the rearview mirror again. "Not good," he said, eyeing the quickly approaching police cruisers.

Jacob was traveling south along Victoria Street. He needed to be going in the other direction, but he didn't want to draw even more attention to himself. The single-lane street was barely that. To Jacob, it was more of a cobblestone footpath that, for some reason, allowed cars to be driven on it. Walkers hustled around slow-moving vehicles. The shops were right on the road and were so close that if you didn't see a vehicle coming, it could take the shop's front door right off the hinges. Because of the construction of the town, one that had never been meant to handle any kind of automobile traffic, there weren't many side streets that cut to the east and west.

Come on, Jacob thought, needing one of those side streets more than ever.

The police cruisers were gaining on him, but at what was a slower pace than most police-involved situations. Jacob came up to a toy store and discovered Church Road. It was even narrower than Victoria Street but was passable by a car. Jacob casually flipped on his blinker and eased through the turn. He gave the police cruisers a glance before disappearing around the corner.

Church Road angled up hard. Jacob had to give the Astra a little more gas to make the climb. When he did, he watched behind him, readying himself to stomp on the pedal.

The pair of police cruisers passed through the quaint three-way intersection without giving Jacob so much as a glance. They hadn't been here for him. He closed his eyes for a moment and let out a long breath. He'd seriously dodged a bullet.

For now.

In Jacob's experience, he knew that the next bullet aimed would be at his back.

4

Jacob arrived safely, much to the relief of Joseph. They had all been worried for him since the news had falsely accused him of being a terrorist. Thankfully, Stromness was a small town. Getting to places was easy, as was escaping those same places. Jacob had just proved that by driving from the center of town back to William's estate in under ten minutes.

Joseph met Jacob at the door, finding the former Mossad operative in an irate mood. They were all mad. How were they not? They'd been publicly accused of being something they weren't, bloodthirsty murderers. Replace the mentioning of the Army of God with the Acolyte and the description would've been perfectly acceptable.

"We'll figure this out, Jacob," Joseph immediately said when opening the door. Jacob's mouth was open, apparently ready to say something, but Joseph had beaten him to it.

Jacob's face softened. "I know…"

Joseph held out his hand and stepped aside. "Come on, everyone's waiting."

The two men headed deeper into the grand entry. As they

neared, Naomi and Gabriel stood and faced them. William was already standing, and his eyes were as intense as ever. The warmth radiating off the fireplace soothed Joseph's nerves. It seemed to do the same for Jacob too.

Joseph returned to his place on the sofa. He sat next to the left armrest. Naomi shared the wide piece of furniture, but had her back against the right armrest, sitting sideways with her knees tucked into her chest. Jacob continued around to the fireplace, gripped the edge of the mantle, and leaned in closer. William leaned against the wall to the right of the fireplace, staying silent. Gabriel plopped into an armchair nearest to Joseph and let out a long, exaggerated breath.

Everyone's attention turned on him.

"What?" he asked, shrugging. "The still air is awful."

Joseph agreed. "So, what is everybody thinking?"

William pushed off the wall and stood tall. "It must be Bailey."

"Bailey?" Jacob asked. "Liam Bailey?"

The big man nodded. "We've suspected that he's been a key figure within the Acolyte for some time now, possibly even one of the Hexad leaders, the Beta."

"How do you mean?" Gabriel asked, sitting higher.

"His news channel and social media network have both spread some blatantly false information about Daniel Laird and the Graal Foundation for years," Joseph explained. "We seriously doubt anyone else could pull it off besides the man himself."

"Are you sure?" Naomi asked, bringing her knees down and folding her legs Indian style. "I mean, is this similar to Hirsch's involvement as far as his lineage is concerned?"

"We believe it is," Joseph replied. "Though, unlike Elijah Hirsch, whose ancestor I personally knew, Bailey's family history is extremely clouded. But it's also just as troubling, not that the public is aware of it."

"What does that mean?" Gabriel asked. "Every family has a few crazies in it—someone to be embarrassed about. Once, my Uncle John took off his pants and—"

"Not appropriate right now," Naomi snapped.

"What about Bailey's bloodline bothers you?" Jacob asked.

Joseph decided to give them the condensed version of the man's family history. "His great-grandfather was one of Himmler's top researchers."

"And?" Jacob asked. "Thousands, probably hundreds of thousands, of people have relatives that were Nazis. That doesn't mean they are today."

"I agree," Joseph said. "I, more than anyone, know that not everyone can be defined by those who came before them. But after years of looking into things, we've come to the conclusion that Bailey's Nazi ancestor was also a member of the Acolyte."

Gabriel faced Jacob. "Think about it, Jacob. Himmler and his SS boys were super into the occult, right? They lived for this kind of stuff. What if Bailey's great-grandfather was why?"

"That's a big assumption," Naomi countered.

"It's all we have," Joseph said. "But I am confident in our information, as you should all be too."

"We also believe Bailey's bloodline was the driving force behind the Thule Society," William said, looking grim.

"I know the name from history class," Gabriel said, sitting back. "Enlighten us further, if you don't mind."

Joseph took over the explanation. "They preceded the SS in a way. A large chunk of Himmler's beliefs had come from the Thule Society, like their obsessive interest in the occult and their theory of the Aryan race."

"Oh, I see," Gabriel muttered, looking uncomfortable. "So, what you're saying is that they were bat-shit crazy?"

Joseph simply shrugged.

"Notwithstanding of the facts surrounding Liam Bailey," Jacob said, quieting the room, "I think it's time we begin the next phase of our mission."

No one argued.

"So, which is it," Gabriel said, opening his hands, "—and, by the way, I can't believe I'm even saying this—but is it the Staff of God or the Ark of the Covenant?"

"The Staff," Joseph replied matter-of-factly. "We aren't ready for the Ark yet."

"Not ready?" Jacob asked. "What do you mean?"

William folded his arms across his chest. "The Acolyte have the Ark."

"They do?" Naomi asked.

"Since World War II, yes," Joseph replied. "The Nazis discovered it in Africa, during Rommel's campaign."

Gabriel sat up. "That feels like a game over kind of thing, doesn't it?"

William shared a smile with Joseph, then said, "They cannot open it."

"Why not?" Naomi asked.

Joseph grinned. "It won't let them, and no one knows why."

Gabriel stood. "You mean to tell me that the right-hand man of Jesus Christ and King *Freaking* Arthur are clueless when it comes to the Ark's power?"

William snarled but replied with, "Correct. Although we do know that Bailey's great-grandfather was one of the men who died trying to open it. This was some years later, mind you."

"He died trying to open the Ark?" Naomi asked. Then her

eyes opened wide. "He was there, wasn't he? He was part of the Nazi team that found the Ark."

"You must understand something, Naomi, Jacob, Gabriel…" Joseph pictured the Ark in his mind's eye. He'd never seen it before. The thing he knew about it, besides its ability to kill those not worthy of touching it, was what the Bible said. "The Ark is centuries older than even me. It is truly ancient, and something we shouldn't waste our time focusing on right now. The Staff is our current goal."

"Hang on," Naomi said, "before we shift gears. Tell me, why the Ark doesn't allow just anyone to open it?"

"Because, thus far, those who have attempted haven't been meant to do so," Joseph eyed the three newcomers. "Remember, this is all about *worth*—heart—what's in your soul."

The room went silent.

Gabriel sat again, then shrugged. "Sure, why not? I've seen weirder shit than that since coming to Scotland."

"The Staff," Naomi started, ignoring Gabriel's comment and looking at Joseph, "I thought we were going to wait for your estate to be rebuilt before launching any kind of operation?"

"That was the original plan, yes," Joseph replied, "but I feel that the Acolyte have accelerated things with their latest move. I fear we no longer have the luxury of waiting." He glanced up at the still standing William. "We may need to move from here soon too. I give the authorities a day or two tops before they discover us here. The Acolyte are no doubt feeding information to anyone they see as an ally, even if they are an unintentional one."

"He's right," William added. "We may be safe here for now, but it won't last much longer with the entire world looking for us now. Our resources may be plentiful, but the Acolyte's are deeper and reach longer." He sighed. "It's the benefit of not hiding like we have. The Acolyte have been working to strengthen their allies whereas we neglected such things."

"They know our faces," Naomi said, "well, Jacob, Gabriel, and mine."

"Not for long," Joseph said, running his hand through his styled black hair. "I suggest we alter our appearances before heading out."

"Dang," Gabriel said, stroking his chin, "just when I got my beard right." He stood and stepped up next to William. "Sorry, Goldilocks, but the doo needs to go." He reached for William's blonde, shoulder-length hair, but was stopped when the other man snagged his wrist and twisted. Gabriel cringed and his knees gave out a little. "Ah, uncle, uncle!"

5

Silicon Valley, California, USA

Twenty minutes after the Acolyte-driven broadcast had aired, Liam's private phone rang. This particular line was only connected to Acolyte business. He smiled, activated the device's voice modulation software, and answered the call.

"This is Beta," he said. His voice was now robotic and unrecognizable.

The man on the other end was one of Delta's lead British agents, a man who had taken over as operations supervisor for the area after his superior had died in Torridon. "*Hello, sir, this is Agent Hart, we've received confirmation that Jacob Fehr has been spotted in Orkney.*"

Liam sat straighter. "Where specifically?"

"*Um, let me confirm... Stromness, sir. We have three agents searching for him now. They are in contact with the local authorities acting as MI5 agents.*"

Liam knew Stromness well, not that he'd ever been there. William Strom, Daniel Laird's head of security, was said to be descended from the original founders of the town. It made sense they'd go there after the Torridon estate was destroyed. Unfortunately, the Acolyte had never been able to confirm the Army of God owned a safehouse there. It had only been speculation.

Until now, Liam thought.

"Double the search party," he ordered. "I want them found."

"Yes, sir, though there might be a problem with that."

Liam squinted. "What problem?"

"*Numbers, sir. We just don't have the manpower right now. A lot of our best operatives were killed in Torridon. And with Delta's death...*"

"What about his death?"

"*Excuse me for saying this, sir, but there is a large feeling of uncertainty amongst the other agents. I for one am game, but a lot of the others are apprehensive when it comes to anymore public operations.*" Hart took a deep breath. "*We aren't an army, sir. We don't excel at open combat. Plus, a lot of us have families, sir. We aren't celibate, warrior monks.*"

Liam grumbled. He was angry, but he understood. When Hirsch had ordered the raid on Laird's home, he had overextended UK Acolyte forces. Liam also understood where the man was coming from in regards to tactics. The Acolyte always operated with the utmost care and only from the shadows. Many of the surviving agents had fled and gone into hiding due to their fear of government retaliation.

After taking a long breath to calm himself, Liam said, "Noted. What do you need from me?"

"*Honestly, just more intel. I can't ask my people to kick in doors and start interrogating everyone we see.*"

"So, there's a shared sentiment in a lack of quality leadership amongst the ranks?"

"*Um, yes, sir?*" Hart replied with nervousness in his voice. "*It's not directed towards you directly, sir. The events of the last month have really shaken things throughout our ground forces.*" He cleared his throat. "*May I be blunt, sir?*"

Liam rolled his eyes, but allowed Hart to speak freely. "Go ahead, Agent Hart."

"*Alpha was reckless in the end. Don't be him...sir.*"

Liam glanced at the television. It was still tuned into PGN, but the broadcast had since moved onto another story. Was he being reckless in his pursuit of the Army of God? He quickly decided that he wasn't, not if he took a step back and weighed his options.

"I agree," he finally said. "Have your men keep searching, but I need you to really dig into real-estate records. We need to find out where they're hiding. We'll do what we can from our end, but I need you to do the same from there, is that clear?"

"*Yes, sir. And thank you for understanding.*"

Liam didn't want to play the role of benevolent master. Liam wanted to rule absolutely. But he also wanted the loyalty of his people—every regional branch within the Acolyte. Now more than ever, Liam needed to be careful with the things he had his men do. If he did act as recklessly as Hirsch had, then he'd be seen in the same light as him.

"You're welcome, but when we do find out where they are hiding, I need you to go in and flush them out."

"*Yes, sir. But what happens when they go on the offensive? Are we to retreat?*"

"No, the Army of God must be stopped. If, and when, they do retaliate, eliminate them all. Question them first, see what they know. With Laird dead, it doesn't matter."

Only the Hexad believed Larid was still alive. They had told their men otherwise, for now.

"*And if Laird isn't dead?*" Hart asked. "*I've heard rumblings that he may have survived.*"

Liam chose his next words carefully. "If he is alive, bring him to me. The Grail too."

"*Yes, sir. But how will I find you? Acolyte protocol states that the Hexad keep their identities a secret.*"

"I know our protocol, Agent Hart. Let me worry about that when the time comes. A lot has changed. So must we." Liam tapped his desk, wondering how much of his plan he should reveal. Hart would be a valuable ally. He was intelligent and well-spoken; a natural leader. "Tell me, what would you think if the Acolyte consolidated its forces and reorganized?"

Hart went silent.

"Something the matter?"

"*No, sir. I actually think that would be a good idea. We are in dire times. Like you said, the world has changed and so must we.*"

"Very good. If all goes well, I can see you standing by my side at the end of all of this."

"*I would be honored, sir. Thank you. I'll report back soon. Agent Hart out.*"

6

Stromness, Orkney, Scotland

Naomi had never needed eyeglasses until now, particularly ones *without* a prescription. She was currently sitting on a tall stool in one of two upstairs bathrooms, staring at herself in the mirror. Her hair was pulled back in a ponytail minus a few strands of loose hair tucked behind her right ear. The way she looked now reminded her of a teacher she had back in high school. She also looked like her mother too...

There wasn't much else Naomi could do to change her appearance. She never wore makeup, and she always dressed down in clothes that were comfortable to live in while on the road. Naomi rarely ever wore heels or a dress; only at conferences when dressing to impress was required. Even then, she'd only wear lipstick. She was also like her mom in that way. Daphne Fehr had been a radiant woman without trying to be. Looking back, Naomi was still amazed with how much she and her brother resembled their parents.

She sighed, undid her ponytail, and looked down at the

pair of scissors lying beside the sink. Naomi knew she needed to cut her hair. She didn't want to, but it was necessary. It currently touched her shoulder blades, the perfect length in her opinion. She picked the scissors up, opened them and inspected the blades. They would be plenty sharp to do the job. Naomi grabbed a portion of her hair, placed the opened scissors against it, and closed her eyes.

Goodbye.

"Nice specs."

She opened her eyes, lowered the scissors, and turned her head to the right to find a freshly shaven, incredibly handsome, Gabriel Abrams leaning against the doorframe.

"Think so?" she asked, once more inspecting herself in the mirror. "Be honest."

He entered and slid up behind her. Now they were both visible in the mirror's reflection. He playfully leaned in closer to the mirror, mock-inspecting her in it. He rubbed his chin. "Hmmm..." Then he shrugged. "If you're going for the whole 'sexy librarian' look, I'd say you've nailed it."

Naomi blushed at the comment. She allowed her heart rate to get under control before spinning around on the stool to face him. "Jacob says I look like Evelyn Carnahan."

Gabriel grinned. "I stand corrected. There is no sexier librarian than Evy. Rick is a lucky man." His eyes flashed down to the scissors in her hand. "Need help with those?"

She held them up, her right eyebrow raising in question. "You cut women's hair?"

He shrugged again. "Just call me Zohan!" He got serious. "My older sister is a hair dresser back in Jaffa." He gently plucked the scissors from her hand. "She used me as a test subject when she was in school. In turn, she taught me how to cut her own hair too. Two Guinea pigs are better than one, right?"

"How long ago was that?" she asked, uncomfortable with the idea of Gabriel accidentally giving her a buzz cut.

"Well, I was still in high school at the time, so, almost twenty years?"

Naomi's face paled. "*Twenty* years? Something tells me you might be a little out of practice."

Gabriel folded his arms. "Look, you want my help or not?"

"Fine." She relented and spun around to face the mirror. "But not too much, okay?"

He dramatically stomped his foot and put his hands on his hips. "I am an *arteest*! Let me work!"

Gabriel ran his hands through her hair, inspecting its quality and fullness. Naomi's heart fluttered, causing her to bite her lip. His touch was something magical, and something she hadn't felt in a long, *long* time.

Apparently, her outward display of bliss hadn't gone unnoticed.

"Enjoying yourself?" he asked, staring at her. He released her hair. "Should I leave and give you a minute?"

Naomi rolled her eyes. "Shut up."

Gabriel didn't push her any further. He resumed prepping her hair, wetting his hands, and running them through it. With no spray bottle, it was the only way he could wet it without dunking her head in the sink. Then came the scissors. She squeezed her eyes shut, unable to watch as he began.

After a few minutes, Gabriel asked her a question that she was both anticipating and terrified of receiving.

"So, are we ever going to talk about this?"

Naomi worked up the courage to open her eyes and look at his reflection. "You mean how weird it is that you know how to cut women's hair?"

He snipped another section, then locked eyes with her. "You know what I mean..."

"Yeah, I do," she said looking away.

"Geez, don't sound so enthused," he said, resuming his task.

Naomi's shoulders fell and she covered her face with her hands. "Sorry, that didn't come out as I hoped."

He grinned. "I know. I was just messing with you."

"You're impossible."

He kept working, concentrating on her hair while also talking. "Not all the time. I'd love to be able to show you the real me someday."

"You mean you don't always act like a teenager?"

The corner of Gabriel's mouth rose. "Not always, no. Though he's definitely the dominate personality."

"You have more than one?"

"Don't we all?" he asked back. "You should meet Gerald, he's a *hoot*."

Naomi smiled. "I'd love to hear about them all..."

"But?" he asked, glancing at her.

"Is now the right time?" she asked sincerely.

He cocked his head to the side, thinking. "It is just you, me, and the mirror in here."

Naomi looked away from him again. "I mean with everything going on. With everything that's still to come."

Gabriel paused his work and gripped her shoulder with his free hand. "Which is why it's the perfect time, Nae. How much time do either of us have left? This is a fight we may not survive. You know that, right?"

Naomi slowly reached up and placed her hand atop his. Then she lifted her eyes up to his reflection. "I know." She squeezed his hand a little. "And I agree."

That made him perk up. "You do? Really!"

She smiled. "Well, let's see how this haircut turns out first. If you make me look like I'm about to yell at the manager, you can forget it."

When he grinned, his wide jawline accentuated the movement. "Deal."

Someone cleared their voice in the doorway. Both Naomi and Gabriel dropped their hands away from one another and looked to find William standing in the open doorway. He opened his mouth to say something but was cut off by Gabriel.

The former Mossad operative pointed the scissors at him and said, "You're next."

William closed his mouth, gave Gabriel a subtle nod, then left.

"I don't envy you," Naomi said, twisting her upper body around to look at Gabriel.

"Why?"

She smiled again. "What do you think is going to happen if you screw up King Arthur's haircut?"

Gabriel's eyes opened wide and his mouth opened and hung there. Then he shook his head and exited his stupor. He took a deep breath, grabbed Naomi's hips, spun her around in a one-eighty, and resumed cutting her hair.

7

Thirty minutes had passed since William had come across Gabriel and Naomi in his guest bathroom. This would be the first time in over a hundred years that he'd cut his shoulder-length, blonde hair shorter than it was now.

He turned and re-entered the master bedroom, shutting the doors leading out to his private, second-story balcony. The temperature change indoors was noticeably warmer, and to William, less comfortable. He enjoyed the cold. It kept him on his toes. It kept his mind sharp.

He opened his bedroom door, closed it, and continued down the upstairs hallway. The left-hand side overlooked the main hall of his impressive estate. Most of the doors to his right led into spare rooms. A few currently housed the people staying here with him. In the middle of them, was a staircase that made movement between floors possible. The other, eastern side of the spacious room was a cookie-cut version of this half. To the left of the staircase was his destination, one of two, second-floor guest bathrooms.

Only now, the door was closed.

Hmmm.

He stopped and turned to face it. Williams listened closely, hearing nothing suspicious. Had Gabriel forgotten his agreement to cut his hair? It was possible. They all had a lot on their minds. Gabriel forgetting something as trivial as a haircut wouldn't have surprised William.

He grabbed the doorknob and pushed it open to find Naomi sitting on the sink, facing Gabriel. Their lips were locked with one another's, in the midst of a passionate kiss. All William could do was roll his eyes and clear his throat. They released one another and turned to face him, looking very much like two deer caught in the headlights of a car.

William rested his hands on his hips and said, "It's about time."

"Yes, well, I think so too," Gabriel replied, stepping away from Naomi to allow her the space she needed to slide off the sink and down to the floor. Both were blushing, but Naomi's embarrassment, if it were possible to measure with the Richter scale, would be off the charts. Gabriel's expression changed. "Wait, 'it's about time?'"

William nodded. "When you've been alive as long as I have, you tend to pick up on other people's behaviors quickly."

"How long have you known?" Naomi asked quietly.

"Before we left Torridon for here," William replied. "The way you two looked at each other was pretty telling. I'm honestly surprised no one has said anything yet."

Naomi was mortified. She went to leave the room, but had to stop and let William step aside first. When he did, he noticed her hair. It was now high above her shoulders, framing her face beautifully. Naomi was naturally attractive. The haircut merely accentuated it.

"Nice hair, by the way," he said, complementing Gabriel's work.

She gazed up at him, gave him a sheepish smile, and ducked out of the room, never once looking back. She opened the door to her room and practically leapt inside. William faced Gabriel again. The Israeli was standing next to the stool, holding the scissors.

"Reservation for Mr. Strom?"

William let out a long, annoyed breath then stepped inside. "Let's get this over with." He sat and stared at Gabriel in the mirror. "Promise me you won't kiss me when you're finished."

Gabriel cleared his throat. "Okay, sure... That shouldn't be a problem."

8

Jacob exited the western bathroom, feeling his freshly shaven face with one hand. Ever since high school, Jacob had sported some sort of facial hair, whether it was a layer of coarse stubble or a full-fledged beard. He did not trim his hair any, deciding to use a baseball cap to hide it instead. His training had taught him how to expertly disappear into a crowd, but it had also taught him how to vanish into thin air while in plain sight, like now.

A hat and sunglasses could do wonders.

Not only could Jacob change his looks, but he could also change his physical mannerisms and his stride. He'd always been amazed about how adding something, like a limp, could change someone's opinion of you. God forbid he added in a well-loved jacket in need of cleaning. There wasn't a single person that could ID him as a government agent.

Former government agent...

He'd always been well-versed in speaking with different accents. From now on, when in public, Jacob would speak with a flawless American accent. He also carried a passport that identified him as an American citizen named Jeffery Friedman.

Gabriel's preparations for undercover work were on par with Jacob's, as he figured Joseph and William's were. The two of them had been living this sort of life for a very long time; hiding in plain sight. The only one that would need some coaching was Naomi. She'd never been involved in anything like this, which was understandable. She was an archaeologist, not a covert operative.

As Jacob stepped toward the staircase, he glanced down over the railing. Everyone but him and William were present. He descended them, thinking over their upcoming quest: the retrieval of Moses' staff. Where was it now? Jacob had no idea, but he had a feeling Joseph knew. The guy didn't give up all the information right away. Jacob didn't think Joseph's methods were for dramatic purposes. This was all a lot to take in. Overweight information dumps were hard to handle for most, especially those in their position, living on the lam with a target on their backs.

Compartmentalizing intel was also excellent strategy. People couldn't give up information they didn't have.

Is that what he's doing? If so, Jacob didn't like it. But he also couldn't fault Joseph for doing so. Joseph was still learning to trust mortals again. And so, Jacob didn't take it personally.

He made a one-eighty and headed down the second-half of the stairs, just as William appeared through a doorway to the north that was built into a wall to the right of the fireplace. It led into the kitchen, as did another door built into the wall on the opposite side of the fireplace. William carried a tray of steaming mugs in his hands. Jacob knew it contained an assortment of coffee and tea, depending on the preferences of the present company.

Both men arrived at the fireplace at the same time. Joseph

was standing, studying the flames in detail. Naomi sat where she had before, curled up against the right-hand armrest of the plush sofa. Gabriel also sat where he had before, in the left-hand armchair. Jacob moved to sit between them on the left-hand section of the sofa.

As he fell onto the sofa, William set the tray down on the coffee table, tipped his chin up, and locked eyes with him.

"What?" Jacob asked, instantly stroking his cheek. "Did I miss a spot?"

He shook his head. "Naomi and Gabriel are a romantic item."

The unemotional response, paired with the words spoken, caught Jacob wholly off guard. He snapped his head around at his sister first, then over to Gabriel. He was speechless. Jacob's reaction spoke volumes, though. Naomi and Gabriel shrank away from Jacob, leaning in opposite directions from where he sat.

Gabriel's eyes darted over to Naomi, and he swallowed. "It was...just one kiss."

"In a bathroom with the door shut," William added as he sat in the armchair nearest Naomi.

Gabriel's chin dipped and he shut his eyes. They flashed open and he stared across the long coffee table. "C'mon, man! What about the bro code?"

It was obvious to Jacob that William did not understand what Gabriel was implying. His response confirmed as much.

"Bro code? I am *not* your brother," he replied literally. "Nor did we agree on not speaking on the matter."

"Ugh," Naomi finally said, hiding her humiliation behind her raised hands. She just covered her face, unable to look Jacob in the eye. When she did look up again, it was at Joseph, not her brother. "So, Joseph, tell us more about the Staff."

Jacob grumbled a curse under his breath, but added, "Yes, please do." Then he sat back and gave their leader his undivided attention. He wasn't sure how he felt about Naomi and Gabriel's budding relationship, but he didn't have time to focus on it right now.

Joseph began his lecture while still staring deeply into the roaring fire. "To understand the Staff, you need to also understand the fourteen from Scripture."

"Fourteen?" Gabriel asked, glancing at Jacob while he spoke.

"Yes, fourteen," Joseph replied. He pushed away from the fireplace and faced his people. "The two most famous staffs belonged to Moses and his brother Aaron."

"There were two staffs?" Gabriel asked.

Jacob nodded. "Yeah, well, I guess it all depends on what source you believe. Record keeping back then was mostly nonexistent. A large portion of everything we know comes from verbal testimony, not written documentation."

"Aaron's staff is supposed to be inside the Ark of the Covenant, right?" Naomi asked.

"Correct," Joseph replied. "That is, if you believe the Rabbinic midrash interpretations, which I do. Particular ones, anyway." Jacob wasn't so sure, but he knew to trust Joseph when it came to things pertaining to this subject. He had lived through it, after all. "The other twelve staffs belonged to the chiefs of the Twelve Tribes of Israel." He held up his forefinger. "However, only one was the true Staff."

"And I'm guessing that belonged to Moses," Gabriel said.

"Indeed," Joseph said.

Jacob sat forward with his elbows on his knees. "Is it true that the Staff is made of sapphire?"

"Sapphire, really?" Gabriel asked.

"Yes and no," Joseph replied. "Legends state that the Staff is made of sapphire, but everything I've read, and the people I've talked to over the centuries say that only parts of it are, that it swirls with the most gorgeous blue sapphire you've ever seen." Joseph seemed to get lost in his own head. He blinked. "The other parts are regular stone, possibly igneous or something similar."

"I'm confused," Gabriel said. "I thought Moses' staff was supposed to be something like a shepherd's crook or a basic walking stick?"

"There are varying descriptions of it," Joseph replied. "The one I described is the most consistent variation, so it's the one I'm choosing to believe...for now."

Gabriel shrugged. "Fair enough."

"Moses is said to have come across it while walking through his future father-in-law's garden," Naomi added. "It was planted on its end and impossible to withdraw except by someone of God's choosing. On the side of the Staff is the name of God. When Moses called out his name, he gripped the Staff and pulled it free."

"Exactly," Joseph said. "It signified that Moses was the chosen one; a man who would lead his people. Again, this is all from Rabbinic literature, so it's not commonly known or believed. The Staff was supposedly made by God, during the twilight of the sixth day of Creation, then given to Adam in Eden. After Adam and Eve were exiled, the Staff was handed down to important Biblical figures such as Shem, Abraham, Enoch, and Joseph—not me, of course." He began to pace. "When the other Joseph eventually died, Egyptian nobles stole many of his possessions, including the Staff. Eventually, it made it to the hands of Jethro."

"Father of Zipporah," Naomi said, "Moses' future wife."

Jacob had always been impressed with his sister's familiarity of the subject. Then again, she adored Biblical artifacts like the Staff of God. Her depth of knowledge shouldn't have surprised him.

Joseph gave her a nod of confirmation.

"All of this sounds an awful lot like the Sword in the Stone," Gabriel muttered.

"That wasn't us," William quickly argued. "Many had heard of the Staff and began creating their own stories surrounding it."

"And the reason I brought up the other staffs is because of where one of them is now."

Jacob had stayed mostly quiet. He liked others to do all the talking. He preferred to take in all the information before adding something to the conversation. This was one of those times.

"Where is it?" he asked.

"In the Tokapi Palace in Istanbul. For years, they have believed that their staff is that of Moses."

"How long has it been there?" Naomi asked, apparently not knowing this side of the Staff's history.

Joseph stopped pacing and took in the group. "It was first put on display in the 1960s, though I know for a fact that it has been on location since the 16th century, after Sultan Selim I, king of the Ottoman Empire, conquered Egypt in 1517."

"Hang on a second," Gabriel said, holding up his hand. "Why wait until the sixties to show it off?"

Joseph grinned. "Yes. Why indeed?"

"Because it's not the true Staff," Jacob replied. "They never had it."

"That is my hypothesis too," Joseph agreed. "And after years of searching, I finally tracked it down, though that was hundreds of years before the false staff was revealed."

"It's back in Egypt, isn't it?" Naomi asked, sitting straight. "It's been there since the sultan's conquest."

"Impressive," Joseph said, beaming like a proud father, "but I'm not surprised."

"Which staff is in Istanbul?" Jacob asked, keeping the train rolling.

Joseph rubbed the back of his neck. "Honestly, I have no idea. Once I figured out that it wasn't Moses' staff, I stopped looking into it. Best Guess, it's a complete forgery or perhaps it's one of the chiefs' staffs."

Naomi asked the next obvious question. "Why didn't the sultan take the Staff with him when he conquered Egypt?"

"I was thinking the same thing," Jacob said. "If he knew where it was, why leave it?"

Joseph stuck his hands in his pants' pockets and began rocking back and forth in place. "Unfortunately, I have to answer your question with another history lesson."

Gabriel shrugged. "It's not like we have anywhere else to go right now."

Joseph nodded. "Sultan Selim I discovered the Staff in an undisclosed location. It's said that when he touched it, he became incredibly ill. He saw it as a curse and ordered his men to leave it be and never speak of its location to anyone."

"Did anyone eventually reveal the location?" Naomi asked.

"Of course, they did," Joseph replied. "As you'd expect, it didn't go well."

"The curse?" Jacob asked.

Joseph nodded. "Yes. I've heard different estimates, but it's believed that hundreds of people have died trying to retrieve it until the Staff itself disappeared."

"Wait, it's gone?" Gabriel asked.

"Yes, shortly after it was discovered, a group of the sultan's men went to, once again, retrieve and found it missing."

"Back to the curse," Naomi said. "What do you think it is?"

Joseph scratched his chin. "Do I think it's cursed? No. I think there's a higher power protecting it, same with the Ark of the Covenant."

"Only the worthy, huh?" Gabriel asked.

"Yes," Joseph replied, glancing at Jacob, "only the worthy shall wield the Staff of God."

9

Gabriel wasn't a scholar like Naomi, or even a mental sponge like Jacob. Gabriel's entire life had either been spent playing soccer or killing terrorists. He was here to support the Fehrs. He was their grunt. But he was very good at being a grunt.

He glanced at Naomi. He was *her* grunt. Like most people in his situation, Gabriel never had time for a relationship. Things were different with Naomi, however. The two of them were going through this together. It had bonded them. They all had bonded, actually. Even him and William were close, but more like brothers that picked on one another.

Jacob was the brother that everyone got along with.

William was the older brother that everyone looked up to.

Gabriel was the younger brother that annoyed the hell out of them both.

He took his eyes off Naomi for a second before Jacob glanced at him. "So," Gabriel said, "when exactly did Moses live?"

"Depending on the source, around 3,600 years ago," Joseph replied. "That's 1,600 years before even my time."

Gabriel let out a low whistle. The age difference between the two men was shocking, though, he guessed it shouldn't have been.

"And no one has touched the Staff since?" Naomi asked.

Joseph shook his head. "As far as I know, no."

She reached her hands over her head and stretched like a lithe cat. Gabriel did everything he could not to stare at her.

Naomi spoke again, this time, mid-yawn. "Sounds to me like the Staff is only meant to be wielded by Moses' bloodline, like how the Grail is connected to Jesus' ancestry."

"The line of Levi, correct, or," Joseph drew in everyone's attention, "maybe someone who's been preparing for this his entire life?" He looked at Jacob. "What about it, Jacob, descendent of Jesus Christ, are you not worthy to wield such a powerful artifact?"

Jacob sat back. "I don't know, am I? Does being related to Jesus make me suited for the job?" He tipped his chin at Joseph. "What about you? You're related to him too."

"No, it's definitely not me. I'm fairly certain I would've noticed if it were me holding one of the relics in my vision. I didn't feel it when I watched the scene unfold. I was merely a witness; three people, three relics."

"I'm confused," Naomi said. "Jesus and Moses were *not* of the same bloodline. Jesus was from the line of David. Moses was, as Joseph explained, from the line of Levi."

"Yeah," Gabriel said, "how does that work then?"

Joseph stared at the coffee table, his eyes growing serious. "Because it's what I believe." He looked up at his people. "It's what I saw."

"Oh, right..." Gabriel said, sitting back. He was way out of his league right now. So, he decided to just sit back and allow the experts to talk it out. He did have to admit, this was an incredibly interesting situation to be part of. Best of all, it was real. It was beyond amazing.

"You guys are forgetting something important," Jacob said. Gabriel impatiently waited for this *important* factoid. "Jesus was also said to be from the tribe of Judah."

"Of course, yes, the tribe of Judah..." Gabriel said, voice trailing off. "And why is that significant?"

"Because it fulfills an Old Testament prophecy that states that the coming Messiah would come from the tribe of Judah."

"Really? It does?" Gabriel asked.

Joseph nodded, pulled out his phone, and tapped. Five seconds later he read, "*The scepter will not depart from Judah, nor the ruler's staff from between his feet, until he to whom it belongs shall come and the obedience of the nations shall be his.*" He held up his phone. "Bible app. Handy to have sometimes. That's from Genesis 49:10, New International Version."

"All of this is the reason I'm so confident that the man who is supposed to wield the Staff...is Jacob. He meets the criteria—check all the boxes, if you will."

Based on Jacob's face, Gabriel could tell his friend didn't believe it.

Gabriel watched the Fehrs interacting with one another. He could see the wheels turning in both their heads. Jacob didn't reply to her. He just looked up at the standing Joseph. Their leader simply nodded.

"Having lived through all of this, I know from experience that it's one of the main reasons Jesus wasn't accepted as the Messiah by much of the Jewish population," Joseph explained. "It was downright blasphemous to even think it, let alone live like it. *I am the Son of God*! The first time I heard it, I didn't know what to think."

"Does that mean you could handle the Staff if you needed to?" Naomi asked.

"I suppose so, though I'm not really sure," Joseph replied. "Also, I would only act as a steward if I had to, and that's all. I would never dare attempt to implement its might."

That surprised Gabriel. "Why not?" He asked, forgoing his vow of silence. "I'd think someone like Joseph of Arimathea would get a free pass in all this."

Joseph did not answer right away. He turned away from the others and faced the fire again, keeping his hands in his pockets as he stared intently at the flickering flames. Gabriel watched as the man's shoulders rose, then fell.

"I fear I would attempt to make amends for my past—my misdeeds. As you know, for a number of years, I did not live a righteous life. I wasn't always a strict man of God." He turned around, but did not meet anyone's eyes. He looked past them, lost in a memory somewhere—some*when*. "Untold power in the hands of the greedy is dangerous. We all know what my greediness led to."

They did. Joseph hid the Grail away for centuries instead of sharing it with the world. He had the choice to heal the sick and transform the hearts of nonbelievers, even those filled with hate. Instead, he locked himself away from the world and drowned himself with regret.

"What about Arthur over there?" Gabriel asked, motioning to William. "He was a hero back in the day, right?"

The bigger man said nothing. All he did was give Gabriel a venomous stare.

"While noble in many ways," Joseph replied, "William does not possess the Holy Blood other than receiving it from the renewal ritual." He pointed at the Fehrs. "These two were born with it. It's in their DNA."

"It's why the Grail is mostly useless," Jacob explained. "The only one in the world right now that can access its power is Naomi. To Bailey, it would be nothing but a trinket to collect."

Gabriel looked at her, before returning his attention to Joseph. "Sounds like we need to keep the lock and key far away from one another then."

"That would be wise," William said softly.

The room went quiet for a bit. Gabriel studied everyone. The only one he couldn't read was his IDF and Mossad brother, Jacob. With him, it was never easy. Joseph began pacing again, William was still fuming over being called Arthur, and Naomi looked worried.

"And you know this'll work?" she asked. "That it won't kill Jacob like it did the sultan and his men?"

Joseph stopped and faced her. He removed his hands from his pockets and clutched them around his back. "I do not. But like I've done so many times before, I have faith in what I believe."

"Says the man that won't be testing his theory on himself," Gabriel mumbled.

The entire room stared at Joseph. He held up his hands in surrender. "Look, I'm not asking Jacob to blindly follow me. I'm asking him to trust in himself, in his father, and those who came before him. I know what I saw in my vision." He closed his eyes and took a deep breath. "I can see it now. Each key must have a human conduit. I'm not sure why, but they do." Joseph opened his eyes, meeting Jacob's. "I know that you are one of those keys." He shifted his gaze back to Naomi. "Just like you were always destined to watch after the Holy Blood, I believe it is your brother who is meant to look after the Staff of God until the time is right."

Joseph turned around and, once more, stared at the fire.

Gabriel looked around at all the worried faces—minus William, of course.

He shrugged. "Sure, I mean, what's the worst that can happen, you know, besides dying a horrible death?"

10

Naomi couldn't stop herself from rolling her eyes at Gabriel's comment. The longer they were all together, the more the guy had opened up to show his boyish sense of humor. Honestly, it was refreshing, to a degree. Everyone was on edge, and their mission was as serious as it got. In her heart, Naomi knew that the best way to keep the Acolyte from finding and entering Eden was to hide herself and the Grail away until her supernatural extension on life faded. Joseph had said from the beginning that those who have taken part in the ceremonial drinking of the Fisher King's blood would be given brief immortality, fifty years of invulnerability.

Joseph believed that Naomi could replicate the ritual if needed. Naomi wasn't so sure, but that was just a feeling she had. She'd been given the gift from Joseph, who had received it directly from Jesus. She figured that it had been diluted since she had not received it from the source. It was all too much right now. She pushed aside the "what if" and focused on more pertinent matters.

She looked at William and yet another thought popped into

her head. Joseph had also relayed that William was not part of Jesus' ancestry. What about someone like herself, or even her brother. Did being part of Christ's bloodline increase the length of her gift? Could it be for longer than fifty years? If it could, she was sure Joseph would've said as much.

Questions for another time, she decided.

"None of this even matters unless we find the Staff," Jacob said.

Her brother's statement produced a flurry of additional questions within Naomi's mind.

"Speaking of which," she said, "Joseph, you haven't yet told us what the Staff of God actually does. We know about the miracles Moses performed with it, but I'm guessing that's only half the story, isn't it?"

Joseph glanced away, looking very uneasy. "Scripture says that, at first, Moses wasn't an eloquent speaker, that he wasn't comfortable with public rhetoric. It's why Aaron was such an important part of what happened. Aaron served as Moses' prophet and was given the same abilities as his brother."

"Like turning staffs to snakes," Gabriel said.

"Exactly," Joseph said, "but still, he wasn't Moses. It wasn't until after the plagues began that we believe that Moses started to speak and act for himself without the help of Aaron, not that Aaron still didn't do some amazing things."

"Very inspiring," Naomi said, staring off. "A man who wasn't perfect in many ways still became synonymous with law, order, and true belief."

Joseph nodded. "Moses was an amazing man, one of the most influential people in human history."

"The other being Jesus," Gabriel added. The ancient man gave him a curt nod. "What fixed Moses' shortcomings?"

Naomi grinned. She had already worked it out. "It didn't fix anything, Gabriel. The Staff gave him the ability to win people over, to command their attention."

Her brother faced her. "Are we talking mind control? If so, this just got a whole lot more dangerous."

"No, no, no..." Joseph replied, quickly stepping in. "Well, at least, I don't think so, not in the classic sense, anyway. But, remember, the Staff was often described as a shepherd's crook."

"And crooks are used to herd sheep," Naomi added.

"Of which us normies are referred to as several times," Gabriel said. "Even I know that."

Joseph took a moment to collect his thoughts. Everyone allowed him to do so, staying silent and patient.

"Do I personally believe that the Staff of God is some science-fiction instrument used for mind control? No, I don't. But what I do believe is that it does, in fact, enhance the user's ability to communicate with people, to get through to those that do not want to hear or understand."

Naomi sighed. "Ignorance is most definitely bliss sometimes." She let out an exhausted laugh. "Look at us just a few weeks ago. We were completely unaware of this 2,000-year-old war until that inscription was found beneath Safari Ramat Gan."

"What happens if someone evil wields the Staff?" Jacob asked softly.

"Yeah," Gabriel said, "aren't the Acolyte heads all descended royal bloodliners too? Won't they also be able to use it?"

"Technically, yes, though I don't think God will allow it," Joseph replied. "Again, that's just what *I* believe. But that is precisely why we need to find it first. We can't take that chance. The power of influence is a mighty weapon, as we all know, especially in today's world. You've seen what the Acolyte is doing now." He motions to the muted TV hanging above the fireplace. "Imagine if they were given a boost. Imagine if their influence grew, became supernaturally limitless."

"Free will would go extinct," William said, speaking for the first time in ages. "Our world would turn into their *perfect* utopian society." He eyed every member of the group. "Where people like us don't exist."

"They really did influence the Nazi Party, huh?" Gabriel asked, dipping his head and shaking it. "The Acolyte, Bailey's great-grandfather, is to blame for a lot of what happened during the war."

Naomi had never thought about it like that, but she supposed it was true. If Bailey's great-grandfather had, in fact, been one of Himmler's closest advisors and researchers, then it would've been very possible for his beliefs to seep into those of what would become the SS. His core values had ballooned into imprisonment and extermination.

"That's what the Acolyte is trying to do now," she said, eyes watering. She gazed at her brother. "They are hunting down whom they oppose—those that believe something they do not—all in the name of making a better world. Bailey's great-grandfather birthed the Schutzstaffel's mindset. He instilled their mentality—their outlook on humanity."

"Oh, man," Gabriel said, face falling. "I think she's right. Their obsession with hunting and killing Jews could've been their way of trying to wipe out anyone who opposed the Acolyte's mission to collect and use the Relics of God. We already know that the keys can only be activated by a specific royal bloodline." He looked around the room. "What happens if they wipe everyone out…except themselves?"

William shifted uncomfortably in his stance. "What of the rumors about Hitler having a small amount of Jewish blood in him?"

"That had never been confirmed," Joseph replied. "But...as we've all seen, the truth can be swept under the rug when the man with the broom has all the power."

Jacob held up a hand. "Wait, are we really saying that the Nazis were really the public war machine of the Acolyte?"

No one answered, because they all believed it.

Naomi sat straighter, wiped her eyes, and took in their leader. "So, Joseph, where in Egypt is the Staff." The subject needed to be changed as quickly as possible.

Joseph released his hands from behind his back and shoved them back into his pants' front pockets. Naomi watched as sweat developed on his forehead.

"What's wrong?" she asked. "What aren't you telling us?"

He blew out a long breath. "The Staff is currently being watched over."

Jacob looked around, then returned his attention to Joseph. "By whom?"

"The Medjay."

"The Medjay?" Naomi asked. "A band of ancient Egyptian warriors protect the Staff of God?"

"Their descendants do, yes," he replied. "They settled around 1,000 BC. From what I know, they married women in Moses' bloodline, giving them the best of both; warrior and Holy blood. And their leader... He isn't overly fond of me."

Naomi sat back and folded her arms across her chest. "Why? What'd you do, try and steal it?" She grinned. Joseph did not. "That's exactly what you did, isn't it?"

Joseph looked down at his feet. "Who would've thought

they'd still hold a grudge against me, even after three hundred years?"

William stood and pulled his phone out of his pocket. "I'll call our pilot and get us underway."

As he dialed, he stepped back into the kitchen area beyond the fireplace.

"Who brought the Staff to Egypt?" Gabriel asked.

"Even I don't know that definitively," Joseph replied. "The First Temple, Solomon's Temple, was destroyed more than five hundred years before I was born in 587 BC. But, based on everything we've come to know, I believe it was the Children of Moses, a legendary tribe of Moses' most devout descendants who were said to flee Jerusalem during the Roman siege of 70 AD, when the rebuilt, *Second* Temple was razed."

"Wait," Naomi said, "so what happened to the Staff during the six hundred years between the two temples being destroyed?"

Joseph shrugged. "I'm not sure. I was more focused on keeping the Grail safe at that time. I was still newly immortal too. There was a lot going on."

"And the Children of Moses..." Jacob said. "Were they the result of the Medjay and Moses' descendants procreating?"

"Yes, ancient warriors and Moses' heirs—together." He explained it by holding up both hands one at a time then lacing his fingers together to become one unified entity. "And now, the same group watches over the Staff today."

Gabriel sighed. "The same people you tried to steal from."

Joseph adjusted his shirt collar, pulling on it slightly. "It was for a noble cause."

William returned to the room. "They were also once allies of the Army of God." Everyone stared at Joseph. William did too. "Until the first time he tried to obtain the Staff."

"The first time?" Gabriel asked. "So, three hundred years ago—"

"Was merely the last time I made such an attempt."

"How many times in total are we talking about?" Naomi asked, unable to properly comprehend what Joseph was telling them.

Joseph turned away from them. "Several, and, once again, because of my selfishness, I lost a great ally in this war. Now, we are just two opposing forces fighting the same battle against the Acolyte."

Gabriel wrapped his hands around the back of his head. "Imagine where we'd be now if you hadn't been so greedy?"

No one said another word. Naomi glared at Gabriel. He shrank back under her gaze, cleared his throat, and apologized. "Sorry…"

William checked his phone and frowned.

"News?" Naomi asked, seeing his expression change.

"Bad, unfortunately," he replied. "A storm is coming in from the north. All flights are grounded until it clears."

Joseph grumbled something in Hebrew under his breath. "Well, at least that'll give us some more time to check over our gear." He gave everyone a solid look. "See to your things. We leave as soon as Mother Nature allows it."

Naomi gazed out a nearby window. "Well, at least it's still early in the day. Hopefully, it'll clear up before nightfall."

11

Kirkwall, Orkney, Scotland

It had taken some serious digging, including a dozen phone calls, but Agent Frederick Hart of the UK Acolyte branch finally discovered a possible location associated with the Army of God. It was thin, at best, but it was better than nothing. The odd sales history of a specific property in the north of Stromness had caught his attention. Though it had no official link to anyone the Acolyte knew, it was still worth checking out.

There was a single portrait of the man who had supposedly founded Stromness, William Strom. Coincidentally, the man who had protected the possibly dead Daniel Laird looked eerily similar to the current Strom. He went by the same name too. If the prospect of immortality hadn't been in play, Hart would've thrown out any chance of the two people being one and the same. A distant relative, maybe, but not the same person. Yet, here they were, hunting the followers of the Fisher King, a legendary immortal royal who had watched over the Holy Grail for centuries.

Hart relayed his suspicions to Beta, who then looked into it further himself. Hart knew that the Acolyte had nearly unlimited resources. In this case, Beta was going to use his connections in America, specifically a loyal confidant within Prophecy Global Inc., to run the information through Delphi's AI system and see what it spat out.

The contact must be Bailey.

Hart still found it incredible that the founder of Stromness was still alive. There were also rumors that the man had once been the real-life King Arthur, though not the romanticized version of the man.

Fourteen armed men stood around Hart inside an undisclosed warehouse outside Kirkwall Airport, twelve miles from Stromness. Once they were ready, mobilizing his unit and getting them on location wouldn't take long. But they needed to be careful. Strom's people weren't pushovers. Two of them were very dangerous in their own right. Both Jacob Fehr and Gabriel Abrams had military experience. They'd each worked for the Mossad too. Naomi Fehr was a different story. Based on their intel, she was nothing more than a normal civilian caught in a shocking situation.

Hart remembered the first time his father had told him about the Acolyte and what they did; what their goal was. Hart had been a teenager at the time and had already been eyeing a career in the military, same as his father. And like his father, Hart had spent twenty-five years serving England as a member of the SAS, and later, their external intelligence agency, MI6. When retirement came calling, so did a high-ranking spot within the Acolyte UK branch, not that he didn't also serve them while he had been fighting for England.

With half the Hexad now dead, and with Beta announcing

his plans to shakeup their leadership structure, Hart knew that this was his time. He had faithfully done what was asked of him for ten years since retiring from the military. Now in his fifties, Hart could clearly see a path to the top, and he'd do so while standing alongside Beta, whomever he truly was.

Rumors had always swirled around all of the Hexad's identities. Even he had no idea that Delta, leader of the UK branch, had been Prime Minister Peter Hughes. The news had shocked him to his core. He knew the organization's secrets were deep, but he had no way of preparing himself for just how deep they were.

Secrets within secrets, he thought, closing out their battle plan.

He checked his watch. They'd strike when the storm was at its worst, using it as cover. He would've preferred it to be later in the day, but the cover the storm would give them would do.

"Remember, question then kill. In the end, there are to be no survivors, unless we spot Daniel Laird." He gave his troops one final look, then said, "Move out!"

12

Stromness, Orkney, Scotland

The storm was punishing, as were most that originated to the north of Orkney. Not only did the tempests bring strong winds, but they also unloaded torrential rainfall that routinely produced localized flooding. Luckily, William's estate sat above the rest of Stromness, in the rolling hills north of the more populated township. He didn't mind the cold, but he did despise being wet *and* cold.

He took a deep breath and relaxed, staring down at his favored weapons. Each were a marvel of engineering in their respective timeframes. Of course, he had Excalibur, or *Stonebreaker*, its true name, one given to it by its original owner, Joseph. The power within the blade existed because of supernatural forces and was nothing science could explain. The steel had been made by combining remnants of the bluestone quarries responsible for Stonehenge, as well as those from a Holy site in Jerusalem, the tomb of Jesus Christ. The results were something that couldn't have ever been predicted. The sword could, quite literally, break stone.

The blueprints for the design had been destroyed, per Joseph's orders, never again to be produced. Then, with great sorrow, he had ordered Jesus' tomb, as well as the physical landscape surrounding it, to be flattened.

William's other preferred armament was a SIG Sauer MCX. The 11.5-inch barrel, suppressor, and .300 Blackout ammunition, made the select-fire assault rifle the *perfect* close-quarters combat weapon. Because of the inherently "slow-moving," subsonic velocity caused by weapons of its nature, the only real downfall of the short-barreled MCX was hitting targets at distance. William had other rifles for that, though. So far, in his long life, most of the many conflicts he'd been involved in had happened up close. Like his choice in cars, William was always playing the odds. There were too many ways that the Acolyte could hit them. He could only prepare for so much.

The perimeter of William's property was similar to that of Joseph's in Torridon. Thousands of feet of iron fencing formed an imposing boundary protecting the land he had owned since the 1500s. The public ownership of the land had changed dozens of times since then, mind you. Selling and re-buying his own property over the years, using fake identities and companies to do so, helped keep the Acolyte off his scent. Newer additions to the property had occurred over time too. Sensors of various designs and purposes dotted the fence line, allowing those inside it a heads-up if someone were to cross without permission.

Once he had moved south to Torridon, his and Joseph's shell companies continued to sell and repurchase the property in absentia. But William Strom had always hoped to return some day, but never in his wildest dreams would it have been like this.

He had always figured it would be further into the future, long after the war between the Army of God and the Acolyte was over.

Not at its climax, he thought, sighing.

It was starting to get late and the storm raged on outside. The wind whistled past the home's thick windows and the rain pounded the reinforced roof. Nothing short of a cataclysmic asteroid or a healthy chunk of C4 could penetrate the sound structure. The heavy stone walls, along with the hidden steel siding, made William's home even stouter than Joseph's had been. The Stromness estate was rightly described as a fortress. William just thought of something. He'd had the upgrades done, even while never planning to return. That made him smile. Maybe his paranoia had been fair, or perhaps, it was something else—someone else—telling him to do it because it was going to be needed later on.

The wall above his bed clicked and slid down to reveal a collection of forty-two-inch monitors arranged in two rows of four. There were eight in all. Each one depicted a different section of the property. Right now, the upper-left monitor was going nuts, showing sparks at the front gate. Then the camera winked out.

William growled, leaned over, and pressed a speaker call button on the phone next to his bed. When activated, his voice would be heard in every room in the home.

"We have company," he said simply.

He released the all-call button, slipped into Stonebreaker's back harness, and tightened it down. Then he picked up his MCX and quickly looked it over. He ejected the thirty-round magazine, verified that it was loaded, and slammed it back home. William didn't bother with a plate carrier. As for now, he was still immortal. All he did was pocket a spare magazine instead.

William stepped over to the French doors leading out to his private balcony. He took one last deep breath, forcing himself into a very dangerous, mental state. William had been such a successful combatant because of his ability to remove his humanity while he was in battle. Some called him a *monster*, or a barbarian.

He just called himself *effective*.

He swung open the doors and stepped out into the gray deluge. He placed his left hand on the top of the stone wall that acted as a railing, vaulting over it in one motion. William landed thirty feet later, feeling multiple bones and ligaments break and tear. But before he could react to the injuries, they mended and he stood as if nothing had happened, because, as he knew, x-rays would show that nothing did happen.

He faced south, toward the front of the property, and his eyes narrowed.

"It's time," he said, sprinting west across the open decline. Fifty yards away was a wooded area. He'd use his all-black attire and the cover of the trees to his advantage.

It was here that William would begin his hunt.

13

Jacob was still downstairs with Joseph. The two men had extended their conversation, and had moved it into the kitchen for a late-night snack. They sat at the bartop, one built into the centralized, marble-topped island. Before them was a plate of meats and cheeses that both men lazily picked from. They were hungry, but they were also tired, despite the relatively early hour. Dinner was still hours away.

They had ended their group briefing, in which Joseph had revealed their destination. Once the storm let up, they'd be on their way to Alexandria. The location of the group's leader was all the intel Joseph had. Since his falling out with the group, Joseph had lost all trace of the rest of the Children of Moses—the Medjay—and the Staff.

"What if they don't agree to help us?" Jacob asked, popping a cube of Swiss cheese into his mouth. "Are we going to try and steal it?"

"No," Joseph replied. "We don't have the numbers. We'll need to convince them of the incoming threat."

Jacob popped a second cube of cheese into his mouth.

"Won't they see you as a threat too?"

Joseph didn't reply. Jacob knew they would, most definitely, see the Army of God as a threat to their prize. Who knew what would happen once the Children of Moses hear that they've mobilized? Things could get very ugly, and Jacob had no interest in getting into a second war, especially with people who were doing good. They weren't the enemy. Hopefully, they'd come to see that Jacob and the others weren't the enemy, either.

"How will we convince them, Joseph? What can we offer them as proof that there's something worse coming than us?"

Joseph took a deep breath, sat back in his stool, and lifted his shirt. "I'll show them this."

Jacob looked down at the ragged scar in Joseph's gut. He'd been impaled, just off center, by Mizrahi. While the lethal wound had healed almost immediately, it left behind something Joseph hadn't expected. A scar. Shortly after being stabbed, Joseph had nearly died. Even now, Jacob could see that his friend was exhausted. It was another side effect of not being immortal anymore. Joseph and William had talked about how they'd been able to go weeks without sleep. When they stayed awake long enough, their bodies eventually "healed" their physical and mental exhaustion.

Must be nice, Jacob thought, holding in a yawn.

His exhaustion was one-hundred percent mental. The stress of everything going on, compounded by the knowledge he'd gained, made it impossible to relax and properly take it all in. His mind was constantly in motion, like it always was, but this was something he had no real control over. This was more of a movie than anything real-life usually served up. The laws of physics were easy to navigate. Their battle had already neglected several of those laws.

Like Naomi now being immortal.

Suddenly, a soft chime sounded overhead. Jacob and Joseph looked at one another, puzzled by the noise. Then they looked up and waited. William's voice replaced the chime.

"*We have company.*"

Jacob and Joseph snapped their eyes back down to one another. They leapt out of their stools and ran for the main hall. Joseph dragged Jacob to a stop.

"What are you doing?" Jacob asked.

"They can't know I'm alive," Joseph responded. "I'm still dangerous to them solely because of my knowledge. If they find out, the ramifications could be catastrophic to our mission."

"I know," Jacob said, biting his lip. He wanted to rush back upstairs and grab his rifle, at the very least, but he also needed to help Joseph. Currently, the only weapon he had on him was the tactical knife sheathed at the small of his back.

This attack was not the war, one they'd surely lose without Joseph's guidance. "Come on," Jacob directed. He pulled Joseph's arm toward the back of the house. "Let's see if we can find cover out in the storm."

Joseph nodded, then it looked as if a lightbulb went off. He didn't go for the doors leading to the rear patio. Instead, Joseph headed for the sink. Jacob kept pace with him, and just when he was about to ask Joseph what he was doing, the other man showed him. He pressed on a seemingly random tile on the backsplash behind the sink. Instantly, a two-by-four-foot section hinged up to reveal a hidden cache of weapons. There were only three pistols and six magazines, but it was better than nothing.

Jacob grabbed one, looking over the Glock 17. It was an older Gen 3 model, but hey, a Glock was a Glock. He liked the finger grooves too. There were three main reasons that made Glocks the most popular handguns in the world: reliability, performance, and affordability. Jacob snagged two mags, swiftly slamming one into place in the bottom of the handgrip. He pocketed the other magazine, then racked the slide. It wasn't a rifle, but it was something.

"Let's go," Jacob said, heading to the rear doors.

"What about the others?" Joseph asked, loading his weapon as they moved.

Jacob looked toward the front of the house, not that he could see it from here. He visualized his sister, Gabriel, and William. "They'll have to make do without us." He tipped his head back toward the double doors. "Besides, just because we're retreating doesn't mean you and I are completely out of this fight."

"But I can die now," Joseph retorted, looking unsure.

Jacob slapped him on the shoulder. "Welcome to the party, my friend!"

14

While Jacob and Joseph had moved their side of the conversation into the kitchen, and William had retreated to his bedroom, Naomi and Gabriel had just been hanging out upstairs, leaning on the railing that overlooked the first floor. They talked about random topics, unconsciously getting to know one another better. Their actions inside the bathroom had been those of pure passion.

The way his hand had slid up from her hip and to her...

"Seriously," Naomi said, "you can't be—just no!"

Gabriel shrugged. "Why not?"

Naomi pushed herself off the railing and faced him. "*Temple of Doom* is NOT the best movie of the original trilogy! I mean, it's a great film and all, but it's nowhere near the best of the three."

"Are you trying to influence my personal thoughts?" he asked, eyebrow raised.

"Yes, I am!" she snorted. "Where's that damn Staff when you need it?"

They both laughed.

"Fine, Miss High-And-Mighty, if *Temple of Doom* isn't the best, which one is?"

She turned and leaned her butt against the rail. "Honestly, it's a tossup between *Raiders of the Lost Ark* and *The Last Crusade*." She expanded further. "Raiders is what started it all. The nostalgia oozes. But Crusade is special too, mostly because of the banter between Indy and his father." She looked down at her feet. "*The Last Crusade* was Dad's favorite because of that…"

Gabriel, still leaning on his elbows, reached his hand over to hers and clutched it. "Still hurts that bad after twenty years?"

She nodded. "Even more now that I know he was involved in all this. I… I sometimes dream of him and Mom being here with us, battling evil along with Joseph of Arimathea and King Arthur." She sighed. "You have to admit, it's all nuts, right?"

He stood and matched her posture, sliding in close to her. "Not all of it is *nuts*."

The corner of her mouth curled upward. "Oh, yeah, which part?"

"Your brother." He shrugged. "He's always been the levelheaded one."

Naomi gave Gabriel a mock look of hurt, then cracked a smile. "I'll have you know, that both of us are pretty damn levelheaded."

He raised his free hand and waggled it, keeping his left hand on her right. "Eh. You are a woman, after all. It doesn't take your kind much to go crazy."

She ripped her hand out of his. "Excuse me?"

Gabriel just smiled. He had an amazing smile. It reminded her of Indy's cocky-ass smile. The boyish confidence overflowed from him, as it did from Gabriel. His now beardless face accentuated it.

Gabriel's eyes caught hers. She locked in on his stare, and was about to move in closer, but something unexpected happened. The peaceful quiet of the home was interrupted by a soft chime. It was followed by William's voice.

"*We have company.*"

They looked at one another, then sprinted in opposite directions. Naomi skidded to a halt in front of her room and leapt inside. She continued across the space to the dresser running along the northern wall. Resting atop it was a Benelli M4 combat shotgun. She had shot skeet back in college, and had recently used an M4 during the battle in Torridon. But she would've been a fool to not accept a proper rundown of how to operate the semi-automatic weapon. Plus, it gave Gabriel and her some alone time, too, so she had happily allowed him to ramble on.

"Just point and pull," Gabriel had said. "Easy enough. It'll kick, and the reloading is annoying."

"You're making me more and more happy to have one," she said, grumbling.

He placed a reassuring hand on her shoulder. "Look, it's easy to fire, you know that. And that's what's most important. We even attached an enclosed reflex sight to it."

"English?"

He rolled his eyes and tapped on the odd-looking object mounted on top of the shotgun. "This is an EOTECH XPS2. When you look through it, you'll see a red reticle projected onto the glass in the form of a circle and a dot. Hover it over your enemy and pull the trigger."

"That's it?" she asked. "Just line up the sight and shoot?"

She didn't have any experience with red dot sights or scopes. This was all new to her. She'd only ever used traditional iron sights until now. And she had only handled a firearm once since her skeet days, and that was a month or so ago.

Gabriel nodded. "Yep, point and pull. It's loaded with high-power, double-aught buck. Each shell contains nine, nasty little lead balls that travel upwards of 1,300 feet per second. If you can get within thirty to forty yards of your target, it'll instantly be bad news for them."

"Shouldn't be too hard since we're indoors," Naomi replied, understanding the choice, "which is why you picked it for me."

He winked. "Bingo." His tone softened. "You have seven in the tube and one in the chamber, along with six more shells in the saddle carrier Velcroed to the left side of the weapon. There are four additional saddles in this bag." He held up what looked like an oversized fanny pack. "Buckle this around your waist. If you don't—"

"I'm screwed."

"More or less, yeah." He continued his training. "When you run dry, the bolt, that's this thing." He gripped the charging handle and racked it back to reveal an empty rectangular slot built into the right-hand side. "It'll lock back. To load it, flip it upside down." He showed her. "Take your shells and slide them into the loading gate, one by one."

"Seven plus one, right?" she asked.

He gave her a subtle smile. "Right. The eighth shell can be loaded directly into the chamber through the open ejection port. Once you do that, press this button and the bolt closes." He did. The bolt and charging handle slammed forward, shutting the ejection port with gusto. "Now, you're ready to rock."

He handed her the M4.

"One more thing." Naomi glanced up at him. "Shotguns, specifically one's like this, have very light triggers, so be sure that what you're aiming at is something you want to kill."

"So, what you're saying is, keep my eyes open and don't flinch."

"It's best practice to just keep your finger off the trigger until the time comes to pull it."

Naomi blinked out of the memory and grabbed the fanny pack-like pouch first. She clipped it around her hips and tightened it down. As she did, she confirmed that it held the four additional saddles. It did. The shotgun was already loaded—seven plus one. All Naomi had to do was depress the safety button attached to the trigger guard. Then it was time to point and pull.

She spun and found Gabriel standing in her doorway. He was armed with what he'd called a Heckler & Koch 416 assault rifle. Instead of having a pouch hanging from his hip, he wore a tactical belt that contained two extra, thirty-round magazines. The first magazine was already loaded into the rifle.

"You okay?" he asked, concern in his eyes.

She met him at the door. "I'll have to be."

Gunfire picked up out front. Naomi and Gabriel exited her room and dashed to the railing. They each gazed toward the front door.

"Keep to the high ground," Gabriel instructed. "Keep them pinned down there." He pointed down to the first floor. Then, he patted a nearby stone support. It was almost three-feet thick, and looked tough. "Use these for cover. And whatever you do, do *not* let them get upstairs, understand?"

He headed for the stairs.

"Where are you going?" she asked, panic laced in her voice.

"Over to the other balcony. We need to divide their attention."

Naomi looked back at the front. "Think we'll be enough if they get in?"

"We won't have to be," he said, grinning. "You know that gunfire out front?"

"Yeah?"

Gabriel continued toward the stairs. "Who do you think they're shooting at?"

Her eyes opened wide. "William!"

"Yeah," he said, chuckling. "Those guys don't know how screwed they are. You think they would've learned something from Torridon. He's still immortal, you know?"

"So am I," Naomi said proudly.

He paused at the top step. "Do you plan on testing that theory today?"

"You would," she said slyly.

Gabriel strode up to her and kissed her hard. When they parted, he stared deeply into her eyes. "Look who's cheeky all of a sudden. Concentrate your fire on the back of the group. I'll aim for the guys at the front." He kissed her again. "Please, be careful."

He spun and hustled down the western stairs.

Naomi sighed and softly said, "You too."

15

William knelt in the trees to the southwest of the front door. He patiently waited for one of the intruders to finish cutting the iron barrier with a blowtorch, all while getting pounded from above by the Norwegian Sea's finest. Orkney sat inside a 600-mile-wide gap between Iceland and Norway and absorbed the initial trauma of every north-originating storm to hit Scotland.

Water drained off William's chin. On the plus side, he no longer had a mop of cold wet hair to contend with. Gabriel had done an acceptable job. The haircut was even styled too. William had to give him some brownie points there. The man had also made it a comfortable experience, had only spoken to him when he required William's input.

Sparks flew into the humid air as the Acolyte agent continued to cut through William's front gate. The destruction upset him, but still, he didn't react. His plan was simple: allow them unmolested access to his property, then pounce from behind. William wanted them to rush toward the estate, instead of trying to flee back through the gate. He'd seen firsthand how effective Jacob and Gabriel were when in combat. William would, once more, trust that they could clean up whomever escaped his wrath here. Even Naomi, the academic, had transformed into a worthy comrade.

In a short amount of time too, he thought. If there was ever another woman he could grow to love, it was Naomi. But she was obviously adored by Gabriel, and she adored him back. William was happy for them too. He really was. Going through life alone was incredibly difficult. He didn't wish it on anyone, even men like Elijah Hirsch and Liam Bailey.

Plus, no one could ever truly replace Guinevere.

William had lived for a long time. He'd seen everything you could imagine. He had witnessed the strongest of warriors wilt under pressure. But he had also witnessed people like Naomi rise to become something infinitely greater. To William, a person's will—their determination and belief in themselves—always outranked their skill.

Always.

Belief was a very powerful weapon, for both good and evil. Strength of mind was paramount when attempting to defy the odds, like going into a battle where you were severely outnumbered. That was the most important lesson that Joseph had taught William. You could hack and slash through the enemy, but did you truly believe in what you were fighting for? If you did, you'd experience something that couldn't be taught. That same belief could, and almost assuredly would, do a number on the enemy's psyche.

Back in his King Arthur days, William had led a small uprising against a tyrant nobleman. His people hadn't been the best or brightest, but they had been the hungriest. They had fought, knowing that they could die swiftly. But they didn't. Yes, some of his men did lose their lives, but their will had outranked their skill, and it had terrified the nobleman's guards, men who, should've easily been able to handle them. But those guards had only believed in their wages, not their cause.

The memory of the heroic display made William smile. Up the driveway were similarly hungry people, though most were much more prepared and understood what was to come. That, in itself, was an invaluable advantage.

The blowtorch went out, and William watched as two men carried the cut section of iron gate away. Once it was dumped onto the ground beyond, armed men filed inside, one at a time. William could've cut down several of them with just his short-barreled MCX, but he kept silent and still. Even when the last of the men had crossed into William's property, he waited.

Their formation changed once they had all entered. Instead of continuing in a straight line, they fanned out. The frontmost pair took off at a sprint, bypassing the front of the house entirely. It was obvious what they were doing. Those two were going to watch the back.

Smart, William thought. The treed area behind the estate was thick, though still navigable. If someone did make it outside via the back patio doors, they could easily vanish into the wooded section. He grinned, amused at their assumption that any of them would run away.

Thirteen of the fifteen men marched up the sloping, gravel driveway, keeping to the lawn on either side of it. It ran straight and true for a hundred yards until reaching a circular parking area. The property leveled off there. As of now, it was empty, except for the car Jacob had used to drive to and from town. The other four vehicles were parked inside the estate's six-car garage.

William raised his rifle, eyeing the back of the lead man's head with the weapon's red dot optic. If he had been armed with a rifle better suited for long-distance engagements, William would've had a scope mounted to the top of the upper receiver instead.

Not that they're far enough away for it to matter, William thought.

He was an expert marksman, having honed his abilities over the years. Still, he preferred the up-close-and-personal-style of battle. He enjoyed seeing the fear in his next victim's eyes. William never got sick of seeing the look of panic on the face of the man who had just shot him or run him through. That was the barbarian in him, one of many flaws that made him unworthy to wield any of the Relics of God.

William enjoyed killing his enemies.

But he also overflowed with compassion, specifically for those who had needlessly died during combat. He'd seen his share of it; women, children, the elderly. It was their deaths that truly fueled his rage. The Acolyte had killed many innocent people over the centuries, and because of it, they must all die. To William, it was that simple.

He pulled the trigger, dropping the lead gunman with the single shot.

Everyone spun around and aimed their weapons in William's direction, but nobody fired. William could've emptied his magazine into the closest men, but that wasn't his plan. Fear was his plan. He stood within the sheets of rain, keeping his MCX held in the low-ready position. He stepped out of cover, illuminated by the gloomy light of a stormy sky. He kept his eyes pointed at the ground, controlling his breathing as he waited for the opportune moment to strike. He needed these men to panic.

"Drop the weapon!" one man shouted.

William gripped the rifle harder, but quickly relaxed. He decided to do it their way for now. He'd give these animals the illusion of control for the time being.

The MCX clattered to the gravel driveway.

"Turn around!" the same man ordered.

William did as he was told. He turned his hulking frame around.

"Now, place your hands on your head!"

He raised his hands and placed them on the top of his head. Then he reached behind it and wrapped his thick hand around Stonebreaker's grip. He slowly pulled the ancient weapon free of its modern sheath.

"What are you—? Drop the sword!" The man's voice didn't sound as in control anymore. It was precisely what William had wanted. If these were veteran agents, then they'd know who he was based on the weapon he now held.

"Do you know who I am?" William asked, keeping his back to them, amping up the men's stress.

"Put the sword down!"

He made a show of turning and facing them. "I asked you a question, worm." He still didn't look up to meet their combined gazes. "I said," his eyes flashed up to the eleven gunmen, "do you know who I am?"

Every one of them took a step backward.

William grinned. "You are smart to fear me. Hundreds of men, more competent than you, have fallen to me." He held up Stonebreaker. "Many to this blade." He hated using its more famous, fictional moniker, but he knew saying it would add to their fright. "Excalibur."

The three forwardmost men, glanced at one another, taking two extra steps away. Now, they were a good twenty yards from William.

A man in the middle of the squad pointed at the three people closest to William. "You, you, and you, do what you must and take care of him. The rest of you, keep moving."

The leader and seven others backpedaled for a moment. Then they turned and hustled up the incline. William glared at them as they retreated. But in the grand scheme of things, it was fine. Killing these three would still take a sizeable chunk out of their numbers.

William waited for the others to distance themselves from him and the three they had left behind to die. He smiled at them.

"What's so funny?" one asked.

"Funny? Nothing," William replied. He took a step toward them.

The three gunmen dug in where they stood and gripped their weapons harder.

"Do not move!" another shouted.

William stepped closer. "Why, because *he* said so? I do not bend my knee to filth. I only have one master." He stood tall and raised the blade in front of his face, turning it so he could see past it. "And even he agrees that sacrifices must be made to win this war."

"Sacrifices?" another of the men asked.

William tilted his head to the side a bit and replied, "You."

The same man, pulled the trigger, sending a round straight into William's sternum. His body exploded with pain, knocking him back and almost to one knee. He growled, tore at his ruined shirt, and slowly stood. His eyes were on fire now. Shirtless, he gazed down at his chest and watched as the gunshot wound began to heal. When it did, the bullet was forcibly removed from his body, dropping to the ground with the tiniest of clatters.

He met the three gunmen's horrified stares. They were visibly shaken by what they had just witnessed. William knew that most of the Acolyte's people blindly believed what they were told, and that very few of them had ever seen anything that held water. Faith was like that—on both sides. Sometimes, you just believed.

William raised Stonebreaker again. He, once more, turned it so he could see past the blade. This time he flexed the muscles in his powerful upper body. William snapped his chin left, cracking his neck. Then he rolled his shoulders, took a deep breath, and charged.

He was hit with a barrage of bullets by the men on his left and right. The center Acolyte agent, the one who had shot him previously, simply turned and fled up the driveway. William pushed aside the agony his body was being put through and continued forward with the sword turned flat and in front of his face. Once he was within striking distance, he lashed out, right to left, and struck the barrel of the left-hand gunman's rifle. The force was otherworldly, stunning the man as his stout, modern weapon folded in on itself.

William rebounded with a slash across the man's throat. He didn't watch the man's head as it was removed from his body, but his comrade did. William's back was struck three times, but then the shooting stopped as the second man's rifle ran dry. William continued his attack, turning, dropping to one knee, then swiping his sword under the gunman's arms and through his gut, clearing his foe's protective plate carrier by an inch.

The second man's eyes went wide and he dropped his weapon, clutching his stomach before his entrails attempted to spill forth. William left him to die and faced the third man. He'd only put another thirty feet between him and the fight. William judged his distance. He was roughly ninety feet from him now.

William raised Stonebreaker over his head, reached it as far back behind him as he could, then launched it, and himself, forward. The momentum sent William to the earth, but he landed gracefully and looked up in time to see the improvised missile strike the fleeing man square in the back. Stonebreaker didn't care what caliber of bullet the armor plating was graded to stop. It could pierce all of them.

He climbed to his feet, stalked forward, and plucked his sword free from the dead man's back without stopping. From where he was, he heard the front door of his home get breached. Gunfire erupted seconds later.

He locked his jaw, fought his rage, and broke out into a sprint.

16

Joseph was half-dragged through the back patio doors and into the storm. In less than a heartbeat, they were drenched and freezing cold. Jacob was taking no chances with his safety, treating him as if he were the President of the United States during an assassination attempt. In retrospect, maybe that's exactly how Jacob viewed himself. If so, Joseph respected the man even more. Members of the Secret Service vowed to protect their leader at all costs. Jacob seemed to be operating in the same way.

Between the intermittent gusts and the rolling thunder, both men heard someone approaching from the west. They quickly descended the steps down to the perfectly manicured lawn, but instead of heading north or east, and away from the incoming threat, Jacob pushed Joseph behind a row of hedges lining the raised patio. There was just enough room between the greenery and the brick facing for them. Not a second after they disappeared, a *pair* of voices arose.

So, there's two of them, not one.

Joseph looked to his left, just in time to watch two armed men slink past the other end of their hiding spot. Had they looked his way, they would've been done for. But they didn't. They kept moving, quickly talking about securing the back of the house. One man spoke in a crisp British accent. The other man's words rose and fell with the landscape of his Scottish roots. He was a Highlander, through and through.

"I don't see anyone!" the Brit said, having to talk over the wind.

"Back doors are shut!" the Scot added, likewise having to shout.

After a moment, the first man added, "I don't see anyone in the lawn, either!"

"You sure?" the second man asked.

"Yeah! There's nowhere to hide back here!"

In truth, there was. Joseph and Jacob were proving that now. But the two intruders had also been correct. Beyond the patio steps, there was only open space, except for a large gazebo built into the very center of the backyard. Beyond that was a wooded area, but the newcomers had no reason to check it. Not even an Olympic sprinter could've run that far in such a short amount of time and not be seen.

"Do we just stay here?" the Scot asked. "What if they made it to that gazebo?"

"That's impossible! Still, I suppose we should check it out, just in case!"

The Scot agreed with a soft, "Aye. Let's go!"

Jacob slowly sidestepped right and leaned out of cover. Joseph was impressed with how quietly he moved. Then he did something that shocked Joseph. Jacob handed him his pistol.

Joseph whispered, "What are you doing?"

He watched Jacob reach behind his back and pluck his

tactical knife free from its place on his belt. Jacob's eyes flashed up to his. Gone was his pleasant demeanor. His eyes were intense, and his face was emotionless. He now resembled a man on a dark mission; an assassin.

All Jacob replied with was, "My job."

He kept low and left Joseph's side. Joseph leaned out of hiding, but did not exit the space between the shrubs and wall. The sky was an unhealthy gray, but it was still plenty bright enough to see through the gusting storm. The back of the estate was lit up with artificial lighting. Even if it were dark out, it would've allowed Joseph to witness Jacob's lethal precision. He'd seen the former Mossad operative at work before, but never like this.

Jacob stayed low and crept forward, holding the knife in his right hand and in a traditional grip. Once he was within range, he launched forward and jammed the tip of his blade into the right gunman's unprotected lower back. Joseph knew from experience what a wound to the kidney could do, not that he had died from one. He had been stabbed there before, however.

Jacob drove the blade in deeper, shoving the writhing Brit to the ground. Then, Jacob spun on the stunned Scot, and dove headlong at him, flipping the knife into a backhanded grip. He bulldozed into the second man, plunging his knife downward and into the Scot's chest, perfectly impaling him just above where his body armor gave him protection. The knife tip punctured the base of the bewildered agent's throat, only stopping when it struck bone.

Jacob yanked the knife free and allowed the gagging, dying man to fall to the lawn. The entire attack had happened in seconds and without a single shot being fired. Then Jacob finished the first man by drawing the blade across his throat.

Joseph stepped out of hiding and made his way down the gently sloping terrain. He slowed as he neared Jacob. He was already stripping the Acolyte agents of their gear, now holding one of the most iconic submachine guns in his hands, the Heckler & Koch MP7. Both agents had been carrying them, and each weapon had been fitted with a suppressor nearly as long as the weapon itself.

Kneeling, Jacob blindly held up a second MP7, offering it to Joseph. He took it and looked it over.

"You know how to use one of these?" Jacob asked, standing and facing him.

Joseph nodded and handed Jacob back his Glock. "I knew Edmund Heckler."

"Really?"

"Yes. However, this was long before the MP7 had been designed." Joseph glanced away. "I may have helped finance his and Koch's early work."

Jacob shook his head. "Why am I not surprised..."

Gunfire erupted on the other side of the estate. Joseph and Jacob looked at one another, then headed for the patio.

"What do you think is going on over there?" Jacob asked.

"If I had to guess, I'd say *William*."

Joseph made it to the doors first. He reached for them, but noticed that Jacob wasn't following him. He turned to find him standing back by the steps.

"What's wrong?" Joseph asked.

"Think you can handle us splitting up?"

Joseph shrugged and held up his MP7. "I do now. Where are you going?"

Jacob thumbed over his shoulder. "To help William. Sounds like our visitors entered through the front gate. I'm hoping I can sneak up behind them and cut off any retreat."

Joseph waited for the gunfire to pause before speaking again. "Good idea."

"Alright, head back inside and see if you can help from this side. I'll go around front and see what I can do there. Maybe we can surround them and pin them down in the main hall."

"Good plan," Joseph said.

"And remember, you can die now. Watch for crossfire."

Joseph nodded. "You be careful too. You may not believe this, but we need you as much as you need me."

"Will do. See you soon."

With that, Jacob left, quickly disappearing around the northwest edge of the home. Joseph gripped the door handle and pulled it open, slipping inside to the sound of war. The heavy windows and doors had blocked the noise coming from the interior.

Joseph needed to hurry.

17

The front door exploded inward. Naomi peeked around her hiding spot, one of several stone supports, and spotted Gabriel tucked around his own support across the way. He looked at her, shook his head, and held up a hand. It was the universal sign for *wait*. So, she did. He was the expert, not her, though she understood his reasoning. Allow them to enter the home, then shoot at them from their higher vantage point, frequently referred to as "shooting fish in a barrel."

She did as Gabriel had wanted and eyed the rear of the group. Eight men in all came rushing inside. Two took up positions just inside the decimated front door and instantly began shooting at something outside.

Not something, Naomi thought. *Someone.*

William was most definitely causing these men some issues, and had no doubt triggered their hasty entry into his beautiful home. She gave Gabriel another look across the room. All he did was shrug. He didn't know what the hell was going on, either. She watched him stand, but he stayed half-hidden. Naomi followed his movements. He held up his hand, but kept his eyes down on the armed men, studying them.

Gabriel spread his fingers and began counting down from *five*.

Naomi matched his countdown in her head, slipping around to the other side of the support, and shouldered her M4 shotgun. She took aim at one of the men guarding the door, picking the one on her right. Naomi examined the armor he wore. It didn't cover the sides of his body all that well. She shifted her aim as a result. When her countdown hit *zero*, she held her breath and pulled the trigger.

Gabriel did too, but Naomi was too busy watching and reacting to what she'd just done. The impromptu doorman was struck in the left side, hip, and thigh with several fast-moving steel projectiles. He went down with a holler and an explosion of blood. Naomi dove back into cover as the men from down below retaliated and tore into her stone support. Luckily, it was as strong as it looked and it held up solidly enough. The biggest problem she had to deal with wasn't the flying bullets, it was the spray of jagged shrapnel.

The battle raging was deafening. Naomi slid down to her butt and took in her surroundings. There was another support fifteen feet to either side of her. If there was a break in the action, she was confident she could make it into new cover without getting hurt.

Oh, wait...

Naomi was about to make a dash for it now, remembering that she couldn't be killed. But that didn't mean she couldn't be hurt. Pain was something she wouldn't outwardly seek. Thankfully, she didn't have to make the choice herself.

William made it for her.

He charged in through the front door, sporting several ragged gunshot wounds in his shirtless chest and a feral, carnal look on his face. In one motion, he impaled the wounded agent, then lashed out at the second doorman, removing the man's rifle from his hands—and his hands from his wrist. Then, Willam stabbed the near comatose man in the gut and continued into his home. The visible destruction sent William into a ferocious rampage.

Gabriel must've sensed what Naomi had. He flagged her down with a wave. "Cover William!" he shouted, sending a volley of rounds at a pair of Acolyte agents.

Naomi followed his example and sent shell after shell toward a man cowering behind one of the supports. She didn't need to hit him. She just needed to keep him pinned down.

William had obviously understood their motives. He willfully charged at the men Naomi and Gabriel were focusing on and, one by one, he cut them down.

"Frag out!"

Naomi froze as a small sphere sailed toward William and detonated at his feet. He was launched backward across the room, crashing somewhere beneath Naomi's perch and out of her line of sight. As he vanished from view, Jacob stepped through the front door and laid into the man who had thrown the grenade with a compact machine gun. He attacked in the same manner that Naomi had and aimed low, peppering the guy's thighs and knees.

Naomi took aim and shot the same man in the side of the head. She turned her aim on someone else as the shell ended his life. Naomi ran for cover behind the next support to the north as another SMG picked up. The only person it could belong to was Joseph.

As the shooting died down, Naomi leaned around her cover and spied three of the Acolyte attackers retreat through the front door. She was about to shout and tell the others what she saw, but Jacob beat her to it.

"Let them go!" he yelled, aiming his weapon at the door.

"What? Why?" Gabriel asked from above.

Jacob looked up at him and dropped his SMG. He was out of ammunition.

Naomi leaned over the railing and watched as Joseph tossed his weapon to the floor too.

"Where's William?" Joseph asked.

"I'm here."

Naomi leaned further over the banister and watched as William limped out from beneath her. He'd already lost his shirt somewhere outside and his remaining clothes were now a bloodied mess. His right arm was mangled and barely attached to his body. She watched in abject horror as his exposed shoulder tissue stitched itself back together until there was nothing except undamaged flesh beneath blood.

Naomi shook, calmed, then headed downstairs. The first one that met her was Jacob. He gave her a quick hug then stepped aside and allowed Gabriel to embrace her next. He patted Gabriel's shoulder, stepped aside, and left them to each other.

"You good?" Gabriel asked.

"Yeah, I'm okay." She looked away from him. "I killed people. I shot that one guy..." she swallowed down her vomit, "in the head."

His face fell a little. "I know, but it had to be done."

"I know." Naomi perked up, but mostly for show. "Yeah, it did."

Joseph slowly walked around the main hall, inspecting the dead, mumbling to himself as he did. Naomi decided to give him some company.

"Something troubling you?" she asked. He looked at her. "Besides all of the death."

"Nothing new, no," he replied. "I just wish there had been a way to get through to these men before they went and needlessly threw their lives away."

Naomi looked around. "There is. We need the Staff."

"I know," he said, turning. His shoulders fell. "I know… We—"

Naomi turned and saw what had made Joseph stop. One of the Acolyte agents was lying on the floor, but had a pistol pointed up at him. Naomi did the only thing she could think of, she leapt in front of the now-vulnerable Joseph and was shot squarely in the chest.

18

Jacob drew his own pistol and shot the Acolyte agent twice. Then he dropped the weapon and rushed to his sister's side. He didn't care if she was invincible or not, he'd just watched Naomi take a nine-millimeter bullet to the chest. He slid in next to her and put pressure on the wound while she gasped for breath. She clawed at his arms, panic in her eyes.

Gabriel joined them next, knife in hand. Jacob removed his blood-soaked hands from Naomi's chest, allowing Gabriel to cut away her shirt. Both men froze at what they saw. Yes, Naomi had been shot dead center in her chest, but the gunshot wound no longer bled. They watched, stunned, as the puncture wound began to mend. The ruined skin surrounding it reshaped itself, returning to the way it had been before. Just when it was about to seal, a deformed piece of lead popped out and settled atop where the life-threatening injury had been.

Jacob lifted his gaze to meet Naomi's eyes. She was still in shock, having also watched her body's supernatural ability respond to the damage. She let out a long breath, then she sat up. Gabriel's hand found hers. Jacob took her other hand, and they helped her to her feet. Neither man let go of her until she proved she could handle her own weight.

"I'm...alright," she said. Jacob released her hand. She used her fingers to inspect the healed flesh. Once she was satisfied, she gave her brother another look. "I'm alright."

Jacob glanced over his shoulder and found Joseph staring at him. The other man gave him a small, reassuring nod. Then he stepped over to the group to check on Naomi.

"You okay?" he asked.

Naomi shrugged. "I guess so, but, man, that sucked."

He smiled, reached out, gripped her arm, and squeezed. "Thank you, by the way."

"Yeah, no problem." William joined them too, but was his typical standoffish self. She looked at him, touched her intact chest, and asked, "How does stuff like this not bother you?"

William placed his hands on his hips. "You get used to it."

Naomi slid into Gabriel's arms, and he held her like a lover would. Jacob stepped away to give them some space. Joseph and William did too.

"What now?" Jacob asked. "We obviously can't stay here."

"No, we can't," William agreed. "We need to be gone by the time the authorities arrive."

"If they arrive at all," Joseph countered. "You're assuming they haven't been swayed to standdown. If I had to guess, the next people we see here will be more Acolyte hitmen, not the police."

"Or both," Jacob added. "We are wanted terrorists, remember? For all we know, the UK is sending everyone after us and this fight just gave the law enforcement a verified location."

William softly nodded his agreement. Everyone did.

"What do you suggest?" Naomi asked.

Jacob looked behind him. Gabriel and his sister were facing them, fully engrossed in what was being said.

Gabriel raised his free hand. His other hand was wrapped around Naomi's back. "I vote for Egypt. Jacob and I have plenty of contacts down there if we need a way in. We know the lay of the land too."

"I agree," William said. He looked at Joseph. "It's time to go see Mosiah."

"Mosiah?" Naomi asked.

Jacob was curious too.

"Mosiah Fayek is the current chief of the Children of Moses," Joseph explained. "He is the one person that has the answers we seek."

"The location of the Staff?" Jacob asked.

"Correct, though he guards it fiercely, as I'm sure you've gathered. He would rather take its whereabouts to the grave than let anyone outside his people obtain it. They all feel that way."

"I get it," Gabriel said. "Better it be lost to time than in the hands of your enemies."

"Just like the Spear," William added. "Better it be buried beneath a mountain than in Acolyte control."

Another question was burning deep within Jacob's gut. "Why would he help us? We have nothing to offer him besides trouble."

Joseph nodded. "Quite true. But we've never seen the Acolyte *this* active. Remember, they think I'm dead, and with it, their quest to produce unkillable soldiers." He grew even more concerned. "Their mission should've died along with Daniel Laird." He stared at Jacob. "Yet, it didn't. Why?"

"He's right," William said. "They came here to wipe out the Army of God. They know we don't have the Staff, and with Laird dead—and in our case with Joseph now mortal—the Grail is all but useless to them. Why are they pursuing us so vehemently?"

"Because of Mizrahi," Jacob muttered, drawing everyone's attention. "He's been too successful. Beta is changing the rules on the fly. He's altered their mission. He doesn't just want the Grail, like Hirsch did."

"He wants to use the Staff to influence the minds of men," Joseph said. His eyes opened wide. "Which means he'll go after Mosiah next." He switched his gaze to William. "We need to leave, now."

William nodded. "Ten minutes." He eyed Jacob, Naomi, and Gabriel. "Grab your gear, change your clothes if you need to, and meet back in the kitchen."

No one argued, but Gabriel did have a question.

"How do we leave? I'm guessing they still have people watching the perimeter. We won't make it a mile before they turn our cars to Swiss cheese."

William grinned. "You'll see."

Gabriel sighed and rubbed his eyes. "It's always a mystery with your people, isn't it?"

19

They rushed across the back lawn, beelining for the wooden area beyond. As luck would have it, the rain had subsided, for now, leaving behind nothing but wind and thunder. It was slowly getting darker too. Gabriel was thankful that the cover of darkness would be soon upon them. It was much harder to get shot in the head if the bad guys couldn't see you.

"Unless they're running thermals or night vision," he mumbled.

"What?" Naomi asked, keeping to his side.

He shook her off. "Nothing. Just thinking aloud."

William was further ahead, carrying another MCX rifle with him. And of course, he had his trusted sword sheathed on his clothed back. Everyone, including Joseph of Arimathea, was armed to the teeth, body armor and all. The only traditional piece of military equipment they were missing were ballistic helmets, not that they did much against a bullet. That type of headgear was designed to protect the wearer mostly against frag, not projectiles breaking the speed of sound. Even a smaller pistol caliber, such as the nine-millimeter holstered on Gabriel's hip, could defeat most helmets.

Everyone's chest rigs were packed with three magazines of whatever caliber cartridge they carried. Naomi's rig did not have what you would call *traditional* magazines. The Benelli M4 shotgun wasn't magazine fed, like the rifles Gabriel and the others carried. In her rig were three, preloaded shotgun saddles. They were identical to the one adhered to the left side of her weapon.

Gabriel would've rather seen her armed with a rifle similar to his, but she had proven herself more than capable with the M4, so he didn't push for a change. Plus, learning to operate a select-fire assault weapon wasn't as simple as "point and pull." That was the beauty of shotguns. They were really *that* easy to operate.

But they do have shit range, he thought.

He watched as William disappeared into the tree line. There was no trail—no discernable entry point of any kind. And maybe that was the point. The trail Gabriel had taken—the one in the back of Joseph's Torridon property—had been cut and maintained, making it very apparent that it led somewhere. Its endpoint wasn't as clear, not that anyone could've guessed that the entrance to the real-life Camelot, the Citadel, had been through solid rock—through a mountain!

William's Stromness property wasn't that. This was infinitely more covert. He didn't vocalize his questions to anyone. Gabriel just fell in behind everyone and kept moving. All except Jacob. He had taken up his position at the group's rear. Jacob either led, or watched their backs, per usual. He was never asked to do either job. He just did it, because that's the kind of leader he was.

In Gabriel's experience, the first person to die in a squad, if something as tragic as that were to happen, was typically the men on the ends of the line. A sniper could easily pick off both positions.

But there was no sniper; no assassin wearing thermals or night vision. The five combatants vanished into the trees without conflict. Surprisingly, William ignited a small, handheld flashlight. Then, one by one, everyone else did too. Gabriel looked up, then back. He understood the man's lack of stealth here. The canopy was dense, and so were the trees behind them. No one would be able to see their lights, and that's if they even knew where to look. There was also little light being filtered in, making it all that much darker.

Gabriel respected William's confidence that they had entered the trees unseen, but his years of training and life experience had made him incredibly paranoid. He knew Jacob was thinking the same thing right now. In reality, you were never truly safe, just safe for the moment. It may have been a bleak way to view the world, but it kept people like Gabriel and Jacob alive. In their profession, if you didn't live that way, you were either a terrible spy, or a dead one. They continued for another two hundred yards before the trees abruptly ended.

The trees did, but the canopy did not.

Gabriel slowed, then stopped, admiring the ingenious camouflage. A large square building had been constructed with nearly zero space between its walls and the forest. An artificial canopy had then been attached to the structure's roof, making it seem as if the wooded area was whole and unmolested.

Sneaky, sneaky, he thought, letting out a low whistle.

"You like it?" Joseph asked.

Gabriel shrugged. "How can I not?"

"It was all William's doing," Joseph explained.

Gabriel gave the big man a glance. "Oh, never mind."

The big blonde didn't reply to Gabriel's playful jab. Instead, he headed for the only door in sight. There weren't any traditional hangar doors present, not that Gabriel could see, anyway, and he didn't have the luxury of scouting the area to confirm. There was no keyed lock or even a door handle. William slipped open a panel to reveal something Gabriel had grown accustomed to by now, a state-of-the-art palm reader. William pressed his hand against it. Gabriel was surprised to see his hand flinch a second later.

"What was that?" he asked. William removed his hand after hearing a click. Gabriel didn't need an answer. He figured it out on his own when he saw a small needle retract into the palm reader. "The door tests your DNA?"

"It does," William replied. "Can't be too careful."

"That's, like, being *really* careful, though," Naomi said. Then she quickly added. "Not that I disagree with your use of caution."

William pushed through the handless door, entering the dark void. A few seconds later, lights bloomed to life inside. Gabriel stepped through as rain began to fall again. He entered behind Naomi and ahead of Jacob, taking in what the building held.

"Um, really?" Gabriel asked, unsure of what else to say.

At the center of the hangar was an honest-to-God helicopter. Gabriel looked around, finally confirming his suspicion. There were no hangar doors, no exit large enough to allow the aircraft to exit, especially with how tight the trees were to the walls.

"Yeah, I'm with Gabriel on this," Naomi said. "I don't get it. How the hell are we taking off?"

"We go up."

William's response was as confusing as the hangar's existence. Even Jacob hadn't followed.

"Up?" he asked.

Joseph nodded his agreement. "Yes, up. Come on now, after all we've been through, you don't think we're just going to tell you without showing you too?"

Gabriel sighed. "Ever the showman."

"It's getting kind of annoying..." Naomi's remark made him smile. Jacob too.

Something else about the prospect of climbing in a helicopter struck Gabriel. "I thought you said it was too dangerous to fly right now?"

"I did," William replied. "Now get in."

As they marched toward the aircraft, Joseph produced a cell phone and quickly dialed.

"Who are you calling?" Jacob answered.

"Isla and Ian," he replied. "They'll need to come by and move the Grail back to Torridon for safekeeping."

Gabriel's introduction to the Scottish siblings hadn't been a pleasant one. He'd been knocked unconscious, dragged to, and dropped at Joseph and William's feet. The two were as fiercely loyal to the cause as William, and had been keeping watch on the area for years.

The last time Gabriel had been to Joseph's estate, the unrepairable sections were being cleared by construction crews. The Army of God members had also checked on the basement level, finding it completely untouched. It was there that they could store the Grail, if the need should ever arise. The secret entrance had been left intact too, so access to the lower level was still possible. The elevator exit, the one the others had driven a car out of, wasn't accessible from the outside. It was another of William's security-first contingencies. No access except through the entrance.

They piled inside the small-ish civilian helicopter and William immediately got it going. Once the rotors reached takeoff power, he flicked a red switch. A low rumble followed.

"No way..." Gabriel said, leaning right and looking up.

The ceiling began to open.

20

Silicon Valley, California, USA

For the second time in less than two months, the Acolyte had failed in delivering a decisive blow to their enemy. Yes, they may have possibly killed Daniel Laird in Torridon, but that was still unknown, though widely believed. They had also failed to retrieve the Holy Grail that day, nor did they retrieve it just now in Stromness. Liam, like Hirsch, had severely underestimated his foe's ability to counter and survive.

"*It's William, sir,*" Hart explained. "*He's too much for us. We lost four men before we made it through the front door! If we continue at this rate, we'll have no one left.*"

What could Liam say? His men did as they had been told and attempted to infiltrate and eliminate the remaining members of the Army of God. And like the Torridon operation, the Acolyte had lost more men than had returned. This time, only three men had survived, including Agent Hart.

"What about the targets?" Liam asked, moving the debrief along.

"*Took off in a damned helo shortly after we left. Saw it lift off from the middle of the woods at the back of the property.*"

Liam didn't like that. "Didn't you do aerial recon first?"

"*Yes, sir. Based on the pictures we have, there is nothing there except trees.*"

"I don't care how they escaped. All that matters now is that you follow them. They cannot be allowed to leave Scotland!"

"*How, sir? We don't have an aircraft in the area.*"

That was true, but a helicopter had limited range. They wouldn't be going far.

"Get to the nearest airport. They won't be staying in the UK. It's too dangerous for them now."

"*That'd be Kirkwall, sir. It's where we set up our field operations HQ.*"

Liam sat forward in his office chair. "Do you still have men there?"

"*Yes, sir. I left two men behind to keep an eye on things, but that won't be enough to stop them.*"

"How far are you from Kirkwall?" Liam asked, praying it was close.

"*Not far, 'bout fifteen minutes with good traffic.*"

Liam stood and gripped his phone tight. "Get there as fast as you can and delay them. They won't be able to takeoff right away."

"*Yes, sir. We'll give it a go.*"

"Do better than that."

"*Yes, sir. We'll stop them.*"

Liam expected Hart to hang up, but he didn't.

"Is there something else?"

He could hear the other man hesitate before he spoke again.

"*If they do make it out of Scotland, what's our next move?*"

Liam grumbled, but answered Hart. "They will go see an incredibly large thorn in our side."

"*Oh?*"

"Yes, this particular group has also been an issue for some time."

"*Like hundreds of years?*"

If Liam had been Hirsch, he would've already hung up on Hart. Alpha had believed in classifying select information. The field agents didn't need to know why, only who this group was. But Liam had always hated keeping the people doing the dirty work in the dark. It created unnecessary blind spots in their operations. Liam believed that the men and women on the ground needed as much intel as possible. So, he revealed what he needed to.

"No, longer. Much longer."

"*Oh. And, sir? There's something else you should know.*"

Liam sat back down in his plush office chair. "Yes?"

"*One of my people spotted another man of Middle Eastern descent with Abrams and the Fehrs. Could he have been Laird?*"

Liam took a deep breath. "Yes, it very well could be, which means you *must* keep them from leaving, anyway you can. Make as much of a mess as you have to. I don't care what or how."

"*Yes, sir. I'll relay it to the men. Hart out.*"

Liam hung up, winded from the conversation. The only plus to Laird being alive is that he was now mortal and finally killable. He could also possess valuable intel. But there was an immense negative that walked hand-in-hand with the good. If Laird could convince the Medjay chief to aid his efforts…

No, Liam thought. *They have hated that man for years. There's no way they'll agree to help.*

Another thought popped into Liam's head, one that could

allow them to cut the heads off two very annoying snakes. He'd need to make a couple of calls to make it happen, but if it worked out, both the Army of God *and* the Children of Moses would be annihilated from this world.

But we still need the Staff of God. Killing them won't solve that.

He closed his eyes and breathed, recalling why the Acolyte had been so successful over the centuries. They had always been experts on playing the long game. If they lost the ability to track down the Staff, then they'd simply keep searching. Eventually, after enough time and money spent, they'd find it. It was how they had discovered that Daniel Laird was also the fabled Fisher King.

If they couldn't stop Laird from leaving Scotland, then Liam would call off the dogs for a few and allow them to continue to Egypt. But for any of this to work, Liam would also need to convince one of Hirsch's contacts within the Egyptian government to help. Loyalty was like currency in the spy world, and just because Hirsch's contact was loyal to him, did not mean he'd be loyal to Liam. Luckily, Liam had an unlimited amount of money to bribe him with if the man decided not to accept loyalty as payment.

Liam also had something else on his mind. With three of the six Hexad leaders dead, did he really need the other two, Epsilon and Gamma? What happened if they too were murdered? Would the Acolyte fall into further disarray, or would it strengthen the only branch that really mattered anymore?

The American branch was powerful, and much easier to control since they operated through money and blackmail, not zealous beliefs. Liam did have to give it to the Middle Eastern arm, though. They had been the most dangerous for centuries. They had been living and breathing this war long before the

United States had become a country. But Bailey saw that as a negative. They were always so caught up in the past. Liam was solely focused on the future. He didn't care about the long-running Acolyte-Army of God battle. This war was merely a bump in the road. All he cared about was where it could catapult him if they succeeded. But to do that, they didn't need to eradicate the Army of God.

They had to beat them to the Staff of God. Then, Liam Bailey would become the next great prophet of God. And when it happened, he'd proudly show it to the world.

21

Kirkwall, Orkney, Scotland

Two weeks ago, Joseph had his pilot move the Graal Foundation's jet from the mainland of Scotland up to Orkney. As it turned out, it had been a genius move. If he hadn't moved the plane, Naomi and the others would've been done for. Getting a regular passenger jet off the ground in this kind of weather would've been impossible. But not your own plane. All you'd have to contend with is air traffic control not giving you the official all-clear and leaving anyway.

Not that anyone can really stop a plane from taking off, Naomi thought as they touched down. Landing during the chaotic weather had been intense. Flying through it had been worse. Thankfully, the fifteen-mile flight had been short and sweet.

Their radio was currently going berserk with questions coming in from the control tower. William ignored them, going as far as turning it off altogether. Gabriel looked like he was about to vomit, which was understandable. Naomi would've been in the same shape as him, but her healing ability kept her from getting that far. Every time she'd grow queasy it would quickly vanish, and she'd feel right as rain.

Kirkwall Airport wasn't all that big, so it was easy for Naomi to spot their ride, even through the cascading rainfall. The wind died down on the tarmac as they exited the helo and sprinted straight for the awaiting jet. Two men came rushing out of the tower, waving their arms, and shouting at them. The Army of God operatives paid them no attention and kept moving.

"They really don't want us to fly, do they?" she asked rhetorically.

Gabriel still replied. "Or it's the fact that we're armed for war?"

Naomi looked down at her M4 as she ran. "Oh, yeah. That too."

They slowed as they neared the plane. The stairs were already flipped open, attached to the inside of the side door. The door itself opened downward on powerful hydraulics. A lone man stood, slightly hunched, at the top of them, unwilling to enter the maelstrom.

The Army of God gathered at the base of the stairs before climbing them.

"Let me go first," Joseph said. "Andrew is going to want a substantial bonus for flying in this mess."

"Same!" Gabriel said, blinking the water from his eyes as it streamed down his face. "Oh, wait, I forgot, we aren't even getting paid!"

Everyone was wet and cold, even Naomi. But she felt different from what she had expected. She was uncomfortable, but she didn't shiver. She watched Gabriel's hands. They twitched. She felt bad for him. Even Joseph looked miserable. The only ones not outwardly responding to the conditions were Naomi and

William. However, even if William were mortal, she didn't think he'd react.

Joseph popped back outside and waved them up the stairs. "Let's go!"

Everyone pounded up the stairs and entered the warmth of the dry, airplane cabin. Naomi entered last. She gave the tarmac one last look before turning and stepping inside. William closed the folding stairs behind her. Gabriel collapsed onto a pristine, white, leather sofa. Jacob fell into a matching chair, but did so with less drama. Naomi was fine. She was still wet, but she wasn't cold or tired. Physically tired, that is. Naomi was mentally wiped from stress and worry.

She sat on the sofa with Gabriel to her right and her brother to her left. Joseph exited the cockpit and was replaced by William. It seemed that he would be Andrew's copilot on their flight to Alexandria, one that spanned 2,500 miles.

The jet powered up and they quickly got moving toward the end of the runway. Kirkwall's main airstrip was positioned in an east-west orientation. They were headed west now.

Multiple sets of lights shone outside. Naomi got up and reached to the ceiling for balance as she neared one of the jet's several cabin windows. She leaned in for a closer look and watched as three vehicles came barreling through a simple, chain-link fence.

"We need to move," she said, looking over her shoulder.

Joseph looked around. "We are."

She pointed at the window. "I mean, we need to move faster."

He stepped up next to Naomi and gazed through the window. Three black sedans came screaming onto the tarmac and were in hot pursuit of them.

"Aren't you supposed to be seated during takeoff?" Gabriel

asked.

As if on cue, the plane started forward, its engines powering up and pushing its weight. At first there was resistance, but then it became effortless. She sat in the window seat and tried to keep watch on the three cars. In seconds, they'd be free of the Acolyte's UK branch.

She watched as two men climbed out of one car and immediately shouldered a weapon Naomi recognized. They were famous all over the world.

"They've got RPGs!" she shouted, flinching when both weapons were fired directly at the jet.

"What?" Gabriel shouted, getting to his feet.

The first rocket detonated somewhere behind the aircraft.

The second rocket struck its rear landing gear.

Naomi, Jacob, and Joseph held on to whatever they could as the back-half of the fast-moving plane dropped to the tarmac in an explosion of sparks and the deafening wail of shrieking metal. Gabriel was thrown off his feet and disappeared out of view behind Naomi, not that she had her eyes open.

Everyone cried out. The plane spun sideways and continued off the end of the runway where it ground to a halt in the dirt beyond. The interior lights now flickered like the inside of a haunted hospital.

A voice moaned from somewhere behind Naomi. She climbed out of her seat and found Gabriel between her seat and the one behind her, lying flat on his stomach. She dragged him off the floor, an effort made easier because he hadn't lost consciousness. Besides being ragdolled around the cabin, it looked as if he'd avoided sustaining a serious injury. All Naomi could see was a busted lower lip.

"You good?" she asked.

He nodded. "Yeah." His eyes moved past Naomi, finding Jacob's. "We've got to get the hell out of here before they hit us again."

Naomi faced her brother, and the two men quickly rushed to the side door. There was only one positive thing about their crash. Their exit was facing away from the direction they had been attacked. William appeared next, half-carrying the pilot with him. He set Andrew down and aided Jacob and Gabriel in getting the door open. It screeched in protest, but nevertheless, swung open.

Thank God, Naomi thought. Being stuck inside the jet with the thought of it becoming a fiery coffin—a mass burial—gave her the willies. She didn't want to know what it would feel like to be burned alive, then heal, then burned again. Her skin broke out in goosebumps, but she pushed the dreadful image away, grabbed her stuff, and headed for the exit.

Shotgun in hand, she moved to follow William outside. He'd gone first to secure the immediate area. But Naomi stopped. She stepped aside. "Go," she said, eyeing the others.

"Naomi, no," Jacob retorted. "I—"

"Can die if you stay here too long," she finished. "I can't. Now, go."

Joseph shoved the two men toward the door. "She's right. We are at risk. Trust her, Jacob, Gabriel."

Jacob nodded. "I do." He helped Andrew to his feet and ushered the bleeding man along.

The former Mossad operatives put the pilot between them and rushed down the short flight of askew stairs. Andrew seemed to be coming out of it as he moved, which was good. They didn't need to be babysitting a marginally comatose adult. Jacob and Gabriel shouldered their rifles when their boots hit the earth, and they backpedaled away, spreading wide as they did. Once they were thirty feet from the plane they knelt and waved for Joseph and Naomi to join them. Andrew kept behind Jacob, unarmed and wide-eyed.

"Go ahead, I'm right behind you," she said.

Joseph swallowed down his fear and exited. As Naomi had said, she was right behind him, descending the stairs as quickly as she could. When her feet touched down, she swung her shotgun up but didn't find anything to shoot. The jet was acting as an enormous shield.

"Heads down and follow me," William said, getting to his feet.

No one argued with him taking point. Naomi was about to take Andrew's arm, but Joseph got to him first.

"It's because of me he's in this mess," he explained. "I'll look after him."

Naomi smiled. "And I'll look after you."

Joseph smiled back. Then, everyone fell in line behind William and melded into the terrain. Beyond the eastern leg of the runway, was a bountiful sea of lush farmland. Hiding would become easier and easier as the sun continued to set. Luckily for them, Kirkwall Airport was less than ten miles from the open waters of the North Sea, so keeping direction was a cinch, even in a heavy storm.

Plus, we have William, she thought. He unquestionably knew exactly where they were and where to go from here in the likelihood of an event like this.

Naomi couldn't believe it. *This* was her life now. Only a few short weeks ago, she was just an archaeologist for the Israel Antiquities Authority in Tel Aviv. Her life had been wholly consumed by the past, much of it the ancient past. Now, her life was consumed with the *what if* of tomorrow, but oddly, also the ancient past. It was amazing, confusing, and dangerous, all at the same time.

Would her life ever go back to normal? She doubted it, and she didn't have the luxury to focus on it. Right now, they needed to find a new way out of Orkney.

22

They cut south, through a footpath between properties. At least, that's what Gabriel assumed. There were no fences to either side of him, just tall grass that grew up to his shoulders.

No, not grass, he thought, mistaking the wheat for grass in the dusky light.

The rain had letup again, but had not stopped like before. Still, it was a much-needed respite. William edged southwest, through the wheat. Everyone followed him without question, even though it felt like a random place to enter. But it wasn't. Gabriel slipped through next and discovered a barbed wire fence. There was no gate in sight.

Gabriel winced when William grabbed the barbed wire with both hands and pushed it straight down. He tipped his head to the side, ushering Gabriel along. Gabriel carefully climbed over it, then turned and aided in getting Andrew, the pilot, over. Joseph and Naomi were next, then Jacob. When everyone had safely made the tense entry, William climbed over and released the wire. He didn't once look at his hands. All he did was wipe the blood on his pants and continue forward.

They crossed the farm in silence, but Gabriel had to know.

"Where are you taking us?"

William replied without looking at him. "There's an auto shop just south of the airport parking lot; directly across A960. We can find transportation there."

"You've really done your homework, huh?"

William shrugged. "I've had a long time to plan for something like this, in case it ever happened."

"Thank God for recon nerds," Gabriel said, grinning wide.

William stormed off, distancing himself from Gabriel. Naomi fell in beside Gabriel, chuckling softly.

"You liked that?" he asked.

She shook her head. "No, I was just wondering—laughing at, really—why you think it's a good idea to jab at a man twice your size, and one that can't die?"

"I've been wondering too," Jacob said from the back of the pack.

Gabriel gave Naomi a look. Jacob too. "Really? Oh, come on! He knows I'm just messing with him," Naomi was unamused, "doesn't he?"

"Why don't you ask him that yourself?" Joseph asked back. "I understand why you use humor in dire situations. But William doesn't. He's wired differently." Gabriel glanced back at Joseph. "Put yourself in his shoes. He's been planning for situations like this for decades—centuries even. If you were him, and his worst fears finally came true, would you think any of this was funny?"

"Shit." Gabriel sighed. "No, I wouldn't." He groaned and picked up his pace, muttering to himself. "I can't believe I'm about to have a heart to heart with King friggin Arthur, while on the run from an evil, global organization." He held his hand up to his ear, spreading his thumb and pinky out as if they were part of a phone. "Hello, cliché comic book storyline? Hi, this is Gabriel, can I have a moment of your time?"

23

Agent Hart's men had done well. Both rockets had been on target. The first one barely missed, and the second one hit the jet squarely in the rear landing gear, tearing it to shreds. That fact that either man had gotten close had been impressive. They had waited a few minutes for the battleground to breathe and regroup.

"Take the cars and check the plane. If they've escaped, form a perimeter; one mile in every direction. Do *not* let them slip through!"

"But, sir," one man said, "we can't possibly cover all the farmland. You've seen the satellite images. There are too many places for them to disappear! There are only five of us."

That was true. Hart and the two men that had survived the debacle at the estate had driven here as fast as they could and formed up with the two men watching over the airport. As expected, Hart had received a call that a civilian helicopter had recently landed. Their numbers had waned, but they still had a job to do.

Hart turned on the man who had questioned him. "I said,

form a perimeter. Shall I phone Beta?" The other man stepped back and shook his head. "Then do it."

"Yes, sir." The man made a circular motion above his head. "Move out!" He pointed at the helicopter. "What about that, sir? There could be valuable intel inside."

Hart gave the aircraft a long stare. He had some flight training. Maybe he could get it off the ground and use it to sweep the area from above.

He started for it. "Leave it to me."

24

A quarter of a mile later, William stopped, hearing something that bothered him. It was barely there, buzzing, floating along with the rising and falling gusts. If he hadn't been downwind of the airport, and the sound's origin, he would've missed it. The pastures were relatively flat here, but they were void of all artificial light. And as the sun continued to set, its occupants were becoming very well hidden.

William stopped his attentive march, removed a small pair of binoculars from his chest rig, and lifted them to his eyes. He focused the device and spotted *it*. Someone had powered up his helicopter. It was obvious that the aircraft was about to be used to hasten the Acolyte's search for them. William couldn't let that happen.

A pair of boots stopped next to him. He could just see their owner in his periphery.

"See anything?" Gabriel asked.

"Lots," William replied. The other man didn't speak again, but nor did he leave William's side. "And?"

Gabriel faced him. "And... I'd like to apologize." William's eyes darted over to him, but he didn't lower his binoculars. "I'd like to apologize for the way I've been talking to you. When I get nervous, I tend to joke around a bit."

"A bit?" William asked, looking through his binoculars again. He watched his helo drunkenly lift off. Whoever was flying it knew his or her way around a helicopter, but was no expert.

"Okay, a *lot* a bit. Look, it's nothing personal, William. I think you're a great guy. I mean, you're King Arthur, right? I used to love the stories about you when I was a kid. They were so unbelievable, and in the best way possible! By the way, was Guinevere hot?"

William became increasingly uncomfortable with Gabriel's display of honesty. He honestly liked it better when the man acted like a clown. Still, humility was an admirable quality. The world would be a much better place if everyone showed it more often.

"She was," William heard himself reply. "She was an amazing woman." He turned his head toward Gabriel. "Apology accepted too. But would you do me a favor?"

Gabriel stood tall. "Anything, my liege."

And there it is...

William dug into his pocket and pulled out an object the size of a thick Sharpie marker. He flipped open the top, revealing a small red button, and handed it to Gabriel. "When I tell you, push it."

"Okay... What's it for?"

William grinned, then gazed back through his binoculars. "You'll see."

Now, everyone joined William and Gabriel, curious what the pair was up to. He traced the movements of the aircraft, willing it to continue further away from any and all buildings.

"What are you two—"

William interrupted Jacob and said, "Now."

Gabriel depressed the red button. Over to the northwest, a fireball was birthed in the night sky. The flaming debris fell fifty feet, smashing into the empty tarmac.

"What was that?" Naomi asked.

William removed the binoculars from his eyes and pocketed them. "My helicopter, as well as the poor bastard flying it."

Gabriel looked down at the detonator, then back up to William. "Our helicopter—the one we flew to get here—was wired with explosives?"

"Yes, it was," William replied.

Gabriel's stunned confusion quickly morphed into childlike excitement. He held up his fist, extending it out to William. The other man rolled his eyes, but gave into Gabriel, and softly *booped* it with his own.

As expected, Gabriel created a series of immature, explosive noises with his mouth. This time, it didn't bother William in the least. He didn't let the man's over-the-top expression bother him. Gabriel had done the manly thing and owned up to what he does, and who he was. William decided that it was now his turn to man up and not knock him for it. Some people were just *different*.

"You two BFFs now?"

William and Gabriel snapped their heads around at Naomi, and before anyone else could comment on the brief display of brotherhood, William stomped away, grumbling to himself.

25

Even Jacob was impressed with William's preparedness. Jacob had always thought that he'd been an over-the-top prepper in his own life, but that wasn't the case with William around. He was the ultimate spy in a way. His greatest mastery was doing what he did, while also staying out of the spotlight for eons. Jacob was curious how many identities William had used since meeting Joseph.

Probably more than he can count, he thought. Jacob had also lost count of his own aliases over the years.

He looked up, seeing the first star peek through. Night fell fast here. The storm had all but dissipated now too. Flying out of Stromness was now a viable option, except for the fact that their plane was currently being swarmed by Acolyte assassins and in ruins. The prospect of finding safe passage was very favorable since the enemy had no idea where they were. Still, being on foot was a serious disadvantage. Eventually, Jacob and the others would be found. There were only so many places they could go without proper transportation. This wasn't a bustling metropolis. There weren't infinite places to hide.

"What happens when we secure our rides?" Gabriel asked, getting Jacob's attention back on the mission in front of him.

"We head into Kirkwall and make for the marina," Joseph replied. "There are ferries that travel between there and Hirtshals."

Jacob glanced at him. "Hirtshals?"

Joseph nodded. "Yes, it's in Denmark."

"We are sailing across the North Sea on a ferryboat?" Naomi asked, sounding as shocked as Jacob was. That didn't feel like a very secure way to travel or a practical way to disappear.

"We are," Joseph replied. "At this rate, the Acolyte are running out of men in this region. We need to do whatever we can to slip past them and get out of Scotland."

Gabriel scratched his chin. "I mean, yeah, I guess." He looked at Jacob. "Hiding in plain sight is often the best way to do it, right?"

Jacob nodded, but didn't verbally reply. Gabriel was right too. Sometimes not hiding, in the classic sense, was the best thing to do. It was one of the reasons they all got subtle makeovers, so they could hide amongst the crowds as if they were wearing masks.

"But first," William added, "we need transport into the city."

"Yeah," Gabriel said, "where's this auto shop you mentioned earlier?"

Jacob saw it. "There," he said, pointing ahead. There was an aura that stuck out against the veil of growing darkness to the south of the airport. It wasn't much, but it was noticeable in the dimming light.

"Are they still open?" Naomi asked. "I thought they'd be closed this time of night?"

William answered while also keeping them moving. "The

McBriars are widely known as the best mechanics in Kirkwall. They routinely work long shifts, deep into the night."

"You've met them?" Jacob asked.

"No," William said, "but we had Ian do some recon on them a couple years back and have kept tabs on them since." He looked down at his watch. "We need to hurry, though. It's getting late, even for them."

And with that, William picked up his pace. In turn, so did everyone else. Jacob, once again, fell to the back of the group. Joseph continued to help their pilot along. They needed to dump him somewhere before leaving for Denmark. Having him around was already a risky move, though a necessary one. Jacob had no doubt that the Acolyte would've killed him had they left him behind with the plane. But would the Acolyte just up and leave once they realized that their prey had left?

That's what Jacob and the others were counting on. Scotland had seen enough bloodshed in the last month-plus. The beautiful country needed a break. It made Jacob feel terrible when the people around his operations were likewise affected by his or his enemy's actions.

Scotland had been through a lot, so had Israel, for that matter. But the people the Army of God had killed would give the affected areas some relief in the long term. If they could rid the world of the Acolyte, the world would absolutely notice, but not as to exactly what had happened. There would be a respite, but would the innocents understand where it had come from, and who had given it to them?

William slowed up ahead. They had arrived at highway A960. A little further to the southwest was their destination. William gave the road a long look before rushing across it. Everyone quickly followed him and ducked into the brush on the side of the road as a random car whizzed by.

William faced the group. "Okay. When we arrive, we don't dawdle. We go straight in, weapons up. We need the McBriars to give us exactly what we want—and quickly. Understand?"

"Are we really stealing vehicles from civilians?" Jacob asked.

"Yes and no," Joseph replied. "I have enough cash in my pack to buy the business, let alone the cars we need."

"You're going to pay them off?" Naomi asked.

Joseph shrugged. "Everyone has their price. Just because the McBriars are successful doesn't mean they can't use a quick economic boost too."

"Let's move," William said, ending the discussion of the matter. This was happening regardless of whether Jacob liked it or not.

The next wheat field grew up to their knees and was flat. It cut down their travel time significantly. They arrived at the rear of the business in no time. Again, William paused.

"Jacob, Gabriel, with me," he said, looking back at them.

The two men stepped up to either side of William, weapons hot but fingers off their triggers. The next part of their mission was to be strictly a scare tactic. They were Joseph's shock troops right now.

Naomi leaned in close to Jacob.

"I'm not pointing my gun at these people," he looked over at her. "Doesn't feel right."

"I know," he agreed. "But sometimes we have to do things we don't like."

Gabriel leaned around William. "I mean, they *are* getting paid..."

That was also true. The McBrairs were about to get handsomely paid by them...after they held them up and stole their clients' vehicles. Jacob definitely didn't like this, but what else could they do?

William edged up to the rear of the property. All that was between them was a chain-link fence. He pulled a pair of wire cutters out of his chest rig and got to work snipping a flap in the barrier. After replacing his cutters, William peeled away the section of cut fencing and held it for everyone. Jacob gave the field behind them one last look before he ducked through.

Gabriel got down on one knee, eyes forward. Naomi, Joseph, and Andrew mimicked his posture. Jacob was impressed by the pilot's ability to keep his mind in the game and keep from turning into a blubbering ball of mush. Jacob also wondered if there was more to the man than just him being the Graal Foundation CEO's personal pilot.

Doesn't matter, Jacob thought, eyeing the grounds at the rear of the auto shop.

They knelt in a junkyard of sorts. Not only did the McBrairs work on people's vehicles, but it looked as if they also dealt in junkers. It made sense in some ways. They could strip the wrecks for parts and sell them, or possibly install them into the cars they worked on. New parts were expensive. It wouldn't have shocked Jacob to learn that the McBrairs offered used parts at discounted prices. Orkney wasn't exactly low class, but nor was it all that ritzy. Money was bound to be hard to come by for some.

William waved them forward. Jacob and Gabriel moved swiftly alongside him. Everyone kept their weapons visible, but they kept them aimed at the ground. Music could be heard somewhere inside the garage. The building was metal and perfectly suitable to store a small plane, or in this case, house the inner workings of a family-owned auto shop.

They followed the music and soon heard voices. William

slowed and straightened his hunched posture. He stepped into the main building, immediately getting a reaction out of the individuals inside.

"Who are you?" one man asked.

Jacob entered next.

Then Gabriel.

There were three men, all around Jacob's age, ranging from their mid-to-late thirties. They looked nearly identical except for their subtle age differences. Jacob figured they had to be brothers. Each one of them eyed the weapons being carried. Neither asked another question about who had just arrived uninvited, or why they were here. They each slowly raised their hands and took a step back.

Joseph stepped around Jacob, Gabriel, and William, putting on his perfected charm.

"Gentlemen, good evening. We are in need of transportation, and we've selected your fine establishment to acquire it."

"You want to steal our cars?" the middle, older local asked.

Joseph shrugged. "We need cars, yes. But I never said they have to be yours."

The trio looked at one another. The guy in the middle shrugged. "Alright. Sure. Just don't do anything rash with those, okay?"

This was the part that Jacob hated. These men were scared for their lives even though they truly had nothing to worry about. Their lives were not in any danger.

Joseph stepped closer to them. Jacob realized that he had no weapon visible. The only thing he had in his hands was his backpack. He slowly unzipped it and reached inside. He stopped three feet from the cautious McBriars.

"For the trouble," Joseph said, pulling out a thick stack of bundled bills. He held it out to the brothers. All three of the McBriars just stood there and stared at the money. Jacob had no idea how much they were being given, but it must've been a fortune to them considering how wide their eyes had gotten. "Go on, take it. No strings attached."

The middle brother carefully reached for the money. He took it and looked up at Joseph. "Besides the vehicles you've requested."

Joseph smiled. "Naturally. We don't mean to cause problems. We are just passing through, and in a bit of a hurry."

The elder brother glanced at the youngest one. "Give them what they want. Quickly."

"In good condition too," Gabriel added. "We can't be breaking down a mile out."

The third McBriar gazed at the cash, then back to his older brother. "What will we tell the cars' owners?"

"The truth," Joseph replied, "well, part of it. You'll contact them and the authorities and tell everyone that they were stolen in the middle of the night after you closed for the evening." He reached into his bag and produced another fat stack of bills. "You'll, of course, leave our involvement out, yes?"

The younger brother returned with two sets of keys, skidding to a halt when he saw the second stack of money. The older McBriar snagged the keys away from his frozen sibling and traded them for the second stack of cash.

He looked up at Joseph. "Who was where?"

Joseph gave him a wink. "Exactly. Goodnight, gentlemen." He tossed a key to Jacob. "Let's go." He stopped after a step. "Oh, where are the vehicles?"

"Out front," the older brother replied. "Can't miss them."

Naomi gave them a small wave before joining the others in

their retreat. "Sorry about this."

The trio was lost in thought, gazing down at the twin bundles of cash they had just received. The older one blindly waved in her direction. "Yeah, n-no problem. Happy we could help."

I bet, Jacob thought, rolling his eyes as he hurried along with his sister. "It's amazing what money can do to some people."

"All people," Gabriel added. "Everyone has their price."

Jacob wasn't so sure about that, but he did believe that most people did, in fact, have a threshold they wouldn't cross...until the right offer was made.

They rushed outside. Jacob unlocked the silver SUV with the key fob and climbed in the driver's seat. Gabriel joined him up front on the passenger side, and Naomi slid into the backseat. She'd stayed mostly quiet during the group's encounter with the McBriars, which was expected. Jacob was happy that she'd stayed out of it too. The less she got herself involved in any and all illicit activities the better.

Any more than she already has.

William drove Joseph and Andrew. He backed out of his parking space first and led the way. The later hour gave them the road mostly to themselves. As they traveled north, up to A960, Jacob took in the multiple sources of light radiating from the runway. Their plane was still on fire, spreading up into the fuselage now. There were also the lights of fireteams, he could barely see the people from here, but he knew they'd be furiously attempting to put out the blaze before it could get even worse. Then there was their helicopter.

What a day.

Gabriel fiddled with the GPS, pulling up their destination, Kirkwall Marina. Jacob gave him a questioning look. "What?" Gabriel asked. "It's not like you know where you're going."

Jacob took a left onto A960, keeping pace with William. He relented, agreeing with Gabriel. Jacob planned on sticking to William's bumper, but knew that they could also get separated. They could also have a need to separate should something unfortunate happen, like being discovered by the authorities.

"How far is it?" Naomi asked from behind.

Gabriel twisted his body around. "About four miles."

"Oh," she said, "well, that's not bad."

Jacob looked at her in his overhead mirror, not feeling as optimistic. "A lot can happen in four miles, Nae."

"What does that mean?" she asked.

Gabriel looked at them both then sat forward. "It means we should all buckle up," he spun around and gave her a wink, "just in case." He looked at Jacob next. "It's the law, you know?"

26

Naomi was thankful that the drive to the marina had been short and uneventful. No one had followed them, police or otherwise. It seemed that the McBriars had kept their word and had not called the "theft" in. Not right away, anyway.

Jacob followed William into the parking lot at the front of the Kirkwall Marina. The sun was almost fully set now. Naomi hoped the ferries were still running. She voiced her concern.

"Think they'll even be a ferry operating right now?"

Her brother pulled into a spot a few down from William, threw the vehicle into park, then turned and faced her. "Not sure, honestly. Some of these lines run after dark. Some don't."

Gabriel spun around and looked at them both. "Yeah. I think we'll be okay, though."

"What makes you say that?" she asked.

He shrugged. "Why would Joseph and William bring us here if there was no ferry?"

Naomi hadn't thought about it that way. They've seen, firsthand, how prepared William had been with everything so far. It'd make little sense for him not to know the ferry schedule too. Coming here, and finding that there'd be no transportation, would've been a serious blunder on the part of someone that never seemed to blunder.

That made her relax some.

The group linked up, even Andrew the pilot. It looked as if he was coming with them. It made sense since he had been seen with them, even before the plane had been RPG'd. Naomi looked around, happy to see very little movement around them. A few people were meandering about. Most were headed toward a sign that read "Kirkwall Orkney Ferry Terminal."

Well, that's a good sign, she thought, no pun intended.

Seeing several people heading for the dock must've meant there was one coming in or getting ready to board. But there was still something they needed to do. She took in each member of their group and confirmed that no one was armed. Metal detectors were common, even in places like this, especially when international travel was involved. They would be making this trip weaponless and would be incredibly vulnerable.

"What do we do with our gear?" she asked, visualizing the trunkful.

"Nothing we can do," William replied.

Gabriel's right eyebrow raised. "What about Excalibur? You aren't going to leave it, are you?"

William snorted a laugh. "Obviously not." He turned and popped his vehicle's hatch. He reached inside and removed a rectangular, metallic case. There was no doubt that it contained his prized weapon.

"How are you going to get it aboard?" Jacob asked, folding his arms across his chest. Naomi was curious too.

William dug into his pocket and removed a billfold. "With this." He set down his case and plucked free a plastic ID card.

Naomi took it and looked it over. "Patrick Burke of the Scottish History Society?"

William grinned and slipped into a flawless Scottish accent. "I'm hoping a Danish historian mate of mine can help me properly date this extremely rare artifact."

"Impressive, once again," Gabriel said.

"Yeah," Naomi agreed, "I'm honestly waiting for the time you don't have a plan for something."

William's face hardened as he took the ID card back. "It's coming." He grabbed a duffle from the open hatch, dug into it, and produced a handful of phones, handing one to everyone. She'd been around this group long enough to know that they were untraceable burner phones. "Take these, just in case."

Naomi knew "It's coming" was referring to dealing with the Children of Moses. That was something no one could plan for. She figured they'd either agree to help them, turn them away, or the more likely outcome was that a fight would breakout and people would die.

"Any word from Ian and Isla?" Jacob asked, looking at Joseph.

"Yes, they messaged me on the drive here. They're already on their way to retrieve the Grail."

The group started for the dock, heading toward the sign for the ferry terminal. The wind was heavily laced with moisture, causing the chill within to glue itself to Naomi's skin.

"You okay?" Gabriel asked, nudging her with his elbow.

She nodded. "Yeah. The, uh, chills come in waves. I can feel them, but then they quickly vanish. Then, I feel warm again until I get cold again."

He cocked his head to the side as they continued to follow William. "You are one confusing woman, Naomi Fehr."

She looked off. "Yeah, I know." Her eyes landed on Joseph. "Are you sure the Grail is safe in Stromness?"

He nodded. "Yes. Since the police didn't show up shortly after the onset, I'd wager they were told to standdown by another party."

"Just like in Torridon," Jacob muttered. The comment was more to himself than anyone. Naomi could see that he was lost in his own head, attempting to put everything together in a way that was manageable and made more sense.

"The Acolyte?" Naomi asked.

Joseph shrugged. "Who else could it be?"

"I don't know, you?"

He smiled. "That would've been a smart thing to do, but no, it wasn't me."

Gabriel stepped into their conversation with a question of his own.

"You can do that—just like that?"

Joseph scratched his head. "If you know who to call, yes. It depends on the city too. Small towns like Torridon, Stromness, and even Kirkwall make it easy to be able to manipulate people when the right pressure is applied."

"You'd threaten them?" Gabriel asked, looking as stunned as Naomi was.

Joseph shook his head. "No, no, no..." That got a groan out of William. "Well, it wouldn't be ideal. Remember, whether you like it or not, money can move mountains. Wealth is nothing but a tool. It still needs to be used wisely, though."

"Like paying people off?" Gabriel asked.

Joseph's reply was quick. "If necessary, absolutely. How do you think I got things done 2,000 years ago? As you can clearly see, I'm not a warrior. I needed to do things differently than

William would in the same situation."

"Mob boss with a heart of gold, right?" Naomi asked, glancing at Joseph, then Gabriel.

"Right," Joseph replied.

Gabriel frowned. "Stealing my lines now, are you?"

She couldn't hold back her smile. "It's not theft if you respect it. I think it's called *admiration*."

"Smartass…" Gabriel replied, voice trailing off. "What happens if someone can't be bought? What do you do then?"

Joseph looked down at his feet, then stopped as they arrived at the terminal building. "You do whatever has to be done to succeed, preferably without involving the loss of a life."

"What happens if even that can't be avoided?" Naomi asked softly.

Joseph didn't answer the question. He simply said, "Excuse me, and entered the front door of the terminal."

Naomi had received the message loud and clear. She knew that Joseph hadn't always been an honorable, clean man throughout his long life. He had his regrets. Most were things he'd never share with even his closest allies. That was the worst thing when it came to immortality. Someone like Joseph, even William, had to live with their mistakes for much longer than the blink of an existence most humans were given. William had dealt with it better, but he was still much younger than Joseph. Plus, William had always been a fighter. His mentality had been different from the onset. William had leaned into the life, quickly accepting it was who he was.

The same thing had made Joseph bitter beyond belief.

Naomi wasn't sure how much time had passed when Joseph exited the ferry terminal. When she looked up from her feet, she spotted the watercraft pulling in, then heard the blast of its horn.

Like a lot of ferries she'd been on, this one featured twin loading ramps, one on the bow and the other on the stern. It also sported two levels. Both were fully enclosed to protect passengers from the harsh elements of the North Sea.

Joseph handed tickets to everyone. The group headed out to the dock and fell in line behind the other people they had seen earlier. Naomi watched her brother and Gabriel closely. Neither were focused on the ferry like she had been. They were eyeballing the people ahead of them.

The life of a spy, she thought. Naomi appreciated their paranoia. It was one hundred percent warranted. *Better to be paranoid than oblivious*, she decided. She looked over her shoulder and watched as two women stepped up behind them. Neither looked dangerous nor intimidating. Still, she'd be wary of them until they proved her otherwise.

The ferry's platform banged down to the dock and a lone deckhand ushered everyone aboard, checking tickets, passports, and suspicious items as he did. He even had a security wand in his hand, not that he used it very effectively. She could tell that he wasn't all that worried about what the passengers were carrying. That told Naomi that he'd been doing this job for a long time. Or perhaps it's that he was new and just didn't give a shit.

As expected, the local asked to inspect William's metal case. William happily obliged, quickly showing the man his ID too.

"Scottish History Society," the man said. "You do great work."

William nodded as the deckhand stepped aside and let him pass. Everyone else was given a quick wave of his wand, as well as a half-glance at their falsified passports, before being allowed entry.

"Good evening, miss," he said, smiling at Naomi.

"Hello," she said. "I bet you guys are happy the storm let up, huh?"

Oddly, the man laughed. His next words, made Naomi smile. "Nah, that was nothing compared to the things we've seen over the years."

So, he isn't new, she thought.

Naomi continued past him but was stopped. "Might I suggest the second level, miss. It's much warmer upstairs."

Naomi glanced over her shoulder and smiled. "Thank you. I appreciate that."

Naomi really did love this part of the world. Too bad she'd been a key part of its recent destruction. She slid around everyone and headed upstairs.

"Where are you going?" Jacob asked.

Naomi turned and tipped her chin to the deckhand. "He said it'd be warmer upstairs." She took in the group. "I don't know about you, but I'm sick of being cold and wet."

"Says the immortal," Gabriel mumbled under his breath.

Naomi just rolled her eyes and continued upstairs, smiling to herself when she heard the others immediately follow her. She headed around to the bow of the ferry, which was about to magically transform into its stern thanks to its double-endedness. Once everyone was aboard that was coming aboard, the ramp was lifted and the ferry began its journey in the opposite direction, sailing without having to turn around.

The six travelers fell into a pair of bench seats that faced one another, but they stayed silent.

Naomi sat between her brother and Gabriel. Having them so close to her gave her comfort, like a warm blanket on a chilly evening. Across from her, Joseph sat in the middle of William and Andrew. Everyone looked fried, even the usually unflappable William Strom.

Gabriel was the first to speak. Naomi wasn't prepared for what came out of his mouth. "Sorry about your home, William."

The bigger man looked up from his feet and eyed Gabriel. After a short stare, he gave Gabriel a nod of appreciation.

"Yeah," Jacob said, sitting back. "Ever since we showed up at your door, you two have done nothing but suffer."

Joseph shrugged it away, but Naomi could clearly see the emotion on his face. It had pained him to see his Torridon home destroyed. And it had deeply hurt William to watch his estate shot up by Acolyte thugs.

Naomi also sat back, finding comfort in her brother's arm as it wrapped around her shoulder. Gabriel's hand slid atop her leg and found her hand. She needed both of them a lot right now.

"We sincerely apologize," she said.

Joseph smiled at her. "It's the fight we chose, Naomi. Jacob, Gabriel, we've known this day would eventually come." He sat forward, elbows on his knees. "We knew our lives would be thrown into disarray at some point in the future, and with the way the world has developed around us, we knew it was coming soon." He folded his hands. "Evil has taken the hearts of many. It was only a matter of time until it organized and made a move on us."

"You believe you're a shield for good—that you represent the world's light?" Gabriel asked.

There was no humor or slyness in his voice. He was genuinely curious. Naomi was too. It was a subject they had yet to cover. Being a close confidant of Jesus Christ should've made anyone a warrior for good in their own personal life and in their communities, but did it also make them a global warrior too? If the Army of God failed and were wiped from the Earth, was evil guaranteed to prevail, even without the Relics of God?

"Did you know that I did not witness Christ's resurrection?"

Joseph's reply threw everyone off, even William. Poor Andrew just sat back and listened. Whether he knew who Joseph really was or not, was now out the window. Now, he knew.

Naomi shrugged. "There's very little written about you at all, but I'm actually a little surprised you weren't there."

"I assumed you were," Jacob added.

Joseph shook his head. "No. As soon as we entombed him, I fled north."

"With the Grail?" Gabriel asked.

"Yes, with the Grail, and my...newfound gift." He looked away. "I panicked. I didn't know what was going on, but I knew I had to get myself, and the Grail, as far away from Jerusalem as possible." He sat back. "It took several years for the news to reach me that Jesus had risen and then ascended to Heaven."

"I'm sorry to hear that you missed seeing your friend again," Naomi said.

Joseph smiled softly. "Me too. But it was then that I realized that my life wasn't one that was meant to build the Church, like his disciples were charged with doing. I was meant to guard the Grail and the Holy Blood." He looked at Gabriel and finally answered his question. "I was meant to be its shield. The Relics of God represent the light, not the people involved with them."

"You successfully shielded them for centuries until we showed up."

Jacob's words had been laced with disdain. Naomi felt them loud and clear. They had been directed at the two of them.

"True, but you did what was necessary. You flushed out the enemy and officially started a war that had been brewing for just as long as I've been guarding the Grail. You may not believe it, but the trouble you've started had to happen. It was destined to happen."

"*Destined?*" Gabriel asked.

Joseph sat back, returning to his usual jovial self. "Come now, Gabriel, don't tell me that after everything you've seen that you don't believe in destiny?"

Gabriel glanced over at the Fehrs, then said, "I'm not sure what I believe, but I do believe that these two were meant to be here, in the middle of this fight."

"That's destiny, my friend," William said.

Gabriel smiled wide. "Wait, we're friends?"

That gave everyone a much-needed laugh.

27

The communal laugh subsided and the group returned to its previous quiet somberness. It unnerved Gabriel. There was so much to learn and plan before they got to Denmark. He wanted to give everyone the time they needed to cope and recharge, but he couldn't help himself. He needed to know.

"So," he started, clearing his throat, "Denmark, huh?"

"Hirtshals, yes," William replied. "It's about five hundred miles east of here, which means it's not going to be a short boat ride."

"And when we arrive?"

"I'm confident we can find a plane and get out of Europe altogether."

Naomi sat up. "Just like that? How?"

"I still don't think you understand just how much money I've accumulated over the last two thousand years," Joseph replied.

Gabriel perked up. "I'm game, how much?"

Joseph turned his attention to him. "Let's just say that I've been invested in every technological advancement you can think of, at one point or another, including Delphi when it was first announced. So, yes, a lot."

"Hang on, you're an investor in Bailey's company?" Naomi asked, rightfully shocked. So was Gabriel.

"I *was* an investor," he corrected, smiling. "That man made his mortal enemy *a lot* of money…and there was nothing he could do about it without arousing suspicion."

Gabriel grinned. "Sneaky monkey."

"Yes, well, I'm never afraid to play a game or two with my foes."

"Joseph is also being very generous with the way he talks about his wealth. If he were to combine his various identities and their accounts, Joseph would be known as the wealthiest man on the planet by quite a large margin." William's eyes met Gabriel. "So, yes, *that* much."

Gabriel glanced back and forth between the two men. "So, when you say that we'll have no trouble finding a plane, you mean to say that you'll simply buy another one?"

"I could, but no," Joseph replied. "This time, I'll just hire a service to fly us discreetly."

"They'll take us wherever we want on a whim?" Naomi asked.

Joseph thought over his next words for a moment, then said, "Remember what I said back on the dock? Wealth is just a tool, but it still needs to be used wisely to succeed. And yes, they will."

Gabriel looked at Andrew. Joseph's pilot had said nothing since they had boarded. "You going to be our flyboy?"

"No," he said. "My job here is done."

Joseph looked at him and nodded. "Andrew has served me long enough. He'll be left in Hirtshals and will do as he pleases."

"I don't understand," Naomi said.

"Is that wise to just leave him on his own?" Jacob asked.

Joseph and Andrew shared a look.

"He'll be fine," Joseph said. "Before Andrew started working for me, he flew 'undocumented missions' for MI6. Then, after he retired, he did a few more in Central Africa."

"You were a British spy, weren't you?" Gabriel asked.

He shrugged. "My past is irrelevant at this point. But my employment was strictly as a pilot, not a ground soldier."

"But you know who he is, right?" Naomi asked. "That he isn't just Daniel Laird?"

Andrew nodded. "Found out after I took the job. It's an interesting origin, for sure. But not for me."

Gabriel looked at Naomi. She opened her mouth to say something, but no words came.

"Okay, sure," Gabriel finally said. "You do you, I guess."

Geez, he thought. *This guy is beyond hardcore.* He squinted at Andrew. *Feels like more of a mercenary...* That's when he realized it's what Joseph had meant when he mentioned Andrew doing jobs in Africa. *He was—is—a merc!*

Naomi sat forward. "I have an idea." She dug her burner phone out of her pocket. "Why not go on offense and use these to spread what we know about the Acolyte all over every online platform? If we call them out, we can put some pressure back on Bailey."

"That might not work," Jacob countered. "We have zero credibility right now. We've already been labeled as terrorists. Why should anyone believe us?"

"Oh, I'm not saying they'll believe us, but it'll still turn some uncomfortable eyes on Bailey's empire. People already don't like his network due to their selective reporting. And don't get me started on Delphi's shadow banning."

"That's the understatement of the century," Gabriel muttered.

Naomi glared at him, then continued. "It shouldn't take much for the predators to pounce."

"It'll give Bailey something else to focus on too," Jacob said, coming around to the idea. "Even he can't afford to have his legitimate companies falter. Investigations could turn up some really nasty stuff."

"And imagine what his competitors will do with the information," Gabriel added. "They'll do anything to tank PGN's ratings. It could also cause a mass exodus from Delphi."

"Especially when Bailey's own network inevitably attempts to suppress the story," Naomi added.

Everyone looked to Joseph for guidance. He was their leader, after all.

He took a long breath and said, "Do it. Apply whatever pressure you can, *but* be careful, please."

Gabriel pulled his phone out and got to work making a new Delphi account.

"One more thing…" Jacob said, getting everyone's attention. "William, do you have remote access to the security feeds around your estate?"

William looked annoyed to even be asked the question. "Of course, I do."

"Good." Jacob looked at Joseph. "When we get to Hirtshals, I'm going to need a laptop with internet access. Video is king, nowadays. If we release the latest attack anonymously, it should catch fire online without much effort." A smirk formed on Jacob's face. "Plus, I have a couple of Mossad contacts who can help spread it further."

"Is that wise to do?" William asked.

"They aren't Mossad agents, if that's what's bothering you. They are civilians that owe me a few favors for some work I did for them."

Gabriel readjusted his sitting position. "Trust him, William. I have the same kind of people. Not all of our contacts are upstanding citizens."

Joseph looked at both men. "Use whomever you must, but do not leak where this information is coming from."

Gabriel snorted. "Now I think it's you who are underestimating us." He thumbed back and forth between himself and Jacob. "Stuff like this is kid's play for Jacob and me."

"I'd love to hear about it sometime," Joseph said.

Gabriel gave him a wink. "Sorry, but that's classified." William groaned, but didn't say anything. Gabriel looked at his people. "So, we doing this?"

Joseph nodded. "Yes."

Gabriel smiled and began typing. "Copy that. Smear campaign commencing in 3, 2, 1..."

28

Pudong, Shanghai, China

Gideon stomped through the puddled sidewalk of Gaohan Road, in a city he'd never visited before. He had exhausted the rest of his Acolyte contacts to discover where Epsilon's chemical plant, one responsible for producing the compounds specifically associated with fentanyl, was located. The Shanghai district was one of China's most vital areas. It contained the Shanghai Stock Exchange, as well as a plethora of impressive skyscrapers. But Pudong also possessed the Port of Shanghai, where Gideon was right now.

Finding the chemical plant was easy enough, once he knew the name. Google gave him the rest of the information he had needed, such as the address. He was on his way now, having used public transportation after parking his rental car several miles away. He didn't want anyone that was looking for him to spot him early, at least not until Gideon wanted to be seen. It was like fishing sometimes. All Gideon had to do was announce his presence, then wait for the fish to take the bait and come to him.

The hour was late, and the rain heavy. Very few people were out and about. Those who'd been caught in the rain rushed around, heads covered, shielding themselves the best they could. Like a lot of port areas that housed factories, or in this case, a chemical plant, the air reeked. The pungent odor was one that would go home with you in your sinuses and clothing. It was a stench that worsened the closer you got to the water.

Gideon was nearly there now. He had no idea if his target would be there. From what Gideon could tell, the man spent very little time in his office, opting to work from home instead. Gideon needed the home address. That was the real reason for him coming here. He planned on interrogating one of the factory workers, a supervising manager perhaps, to get the priceless intel.

If only I had his name, he thought, snarling as he stomped through a semi-deep puddle.

There were several names attached to the chemical plant, but none of them revealed much. To the untrained eye, the clouded information surrounding the names would merely look like those of silent partners, men who preferred to stay out of the public eye. But there was an issue with the plant's list of partners. Based on Gideon's research, none of them existed outside of being on paper. The Acolyte connection to this place had been confirmed. Now, all Gideon needed to do was figure out which of the false identities belonged to Epsilon.

His pocket vibrated. The only people that had this number were those who had helped him get this far. But those contacts had urged him to never contact them again for fear of Acolyte retaliation. Gideon had been shocked to learn how quickly his own betrayal had spread throughout the underground intelligence community. The only contacts that would actually take his calls were the ones loyal to him and not the Acolyte cause. While less reliable as a whole, one of them had pulled through for him, big time.

Gideon stepped beneath the worn awning of a closed dry cleaners. He was two blocks from the industrial region of Pudong. Based on the Google Earth image he had studied earlier that afternoon, Gideon should've been able to see it from here, even in the dark. The factories here ran all night, pumping out their products, packaging them, and readying them for shipment. But the storm was too heavy to see much of anything beyond a few hundred feet.

Now out of the rain, he removed the phone from his pocket and stared at the screen. He didn't recognize the number. Gideon hesitated, but eventually answered it on its sixth ring.

"Yes?" he answered.

"*Hello, Gideon, this is Beta.*" The man's voice was hidden by a voice modulator, making him sound like a robot harmonizing in highs and lows.

Gideon squeezed the device as hard as he could but stayed on the line. He knew he should've ended the call and destroyed his phone, but his curiosity got the better of him. Yes, maybe Beta had been able to track his movements, but no, there was no way for Beta to know where he was exactly.

"How did you get this number?" Gideon asked, hiding his surprise beneath a mask of rage.

Beta had the gall to laugh. "*This isn't the nineties. Don't you know that your phone is always listening?*"

"I've gone to great lengths to keep that from happening."

"*And I've gone to great lengths to circumvent your efforts. It's quite easy, actually, just as long as I know where to look.*"

Gideon thought it over and came to a single conclusion. "*You* knew I'd come to China."

"Pudong too," Beta said. "*I know where your next targets are, and since you're no slouch, I also knew that you'd be able to discover their whereabouts, given enough time.*"

Gideon had been too predictable with his movements. Beta was right. There were only two places he'd go. China or Colombia.

"*China is only a hop and a skip from Russia.*" Beta continued. "*It made the most sense to look there first.*"

Gideon let out a long breath, calming himself. Shouting his displeasures wouldn't solve anything. Threatening Beta wouldn't either. It was clear that the man thought of himself as untouchable. Fear wasn't going to sway him.

"Why are you contacting me?"

Beta replied with something out of left field. "*To help you.*"

Gideon's eyes went wide when Beta offered up Epsilon's name and home address.

"Bullshit. This is a trap." He looked around, but saw nothing out of the ordinary. "Why would you help me?"

"*I can assure you this is not a trap. I've come to realize something. Your success in wiping out the Hexad has actually aided my decision to help you.*" Beta's robotic voice turned more menacing, if that were even possible. "*My brothers atop the Acolyte are no longer needed.*"

"I agree, but that still doesn't explain why I should trust you."

"*Because you want us dead more than anyone, not that you'll ever get close enough to me for it to matter. And no, there's no snarky reply, nor a venomous threat that will change my confidence in that, so don't bother. The U.S. is not Russia or China, or even the Middle East. You can't convince anyone here to help because they have already been bought years ago. American allegiances are locked in with money and power, not ideals."*

Gideon didn't have anything to counter with because he knew, deep down, that Beta was right.

"What about Gamma?"

"Take care of Epsilon first. Oh, and keep your phone on. You'll get what you need in due time."

Beta ended the call. Gideon thought about smashing the phone and walking away, but the idea of being able to take out Epsilon and Gamma without Beta sending anyone to stop him, was too tantalizing. All this conversation did was empower Gideon. But it also made him more paranoid. It was clear that Beta wanted absolute control over the Acolyte, which also meant that he wanted absolute control over the Relics of God.

Gideon didn't have to agree with the Army of God to know that wasn't allowed to happen. No one person should ever have that much power. If Beta possessed the Holy Grail, the Staff of God, *and* the Ark of the Covenant, he could shape the world as he saw fit.

Maybe, at one time, Gideon could've gotten behind that, but not now. The Acolyte were a threat to his survival. Self-preservation was number one on his list. To allow Beta to become an unstoppable, global tyrant would allow him to dictate Gideon's own life.

It meant that Gideon needed to uncover Beta's identity as soon as possible. He sighed and got moving. It also meant that Gideon might have to do something that he never thought possible. Instead of being just an impartial judge and executioner in this battle, he might actually have to pick a side in the coming days.

And no, there was no way in hell he'd be siding with Beta.

29

Silicon Valley, California, USA

Liam's plan was working perfectly. He'd given Gideon invaluable information that should make it easy for a man of his talents to dispose of Epsilon. Once news of his demise reached the airwaves, Liam would contact the assassin again and give him Gamma's precise whereabouts down in Colombia. Soon, everything the Acolyte owned would be Liam Bailey's, and his alone. There would be no appointing of new Hexad members. If the other branches tried, Liam would simply have them executed too. Eventually, the death toll would rise and the other arms would get the point. Either they fell in line, or they would get left behind.

Or worse.

But something else had just happened, something so significant that even his own network, Prophecy Global News, was forced to report on it. Liam had thought about simply suppressing the story, like he'd done countless times before. But, in this case, he allowed his producers to tiptoe along with it. If they didn't report on the allegations, it would make Liam look worse. It'd make him look guilty.

Somehow, the Army of God had sent security camera footage of the attack on the Stromness estate to PGN's competitors. They were running the feeds twenty-four-seven. The headline read that Liam had funded the hit because the owner was one of Daniel Laird's silent partners. Then, the story also *revealed* that the attack on Laird's personal home in Torridon had been linked to him too. Laird, it seemed, had been throwing around the idea of starting his own social media company, one that would rival Delphi.

That was the report, anyway.

Liam knew this was just his enemies attempting to subvert his efforts to acquire the two missing pieces of the Relics of God. This attempt showed their cards, though. The Army of God was going after the Staff. Liam guessed they were on their way now, since his men had failed to stop them from leaving Scotland.

Frederick Hart was dead after the helicopter he'd been foolishly piloting exploded in midair. Bailey had no idea how they had escaped, nor where they were now. Seven people had vanished without a trace, and it enraged Liam to no end. In today's world, with cameras and microphones everywhere, mostly due to people's phones, it should've been impossible for that many people to up and disappear.

But they had.

It's time, he thought. Liam only had one more option in order to stop this adversary from gaining control of the Staff of God.

He picked up his phone. The first call would be to his highest-ranking agent in Cairo, Aten Al-Khafaji. As Beta, and the man in charge until a new Alpha could be appointed, Liam had been given access to the Acolyte's global database. He knew everything and, more importantly, everyone.

"*This is Al-Khafaji,*" the Egyptian said, quickly answering the call. Liam liked that. He also enjoyed the fact that some regions still used callsigns.

"Hello, Mr. Al-Khafaji, this is Beta."

There was a pause on the other end. Al-Khafaji was no doubt wondering whether he should trust that the man on the other end of the call was, indeed, Beta. The robotic voice modulator could've been implemented by anyone, but the phone number could not.

"*Yes, Beta, what can I help you with?*"

Liam stood from his chair and paced. "As I'm sure you're aware, our organization is under attack in a way that has never happened before."

"*Yes, we are aware. Alpha's death has started a landslide of disarray. Then add in the recent assassinations of the other Hexad members...*"

"Yes, I know. It's most definitely a sad day in our history. But I may know of a way to stop it."

Liam waited, then received the desired reply. "*I'm listening.*"

"The Army of God will be going after the Staff next."

Al-Khafaji laughed. "*That's a suicide mission. The Medjay are no one's allies.*"

"True, but I plan on ridding us of both groups with a single blow."

"*How so?*"

Liam grinned. "Leave that to me. What I need from you is to organize every agent we have left in Egypt and prepare to move after we strike the Children of Moses' operation outside of Alexandria."

"*After, sir? Are we not going to be involved in the initial raid?*"

"No," Bailey replied, "we've tried that twice. Both times have failed and have only resulted in our people's deaths. We can't win against a direct assault."

Liam knew that such admission might make him look weak, but it was the truth. The Army of God were organized and strong, despite their small numbers. The trio of Jacob Fehr, Gabriel Abrams, and William Strom was formidable.

"But your plan? You have another option to hit them and succeed?"

"I do," Liam said, smiling manically. "And it will be glorious. Be ready to move by this time tomorrow. I'll meet you in Cairo and we can mop them up as one."

"You're coming here? Is that wise to put yourself out in the open?"

Liam thought it over. He was already being labeled as the bad guy. Soon, he'd happily show it off. His time in the spotlight was coming. Part of him wanted to be on the ground when the Army of God's blood spilled.

No, all of me.

"Don't worry about me, Al-Khafaji. Let's worry about acquiring the Staff."

"Yes, sir. We will be ready to receive you."

Liam looked out his office window. "Good. I'm leaving for Cairo immediately. See you soon."

He hung up and shifted his glance from the view beyond the window, to his reflection within it. He pictured himself holding the Staff high over his head, allowing his Holy lineage to access the power within the artifact. Soon, Liam's will—his desires—would be that of the people of Earth. Soon, Earth would have a unified king.

Him.

There was still one problem that was *not* Army of God related. The people watching over the Ark of the Covenant weren't your typical Acolyte personnel. They operated independently of Hexad rule. They were technically part of the organization, but because of the rise and fall of leadership and the sheer instability of the world, the caretakers of the *Wachturm*, the Watchtower, decided who was given access to it, and who was shot on sight. The Ark's perceived uselessness had led to the radical arm of the Acolyte being given absolute power over the artifact. The former Alphas had decided that if the Acolyte couldn't access its power, then no one could. And if the Acolyte should eventually fall, the Ark would still be safe.

Liam had never been to the Watchtower before, nor had he ever seen pictures of the inside. As far as he knew, none had ever been taken, and if they had, the photographer was never seen, or heard from, again, and the evidence was destroyed.

A long time ago, when Liam was young, his father had told him that he might be headed to the Watchtower after college. Their Nazi lineage had its benefits. Most of the people operating the ultra-secure facility were descended from Thule Society members and the Nazi *Ahnenerbe*, like Liam's great-grandfather, Felix Neumann. Liam once had a chance to be a key contributor at the Watchtower, but had stupidly refused it to follow his passion in media production.

Was it stupid? he thought, looking around. *No. My decision has led me right back to it, but now, with infinitely more power than from simply working there.*

The Ark would be his soon, even if he was forced to eradicate everyone who had sworn to protect it. Once he had the Grail *and* the Staff, no one, not even his brethren in the Watchtower, could stand in his way.

He turned, faced the windows, and narrowed his gaze at his reflection. "*I* am the Acolyte."

30

Hirtshals, Denmark

Hirtshals was a relatively new town, only a hundred years old. Its brother to the south was not. Hjørring had been founded over 750 years ago. Joseph had very little memory of the area, except that he'd been through it sometime in the 1600s, when the Bubonic Plague had ravaged Denmark, killing tens of thousands. The Black Death slew millions more across Europe, as did other variations of the fatal illness. The memory of the bodies lying in the streets gave Joseph the chills. The things he'd done in his long life scarred him deeply, but the things he'd seen hurt even worse.

Like countless other cities along Denmark's long coastline, Hirtshals survived primarily on fishing and tourism. If ever asked, Joseph would describe it as a handsome, quiet place to live. Roads were narrow in places and the people were polite and thankful for what they had. In another life, Joseph could see himself settling down in one of the more-modern homes to the southwest of the center of town, or perhaps one of the coastal neighborhoods to the west. The next time Joseph visited, if there was a next time, he'd like to tour the Bunkermuseet Hirtshals, a museum dedicated to the bunkers left behind after World War II.

They had just pulled away in their mini-van. The group had agreed that splitting up and traveling separately wasn't needed. They hadn't been followed, nor had they seen any news relating to them being labeled as terrorists. The Army of God was safe, for now.

As expected, Andrew had been left at the harbor with nothing but a stack of cash and handshake. The man's involvement was a mystery to Joseph's new friends, and if he could, he'd keep it that way. Andrew wasn't exactly welcome in parts of this world. His past as an MI6 operative, then as a smuggler and mercenary, had made him several high-profile enemies throughout Europe. Luckily, the man was an expert at disappearing. Joseph had wished him well and sent him on his way. Andrew would be fine, that much Joseph was for certain.

But not if he stuck with us, Joseph thought, glancing over his shoulder.

Jacob and Naomi sat in the central pilot seats. Naomi was fast asleep. Jacob was awake, though his attention was elsewhere. Even though he was looking through his window, Joseph could see the man's eyes. He wasn't focused on the outside world. Jacob was looking inward. Gabriel, like Naomi, was sound asleep, but was laid out across the back bench seat. The only hint at his existence was the sound of him softly snoring. They'd only been on the road south for a few minutes, and already two of Joseph's people were unconscious.

The nearest international airport was forty miles to the south in Aalborg. Joseph had already phoned ahead and secured a flight for them, however, there would still be a few hoops to jump through before boarding and taking off. Some airports were stricter than others, even when the client was throwing around exorbitant amounts of money. Sometimes, the money was seen as a risk. Why did the person want to leave so suddenly? Joseph understood why someone would want to cover their own ass.

"Something bothering you?"

Joseph glanced at William. "Nothing new, no. Just the same old worries."

"Care to elaborate?"

"Not right now," Joseph replied. "It's nothing you don't already know."

But that was a lie. There was something Joseph was worried about that even William wasn't aware of. Joseph had told his faithful lieutenant everything—everything except one thing—one feeling. In Joseph's vision of the three keys opening the gates to Eden, he also felt something that he knew, without a doubt, and it was evil. A darkness resided in Eden still. It had been there since the beginning of time, when Adam and Eve had been the only human beings in existence.

There were many interpretations of what that evil was. The most common interpretation was that Satan, the Serpent that tempted Eve into eating the Tree of Life's forbidden fruit, existed in the garden as a balance to God's light.

He pictured Bailey holding the Staff and willing the people of Earth to do his bidding, influencing their decisions, as the Serpent had done to Eve. It wasn't mind control. The people would still have the ability to refuse him. The Staff would just make it infinitely harder to do. Plus, the human mind was different than it was thousands of years ago. In their current form, humanity was weaker than ever, being easily influenced by quick talkers, beautiful faces, and piles of money. It wouldn't take much for Bailey to win over a large percentage of the world's population. All he would have to do is promise to alleviate their struggles. Promise peace. Promise an easy life. That would surely continue mankind's path down the road to contentness.

None of this would've happened centuries ago. Humanity had more to fight for, more to defend. Battling for God and Country had been a common theme. It wasn't all that long ago that mankind used to put those two things above themselves. But comfort bred selfishness, which spread like wildfire, like a plague through the masses, infecting and digging in deep.

Joseph could've potentially stopped it had he not been "off his rocker" and destroyed by guilt, especially in the Dark Ages. War and famine had made people anxious. It had turned them on one another to survive.

There was no truer saying than, *"Hard times create strong men, strong men create good times, good times create weak men, and weak men create hard times."* The cycle was never ending, though the latter portion seemed to be going on much longer than it ever should.

Resilience is in short order. Comfort is now king.

Joseph wasn't sure when, or even if, he should mention the feeling he'd had. He wasn't sure it would even matter. Regardless if he or the others were ever able to enter Eden, they needed to prevent the Acolyte from trying. If they were able to make a deal with Satan...

We must, he thought, focusing his next words into the world around him. *Why would you show me it if we were never meant to enter? What are we to do? Are we to kill the beast? Is that even possible?*

As expected, God did not reply. He rarely did. Usually, he would show you something instead. Joseph needed to remember that this was his plan. Everything that will happen has already happened in his eyes. Like now, if the Army of God did happen to enter Eden, it would've already been preordained to happen.

The destination was set.

The journey, however, was not.

31

Alexandria Governate, Egypt

Founded in 331 BC by Alexander the Great, Alexandria quickly became one of the Mediterranean's most prominent cities, containing such historical marvels as the Library of Alexandria and the Lighthouse of Alexandria. The 330-foot-tall lighthouse was one of the Seven Wonders of the Ancient World until it was badly damaged by earthquakes and eventually decommissioned in 1323 AD. Unfortunately, very little of the lighthouse remained today due to its pieces being recycled to build other structures in the area. The only surviving fragments currently sat underwater, along with Cleopatra's palace and Alexandria's original harbor.

While most visitors focused on Cairo and other spots along the Nile, Naomi had always found Alexandria just as appealing. She had visited the city nearly a dozen times over the years, visiting every historically relevant site she could. She had always planned to take a diving tour of the offshore, ancient remnants but had gotten much too busy with work. Now, she had no idea if she'd ever get to do it.

It saddened her that the airport sat where it did. It had been built twenty miles southwest of the city of Alexandria in Borg Al Arab Al Gadida. Yes, Alexandria was a name shared by both a state and a city. Notwithstanding, the airport sat in the middle of a vast expanse of sand. The juicy parts of the state were back to the northeast, almost taunting her. The drive from here to Mosiah Fayek's place would be a boring one, with nothing to gaze at except more sand and a smattering of uninspiring townships. The airport's location did have a significant positive to the greater goal, though. It was very close to their destination, which sat south of it, out in the Al Hamam Desert.

Fayek Construction Co., she thought, picturing Mosiah and his men operating the business closer to the way the mob ran their own racket.

She really had no idea. Mosiah could've simply been a legitimate businessman with a shadowy, sacred purpose in his back pocket. It might've been similar to the way Joseph—Daniel Laird—had run the Graal Foundation. It was a very prominent organization, but had obviously also been something else entirely.

Naomi had almost forgotten about the heat. She'd been in the cold climate of Scotland, and she'd become accustomed to it. She began to prefer it. But there was something familiar about the heat—something comforting—too. It felt like home.

They had all replaced their clothing with something more fitting for the desert environment that Egypt was known for. T-shirts and cargo pants were the common theme of the group's wears, as were hiking boots and hats. Naomi still wore her fake eyeglasses, needing to hide her true identity now more than ever. They were back in Mossad country. The Israeli counterintelligence agency would still, no doubt, be looking for the Army of God, not just the Acolyte.

They came to a "T" in the road and turned left onto a road Naomi couldn't name, not that she really cared. Small villages and farmland dotted the landscape to either side of the four-laner. There was more green in the area than she remembered. The locals were enjoying a good growing season from the looks of it.

They banked around to the left a mile later. The farms on the right gave way to more villages, but also businesses of an eclectic variety. Bars, restaurants, motels, and gas stations were the more consistent types of businesses. And of course, you had your bevy of mosques. Like a majority of cities in the region, they were everywhere. Some were newly constructed, or possibly refurbished, but most were old and built more than a generation ago.

She continued to stare out her window, deciding to pass the time by counting mosques. It made the uninspiring drive more bearable, except she kept losing focus and count. Eventually, she gave up, unable to make it to double digits without slipping inwardly and dwelling on her own *issues*.

Even though it had only been a few weeks, Naomi was beginning to understand what had driven Joseph to seclusion. God was real, she couldn't die, and she couldn't tell anyone. Not the God part, but the immortal part. They did go hand in hand, however. What could she offer a nonbeliever as evidence besides giving them her word? People did that all the time and it hardly ever worked. *God is real because I said so.* She couldn't show them, like what Joseph had done when he had still been Daniel Laird to them. Naomi couldn't just slit her hand and show the world as it healed in seconds.

How long will it take to drive me mad? She sighed. *Fifty years. I have fifty years until it wears off.*

Her eyes opened wide, and she looked over her shoulder and found Gabriel staring out his window. He was looking south and was turned in such a way that he couldn't see her looking his way. Naomi pictured herself having children, whether with Gabriel or not. She wouldn't age a day over the next half-century, but her partner would. And from what she understood about her ability, her kids would age too. If the father of Naomi's children *was* Gabriel, he would more than likely die before she began to age again.

Not being able to grow old with her lover... *That* would drive her into madness.

She faced forward and eyed the back of Joseph's head. *How many times has that happened to you?* The thought nearly made her weep. The sadness was almost too unbearable to suppress.

"You okay?"

A single tear streaked down her cheek as she looked at her brother. She couldn't hide anything from him. She couldn't lie to him, either. It had nothing to do with his training—being able to read people—it was just because he was who he was.

"No," she replied, "I'm not okay." She held up her hands, inspecting them. Then she met Jacob's soft, loving face. "I don't want this."

But it wasn't Jacob who spoke next. It was Joseph.

"I'm sorry," he said still looking through the windshield. "I know I haven't exactly painted the brightest of pictures when it comes to living an extended life." Now he twisted around and looked at her. His eyes were so sad. "But, please, believe me when I say that there is still good in it."

"What about outliving a loved one?" She couldn't hold back.

"What do I do with that?"

Joseph's eyes moistened. "You..." He faced forward. "You live with it."

"And become bitter and angry?" Jacob added.

Joseph's head bobbed up and down. "That was the path I chose." He turned and faced Naomi again. "But you don't have to follow my path, Naomi. You can choose your own. The real question is, when this is all said and done, how will you choose to live?"

There was no answer to that. Like he said, it would have to wait until it was all said and done.

Naomi's anxiety ramped up to eleven, but fell as they exited the Alexandria Governate. The landscape immediately morphed into nothing but farmland. The patchwork of greens, tans, and browns seemed to call Naomi. Jacob laid his hand atop her closed fists. His touch caused them to open and relax.

"Easy, Nae. We're okay here."

"It's not here I'm worried about." She looked out her window. "It's what's out there that worries me."

That was putting it lightly.

Naomi was terrified of what the future held.

32

Al Hamam Desert, Egypt

Jacob was worried about Naomi, but he wasn't sure he could do anything. Neither could Gabriel. She needed consoling. He doubted any other person could do it besides herself. The problems she was having were internal and something she was going to have to work on as the days passed. All anyone could do was to be present for her; be a shoulder for her to cry on or a rubber wall for her to bounce her words off of.

The most dominant structure in the desert wasn't Mosiah's property, it was the sewage treatment center sitting right next door. Jacob was curious why Mosiah would set up shop so close to something as notoriously putrid smelling as a sewage treatment center. Honestly, it could've been as simple as the land being dirt cheap.

Still... he thought, not looking forward to exiting the van. Even now, down the road and inside the filtered, air-conditioned vehicle, Jacob could already detect an unpleasant odor slipping its way through.

Naomi was the first to outwardly acknowledge it. "Ugh. What is that?"

Gabriel leaned forward and jabbed a finger between the Fehrs. "That. Get ready, this is really gonna stink."

"It already does," Naomi said.

Jacob eyed her. "And it's about to get much worse."

Another mile ahead was the turnoff for Mosiah's property. A simple, weathered sign announced what lay beyond. Jacob half-expected there to be armed guards roaming the perimeter considering the person who owned it. But there weren't. Fayek Construction Co. resembled a stock-standard business. It was surrounded by a razor-wired, chain-link fence and not much else. Jacob didn't even see security cameras. But he seriously doubted Mosiah had nothing in place security-wise.

A rolling gate was pushed aside, allowing anyone that wanted entry access. William guided them through. The atmosphere inside the mini-van had changed from chatting about the stink to deadly silent. It was go-time now. Jacob's hyper alertness was peaked, threatening to blow a hole through the ceiling. He leaned around William and eyed the main building. It was still a way off, but he could see a thickly built individual standing in front of it.

Mosiah?

The left side of a compacted driveway was lined with steel containers. The right side held a bevy of heavy machinery, including bulldozers, excavators, cement trucks, dump trucks, and even a monstrous mobile crane. Personally, Jacob had always wanted to drive a bulldozer.

It should've bothered him that he'd never heard of the Children of Moses during his time in Mossad. Then again, he'd never heard of the Army of God, just the ridiculous rumblings surrounding the Acolyte. Even those were so farfetched that he'd never given them much thought. Secret societies were the stuff of legend and over-caffeinated fiction authors, not real life.

That's what Jacob used to believe.

William stopped them fifty feet from the very displeased local. The man possessed a cleanly shaven head and a thick, salt-and-peppered beard. His scowl was deeper than any William could muster. If this was, indeed, Mosiah Fayek, he was most definitely not pleased with who had just arrived.

"Slow and deliberate with everything you do," Joseph said. "Keep your hands where he can see them."

"Leave your doors open too," William said, looking up into his overhead mirror, "in case we require a quick exit."

Naomi gave Jacob a worried look before he opened his door and climbed out. William and Joseph exited the vehicle too, as did Naomi. Gabriel followed Naomi out her door. As they continued around to the front of the van, several of Mosiah's people appeared from around the containers and heavy machinery. Two more exited the building behind their boss, taking up positions next to him. Thankfully, none were armed, though Jacob figured they were carrying some sort of a weapon beneath their clothing. In a matter of seconds, the Children of Moses outnumbered the Army of God two to one.

And there's bound to be more nearby, he thought.

Jacob and the others were unarmed as well. They had given up their weapons before boarding the ferry in Kirkwall, then decided on not acquiring more before leaving Denmark. They didn't really have time. It wouldn't have been a good look for them, either. Showing up here, unannounced, and armed for combat would've made this conversation even harder.

Jacob, Naomi, and Joseph stood in a line with Jacob at its

center. William and Gabriel hung back a bit. It was clear that Joseph and the Fehrs would be doing much of the talking. They kept five feet between themselves and held their empty hands down by their sides.

Mosiah stepped closer, eyeing everyone. When his sight settled on Joseph, he said, "Get back in your vehicle and leave." Mosiah's voice was softer than Jacob had expected, but it was intense, like he knew he didn't have to speak up to properly threaten someone.

"So welcoming..." Gabriel muttered a little too loud.

"To you, possibly." Mosiah pointed at Joseph. "To him, never."

Joseph held his hands out wider and stepped away from his people. "Come now, Mosiah. It was hundreds of years ago. Things change."

"People do too," Jacob said, earning Mosiah's attention.

He stared at Jacob. "And you are?"

Jacob placed a hand on his chest. "My name is Jacob Fehr," he then motioned to his sister, "and this is my sister, Naomi. We are...descendants of Jesus Christ."

Mosiah regarded Joseph with annoyance. "I see you've gotten your little club back together."

"Wow, this guy really doesn't like Joseph, huh?" Gabriel said softly. Jacob could just make out his words.

"They have been taught that he is their enemy," William replied, "because, in the end, we want the Staff too."

Joseph stepped forward again. Mosiah responded by drawing a pistol from around his back and leveling it at Joseph's chest.

"And what are you going to do with that?" Joseph asked, doing a good job of hiding his nerves. "You know I can't die."

Mosiah shrugged. "True, but shooting you is bound to make

me feel better." His finger tightened on the trigger, but before he could shoot Joseph, Jacob stepped forward.

"The Acolyte are inbound," he said, pausing Mosiah's attempt.

He didn't lower the weapon, but he did take his eyes off Joseph. "Yes, we know."

"You do?" Naomi asked.

Finally, Mosiah lowered his gun. "Nothing in Egypt moves without us knowing about it. I have men all over this land. Every one of them has reported movement in Cairo, as well in the old district in Alexandria." He gripped the pistol hard, but didn't raise it. He just bore holes into Joseph. "Whatever you did, you kicked the hornets' nest, for sure."

Joseph lowered his hands. "They want the keys, Mosiah."

"Let them come. We've defended the Staff for centuries. There is nothing they can do that we cannot overcome."

"That was with Alpha in control," Jacob said. "Beta is not Alpha."

"No, he is not."

Gabriel leaned around Jacob. "He's taking over the Acolyte as we speak. Whatever you know about their methods, it's useless now."

This time, Naomi stepped closer. "Liam Bailey is Beta, Mosiah."

The man's intense stare shifted to her and, for a moment, his hardened face broke. "Is he now?"

"He is," Joseph confirmed. "Could you imagine what someone like him could do with the Staff?"

It was clear that Mosiah was deeply bothered by the fact that Bailey was Beta. That, or he was troubled with the fact that he hadn't known sooner. It was obvious that he prided himself in knowing things as soon as they happened, if not before. Then again, even the Army of God was still speculating. They were confident, though. It made too much sense for it not to be Bailey.

Mosiah didn't rebuke what Joseph suggested. He did quite the opposite. He contemplated it. After giving it much thought, he looked over his shoulder to one of his men. The other man nodded, sharing a common understanding with Mosiah.

"The prophecy is true then," Mosiah said, holstering his pistol.

"Prophecy?" Jacob asked. He looked at Joseph who shrugged.

Mosiah turned to Jacob. "It has been passed down through our families, from the original Children of Moses, and now to us. One day, someone will come seeking the Staff of God to use to spread his falsehoods—a false prophet."

"Holy crap," Gabriel said, stepping up between Jacob and Naomi. "He's right. Look at Bailey's companies." He ticked them off on his fingers. "Prophecy Global News and Delphi. He's practically announced it to the world."

"Unknowingly too, I bet," Mosiah said. "I'd gather he had no intention of going down this dark path. He has unconsciously wandered toward it, perhaps being guided by evil. Now, it's consumed him."

"We can't let that happen," William said, speaking for the first time since exiting the van.

"No, William, we cannot," Mosiah said, quickly agreeing.

Jacob raised his hands in a calming gesture. "Mosiah, we're here to help. We are not your enemy."

Mosiah's head cocked to the side a little and he squinted. "And yet, you are the cause of this all. It is your people's desire to collect the keys to Eden—to have them for yourselves."

"You know that isn't true, Mosiah," Joseph said. "We want

to protect them. We don't want to use them." His eyes darted to Jacob. "I have no desire to see Eden."

That, of course, was a lie.

Mosiah's hands found his hips and he let out a boisterous laugh. "You know, for someone that has lived for two millennia, you are a terrible liar, Joseph of Arimathea." He stepped to within an arm's reach of Joseph. "If I recall, you once had a vision, am I correct?"

"How do you know that?" Gabriel asked, looking at Joseph. Jacob faced him too.

Mosiah happily explained. "Countless times, this man has come for the Staff. Countless times, he has begged, on his knees, to feel its power."

Joseph looked at the earth, awash with shame. "That... That's not me anymore. I've moved on from that."

"Is that so?" Mosiah asked. "And why should I believe you?"

Joseph looked up from the sand, then met eyes with William. The bigger man shook his head. Whatever Joseph wanted to do or say, William already knew about it and disagreed with it.

Joseph held out his hand. "Do you have a knife?"

Mosiah snorted. "Why, so you can run me through?" Joseph didn't say anything else. He just stood there with his hand out. "Fine." Mosiah pulled a knife out of his pocket and snapped it open. He handed it to Joseph and stepped back.

Joseph raised the blade to his palm and nicked it. The wound wasn't deep, but it bled. He then showed Mosiah the injury. The other man laughed, then stopped when the wound didn't immediately heal.

"What is this? Why doesn't your wound heal?"

"Because I'm mortal, Mosiah."

Joseph folded the knife and handed it back to Mosiah

who took it with a look of shock on his face. "The attack in Torridon?"

Joseph lifted his shirt to reveal a scar in his side. "The Spear. I've retained a small amount of my ability, but it'll soon be gone for good. Every time the sun sets, I become more and more mortal."

"And the Keeper of the Holy Blood?"

Naomi gave Mosiah an awkward wave. "Me. I'm the last."

Joseph transformed into a hopeless man. "Please, Mosiah," he begged. "Our people used to be allies in this fight. We used to help one another because of what we represent—what we protect. This is greater than us all. It's greater than old grudges."

"Pool our resources and combine forces," Jacob added, smirking. "We're going after the Ark next."

"The Ark?" Mosiah asked, stunned by the ridiculousness of the statement. "You can't be serious! It's been in Acolyte hands since the Second World W—"

Mosiah's reply was cut off by something in the air. Whispers surrounding the origin of the noise trickled through everyone, but quickly quieted.

"Silence!" Mosiah shouted. He closed his eyes and focused on the sound. As he did, it grew louder.

When he opened his eyes, William was already moving. As was Jacob. He and Mosiah rushed to keep up with William as he sprinted east, vaulting on top of the nearest bulldozer's treads. Then he climbed up onto the cab's roof, digging into his cargo pocket once he had his feet underneath him. He placed his small binoculars to his eyes and carefully spun in a three-sixty.

"What do you see?" Mosiah asked, giving Jacob a worried glance. Jacob already knew what it was, but he was hoping William was about to prove him wrong.

He wasn't.

"Military helos—two of them." He pointed right then left. "Coming in from the east and west. One gunship. One transport." He removed the binoculars and looked down at Jacob and Mosiah. "They're pinching us in."

"Military?" Naomi asked, stopping beside Jacob. "Bailey called the Egyptian military for support?"

"It seems so," Mosiah replied. "We have long suspected that the Acolyte had a relationship with the military." He continued as William descended the bulldozer. "However, this is the first time they have flexed that particular muscle. That tells me they are desperate, which—"

"Which makes them extra dangerous," Joseph finished, joining them.

Mosiah nodded. "Yes, it does."

Joseph faced Mosiah. "Get your people indoors. We'll lead them away."

"You won't make it half a mile before that gunship opens fire," Mosiah warned. He looked back at the main building of his compound before taking in Joseph again. A dozen of his men now joined them near the bulldozer. "We fight." He took in the others. "All of us." His attention returned to Joseph. "While I do not agree with you in respect to gathering the keys, I do share your disdain for the Acolyte." He tipped his head toward the warehouse. "Everyone inside. We will make them come to us."

"What about weapons?" Gabriel asked from further back.

A wide smile formed on Mosiah's face. "You don't think we've survived all these years just by making empty threats, do you?" He motioned to the members of Jacob's team. "Like the Army of God, the Children of Moses are never afraid to get their hands dirty when it comes to protecting that which we care about..." he gave his people a long look, "or those we care for."

33

Hanbal Abdelaal sat in the door of the transport helicopter. He squeezed the handgrip of his PKM, a belt-fed "Kalashnikov machine gun," nervously waiting for his chance to unload into the enemy. Abdelaal was new to the team and had yet to see live combat. He had plenty of hours behind the PKM, however. They had taken several practice runs out in the desert over the last two months. As door gunner, it was his job to protect his fellow squad mates as they descended into battle. And based on their intel, this was guaranteed to be a battle.

They'd been ordered to attack a construction company that was supposedly being run by a splinter cell with deep ties to ISIS. There were also whispers that a small band of extremists had sought refuge with the ISIS affiliate. If Abdelaal had heard it correctly, the foreign unit had recently been hunted in Scotland of all places. Either way, Abdelaal was ready to unleash hell in the form of fast-moving, 7.62-millimeter cartridges. His model of PKM was capable of delivering hellfire at an impressive rate of 800 rounds-per-minute, a veritable aerial chainsaw.

He felt someone slap his shoulder from behind.

His commander's voice came to life in his headset. "*Eyes open! Be ready!*"

"Yes, sir!" he replied, readjusting the weapon's stock.

Unlike some other machine guns, the PKM did not have a two-handed paddle grip. *Spade* grips were more common on heavy machine guns, anyway. The PKM was a more versatile platform, technically being classified as a light-to-medium weapon, and could be fired from the shoulder if needed.

Abdelaal's helo raced in from the east, while the gunship, an Apache helicopter, came in from the west. The plan was to deploy their squad before calling in the gunship. If the Apache was needed, then the operation would have taken a turn for the worse, and the property would be in need of being reduced to rubble.

Either way, Abdelaal was itching for action. In his mind's eye, he was praying for heavy resistance. He wanted to make these terrorist bastards pay.

34

Everyone was just about finished getting outfitted with weapons and flashlights. The majority of the rifles Mosiah owned were AK variants; the AK-12 and the AK-101. Russian-made Kalashnikovs were incredibly easy to get everywhere in the world, minus places like the United States due to their sanctions against the Russian arms industry. They were cheaply mass-produced and their designs were effortlessly cloned by manufacturers in countries all over the world. So, yes, there were technically "AKs" in the U.S., just not ones made in Russia, not unless you jumped through what amounted to months and months of paperwork and whatnot.

Gabriel didn't prefer the AK platform. ARs were much easier to operate and maintain, in his opinion. Still, they were better than nothing. Plus, Mosiah had taken care of his arsenal, unlike some of the "sandbox soldiers" Gabriel had dealt with in the Middle East. To him, the single positive about owning and using an AK was that ammo was prevalent. Rest assured; your AK would never go hungry.

Naomi had already been given a rundown on the AKs

manual of arms. She agreed that keeping it in semi-auto would be best. AK recoil was no joke, especially if it was a bare-bones model. There were parts kits that made them more pleasurable to fire, but that was neither here nor there. Gabriel was very used to the mantra "make do with what you have."

The *whup* of helicopter rotors closed in on them from the east and west, though it sounded like the gunship had either slowed or gained altitude.

"Looks like we're getting ground troops first," Mosiah called out.

"How do you know?" Gabriel asked.

Mosiah gave him an annoyed look. "Because we know how they operate. They will send in their people first to clear us out. If they have been made to believe that we are the enemy, they will do what they can to take as many of us alive as possible. Opening fire with the Apache doesn't guarantee survivors."

"What if that's what the Acolyte wants?" Naomi asked, sticking close to Gabriel.

"The Acolyte only has so much pull," Mosiah replied. "In this case, it's safe to assume that they tipped the military off and came up with some cockamamie story about us."

"Most definitely," Joseph agreed.

Jacob stepped in. "*But* procedure is procedure. The Acolyte can't make them change the way they operate. They can only point them in the right direction."

"Exactly," Mosiah said. "If they want survivors, they will send in the troops first."

"Is that any better?" Naomi asked.

William stepped up. "Yes. People are easy to kill."

"Even if they are just soldiers doing their jobs?" Naomi asked.

No one replied. No one wanted to hurt these men. They

were just following orders, regardless if their intel was false. They didn't know that. They were told to attack, so here they were. Gabriel hated it, but what could they do, surrender? All that would lead to was their transfer into Acolyte hands where they would be brutally interrogated then killed. This was an unfortunate situation. The soldiers were just the pawns, and now, they were in the way.

Gabriel turned and lifted his AK-12 to his shoulder, peering through the mounted red dot. The emitter was from some off-brand Chinese company, but at least it worked…for now. Besides that, the firearm was wholly stock. It'd kick like a son-of-a-bitch, but he was confident he could control it.

"I can't do this," Naomi said, looking like she wanted to toss her weapon down. "I can't kill these men."

Mosiah looked at Joseph.

Joseph looked over the rifle in his hands and nodded. "She's right. How are we different from the Acolyte if we happily murder innocent men?"

"I'm not happy," Gabriel muttered.

Joseph gave him a look like "*you know what I mean.*"

Mosiah sighed. "Fine. Will it make you *happier* if we only go for the legs?" He held up his hand before Naomi could say anything else. "We have to fight them, Naomi. I respect your beliefs, but that doesn't mean we do nothing at all."

William raised his hand slightly.

Gabriel glanced at him. "A question from the class?"

William eyed him before speaking. "Am I allowed to shoot them in the shoulder?"

"Okay!" Mosiah shouted. His voice was laced with frustration. "Change of plan! Non-lethal shots only!" he looked over to his men. "Do you understand?" Everyone either shrugged or nodded. His eyes ended on Naomi. "Happy?"

Naomi nodded, then shook her head. "I guess."

"Shut the doors and find cover!" Mosiah ordered. His men scrambled about. "Incapacitate, but do not kill!"

Gabriel leaned in to Naomi. "Proud of you for standing up for yourself." She faced him. "But you do realize that people will die, right? The army is not operating the same way." He looked at the nearest rolling door as it was pulled shut. "If someone has a gun to your head, I *will* kill them." He looked at her again. "And I hope you'll do the same if it's my head in the crosshairs."

As he expected, Naomi didn't reply. He didn't want to be so straightforward and grim, but he had to be. She needed to know the rules. War was simple: kill or be killed.

Everyone retreated to whatever cover they could find. Everyone except Mosiah and Jacob.

"They only have so many men!" Jacob yelled. "When they breach, fall back to the opposite side of the building if you have to. William!" The big man stepped closer. "Take point if you would."

William understood his assignment better than anyone. He'd draw enemy fire while Gabriel and the others picked off the soldiers from the shadows. Everyone faced east, anticipating attack from the direction of the transport helo. Eventually, Jacob and Mosiah fell back into cover with Gabriel and Naomi behind a muscly diesel truck.

"So, you two have experience in situations like this?" Mosiah asked, eyeing the two men.

"Sort of," Gabriel replied. "Jacob and I were Mossad before joining up with Joseph and William."

"We were IDF before that," Jacob added. He glanced at Mosiah. "We've seen our share of firefights."

"And you?" Mosiah asked, looking at Naomi.

She smiled nervously. "I'm an archaeologist."

Mosiah shrugged. "That explains it then." He gave her a soft smile. "I appreciate your respect for life. Very few still possess it."

"Some things are bigger than ourselves," Jacob said. "Or our country."

Gabriel nodded, staring through the truck as he spoke. "I've never been what you'd call a true believer, Mosiah." He shifted his eyes over to Mosiah, then looked around. "But this is something I can get behind. I believe in this—in my friends."

"Long ago, we vowed to protect innocent lives from evil," Jacob explained. "What we do now is no different, except there are no borders in this fight. It isn't a global fight, either." He glanced at Naomi. "It's much more than even that."

"Spiritual warfare," Mosiah said. "I understand more than most, Jacob. And I agree, some things are bigger than ourselves."

"Question?" Gabriel said, gaining everyone's attention. He looked around again. "Where the hell are these guys?"

Mosiah looked up, then east. "Hmmm... Is it just me, or does it sound like the transport chopper stopped somewhere outside my property?"

"I think they did," Jacob replied. His eyes opened wide, but he never got his next words out.

The troops did not attack first.

With a deafening explosion, the ceiling of the warehouse detonated and fell inward as the Apache gunship opened fire.

Gabriel, Naomi, Jacob, and Mosiah dove beneath the truck. It was a tight fit, but the foursome made it under successfully just as the vehicle was pummeled by debris. Gabriel threw an arm over Naomi's head, shielding her the best he could. The air was filled with dust and heat. Fires broke out in several places.

"We need to get out of here!" Gabriel shouted.

Mosiah agreed. "Yes, we must fall back to the rear of my property—to the other buildings!"

Divide and conquer, Gabriel thought. They would be harder for the soldiers and aircraft to hunt if they separated. He looked up. *If we get the chance to separate.*

The Apache hovered into view above the freshly made skylight, its menacing form backlit by the afternoon sun. The sound of its rotors berated Gabriel's ears, drowning out all other sound. He closed his eyes and turned his head toward the center of the warehouse. When he opened them, he spotted someone standing in the middle of the miasma.

William stood tall, staring straight up at the enemy helo. Then he shouldered a tubular shaped object, took aim, and fired. Gabriel leaned out from beneath the truck just in time to watch the RPG streak through the ragged hole in the ceiling and strike the Apache where the tail connected with its body. The resulting explosion nearly tore the aircraft in half, causing it to bank away, then spin wildly out of sight. Gabriel dropped his eyes down to William. He faced Gabriel and dropped the empty RPG at his feet.

"No fair," he said, squirming out of cover. Once he was on his feet, he helped Naomi out next. Jacob and Mosiah exited cover on their own. They were all covered in dust and were coughing against the noxious air.

"Nice shot," Mosiah said, approving of William's counterattack.

William didn't indulge in the praise. "Is anyone hurt?"

Mosiah's face soured and he took in the state of his business. The building was a mess, but it still stood. Men climbed out of cover, while others lifted debris to retrieve those who'd been buried. No doubt a handful of them had been injured.

"Where's Joseph?" William asked, looking around.

"Here," he replied, stepping around a pile of mangled metal. He was bleeding from a cut to his head. "I'm fine. Just a scrape." He looked at Mosiah. "We need a way out. We can't win this fight, not if they are so willing to shoot first."

Gabriel could see the anger in Mosiah's eyes, the rage within them. He wanted revenge, but like he had said earlier, he also wanted to protect his people. He relaxed some, enough to process a reply.

"We head north, to the rear of my property. There's a way out there." He pointed at one of his men. "Azmi, get Fikri and come with me. Tell the others to fall back and disappear into the city."

Azmi didn't look so sure. "We are miles from the city, Mosiah. Will they make it?"

The leader smiled. "We will make sure they follow us. Go, tell them and get your brother, now."

Azmi nodded and rushed away.

"Uh, what are you planning now?" Gabriel asked.

Mosiah faced the gathered Army of God members. "There is a concealed passage in my northernmost building. If we can make it, we should be safe."

"And your people?" Jacob asked.

"Like I told Azmi, we will keep the military's attention on us, not them. Buy them enough time to get away."

"It should work," William said. "With the Apache down, the troops can only fight on one front. They can't rundown everyone."

"Not yet," Gabriel said. "I bet there are more incoming as we speak."

Mosiah nodded. "I agree. Which is why we need to get

moving."

With that, William shouldered his rifle and pounded north. Everyone fell in line, wary but focused. Gabriel was still under the presumption that the troops would attempt to penetrate the warehouse from their original direction. East. If they could slip away as the soldiers entered, they might be able to lose them now that the Apache was grounded.

That's a huge if, he thought. But what other option did they have?

Instead of going for the roll-down door, they edged over to a traditional door built near the northwest corner. William slowed as he neared. The battlefield had gone silent since the attack chopper had gone down. The soldiers had, no doubt, paused their attempt at infiltration once they'd seen the might of their foe.

Slowly, William unlocked the door. He opened it enough to see east. The coast must've been clear because he pushed it opened wider, stepped out, and glanced west.

He looked back at the group, which now included Azmi and his brother, Fikri. William nodded and exited. Mosiah went next, lifting his hand and pointing north. William understood and moved out into the open, head on a swivel. Gabriel stayed with Naomi. Jacob did too, but from behind. This time, Azmi and Fikri watched the group's backs. This was their turf and they knew it best.

William darted across the fifty-yard expanse of nothing, heading for the middlemost of three identical buildings. Each were the size of the one they had just exited.

Halfway across the expanse, the eastern rolling door of the main building exploded inward. It seemed that they had timed their exit perfectly, accidentally or not. The concussion gave everyone a touch more speed too. William and Mosiah reached the next warehouse first. They threw open the door just as a volley of bullets impacted the metal building's façade. Gabriel and Jacob turned and blind fired back at their exit point.

Gabriel watched two soldiers duck back inside the warehouse. He didn't think either man had been injured, but there was no way to tell. Azmi and Fikri picked up the cover fire, allowing Gabriel and Jacob to leap inside. Once they were *safe*, they resumed their own fire so the brothers could enter.

Mosiah locked the door, took a breath, then marched across the space, heading for a dump truck parked in the middle of what was obviously a repair shop. It was filled with car lifts, workbenches, and anything else an auto repair shop needed.

"Uh," Gabriel started.

Mosiah held up his hand. "You'll see..."

35

"All I see is a busted dump truck," Gabriel replied, getting a nod of agreement from Naomi. That's all she saw too, besides the typical repair shop equipment. What struck her as even odder was that Mosiah was leading them straight to the truck.

As they drew closer, Naomi saw something she had missed earlier. Beneath the vehicle was what was referred to as a *mechanic's pit.* They were especially common in places that offered drive-up oil changes. They made it so the mechanics could work standing up, rather than lying down or having to put the car up on a lift.

Or, in this case, a dump truck on a lift, she thought.

Mosiah Fayek didn't stop. He quickly descended the narrow steps and vanished beneath the monstrous vehicle. Gabriel gave Naomi a questioning look. All she could do is return it with an equally perplexed shrug of her shoulders. She had no idea what Mosiah was up to.

William descended behind Mosiah. He was forced to dip his head, being much too tall to make the climb fully upright. Naomi was next with Gabriel right behind her. Mosiah stopped at the bottom of the pit, creating a traffic jam on the steps. William and Naomi were the only other people that made it to flat ground. She looked up the incline and found her brother watching intently, studying just what the Medjay leader had in store for them.

"Help me with this," Mosiah said to William, motioning to the western wall of the north-south running pit.

"You need help with a wall?" William asked.

"No," Mosiah replied, "I need help with the door built into the wall." He shouldered into it. "Help me push. It's quite heavy."

William did as he was asked, and the two men braced their shoulders on the *door*.

"Push," Mosiah said, putting his weight into it. William did too. The pair were strong enough to get a three-foot-wide section of the wall to sink inward.

Naomi looked back up the stairs, finding Gabriel, Jacob, and Joseph staring in awe. Not that they shouldn't have seen something like this coming. Joseph's Torridon estate contained similar secret passages. Almost as soon as William and Mosiah disappeared inside, they reemerged. The passage's owner waved everyone in, stepping out of the way to do so.

"Quickly," he said, ushering Naomi inside.

She entered, stepping around the moveable section of wall. It acted as a fork in the road. You could either go left or right to get around it. She went left. Gabriel slipped inside and went right. They met around the back, at the top of a second set of steps. Jacob, Joseph, Azmi, and Fikri were next.

"Head down," Mosiah instructed.

They did. Naomi and Gabriel led the way deeper, clicking on their handheld flashlights as they moved. William and Mosiah entered last, then shoved the false wall shut. Not a moment after they did, was there an explosion topside. Everyone paused and listened, but they didn't wait around for long.

"Go," Mosiah whispered. "Keep moving. They will not find us."

"And how do you know that?" Gabriel asked.

Mosiah smiled. "Have some faith."

Gabriel glanced at Naomi. The corner of her mouth arose as she turned and pushed deeper underground. The steps ended twenty feet below where they had started. Naomi walked onto flat earth. The way only to go now was due north, as Mosiah had said.

"How far does this go?" she asked.

Mosiah snaked his way through the gathered crowd, stopping next to her. "Six miles."

Everyone's breath caught.

"Di you say six miles?" Jacob asked from the back.

"I did." He gave Naomi a wink. "We've had a long time to build it. My family has owned this land for generations. It wasn't always what it is now." He took the lead and started them north. "As the world has changed, so have we."

"And this passage?" Gabriel asked.

"Has been used dozens of times for very particular reasons," he replied vaguely. Naomi assumed that meant it was how he got the guns in.

"Where does it lead?" William asked.

"I own a piece of farmland directly north of here. From there, we should be able to move deeper into the city and vanish."

"How?" Gabriel asked. "We going on horseback or something? Gonna ride our way into Alexandria?"

"Or course not," Mosiah replied. "There are a couple of

vehicles parked inside a barn that will do the job."

Naomi shook her head and softly chuckled. "You're just like William; always prepared."

"Yes and no," Mosiah said. "I could've never guessed I'd be in the presence of the Army of God while fleeing the Acolyte."

"Wasn't on your Bingo card, huh?" Gabriel asked, grinning.

Mosiah let out a burst-of-a-laugh. "Not in the slightest."

"Well," Joseph said, "we're here. And we seem to be working together just fine."

"Yes," Mosiah said, nodding. "It seems that we were destined to be here together, in this war."

After a mile of marching north, a single question burned inside Naomi more than any other, and that was saying something, since she was overflowing with them.

"The Staff, where is it?"

"Yeah," Gabriel said, "it's obviously not here."

He didn't answer.

"Mosiah," Joseph said, "cards on the table." The other man stopped and turned to face everyone else. "All of them."

The leader of the Children of Moses placed his hands on his hips and looked down at his feet. "After Sultan Selim discovered the Staff in 1517, my ancestors moved it to a different temple..." he looked up at the group, "in South Sinai. It's been there ever since."

"South Sinai?" Joseph asked, stepping forward. "As in Mount Sinai?"

Gabriel glanced back and forth, then looked at Naomi. "Where Moses received the Ten Commandments?"

"The same," Mosiah replied. "Back in the sixth century, a monastery was built atop our second temple to erase its natural landmarks."

Naomi gripped her hair with both hands, in utter disbelief. "Saint Catherine's Monastery..." Her hands fell away from her head. "Commissioned by Byzantine emperor Justinian I in 548 AD. It's the world's oldest continuously occupied Christian monastery."

"Yes, however, only one staff member knows of the passage within. His ancestry is like the rest of ours."

Jacob leaned over and retied his right boot. "A Children of Moses spy?"

Mosiah nodded. "Correct."

"You said, 'passage within,'" Naomi repeated, swallowing hard.

"Deep within," Mosiah confirmed. "Very deep within the mountain itself."

36

Abu Rudeis, Egypt

Mosiah's plan to get them to safety had worked brilliantly so far. They exited via a false wall at the rear of a dusty barn. Two weathered vehicles, an SUV and a mini-van, awaited them, gassed up and ready to go. The eight-man team of both Army of God and Children of Moses members piled into the vehicles and immediately departed without a word. The six-mile trek had taken them over an hour and they were exhausted.

Then came the next leg of their journey, a 300-mile drive.

Alexandria and Cairo were serviced by only two airports. That's it. The Acolyte were reported to be all over Sphinx International Airport in Cairo. That left Borg El Arab International Airport. The team agreed that a group as large as theirs would have a tough time navigating such a populated spot without being noticed by Acolyte and law enforcement alike. So, they decided on the only other course of action.

They would drive to the South Sinai Governate. The riskiest part of this plan was that they'd need to pass through the heart of Cairo. The one thing they had going for them was the time of day and the traffic. They'd easily blend in. Unfortunately, both of those positives were also huge negatives. It'd slow them down.

William drove the van the entire distance. His immortality kept his mind and body vigil. Joseph, Jacob, Naomi, and Gabriel had argued with him to switch and get some rest. His reply was either to flat-out ignore them, or to just give them a look that shut them up.

In all, the drive had taken almost seven hours to complete. Joseph had stayed awake the entire time, keeping William company while also navigating for him. William had told him three times to close his eyes and get some rest, reminding him each time that he was no longer immortal and therefore in need of sleep.

But Joseph had been too restless for a timeout. Staying busy had been best for him. The others did not prescribe to the same beliefs. Jacob, Gabriel, and even Naomi, had quickly fallen asleep where they sat. The only time anyone behind Joseph had said a word was when Naomi had woken up as they crossed the Suez Canal.

"Not much further, right?"

Joseph turned and looked at her. "No, less than a hundred miles before we stop to stretch." Naomi yawned, then gazed through her window, eyes heavy.

"Naomi," Joseph said.

"Hm?" she replied, staring blankly.

He smiled at her. "Get some more rest, dear."

She smiled, then laid her head back. "Okay."

Joseph wondered if she'd even remember waking up and speaking with him. Even now, as they passed the Abu Rudeis Airport on their right, he wondered it. He also wondered how she'd been able to sleep so soundly. Joseph only slept like that when he'd had too much to drink. Now, he hardly slept at all, except for recently, when his body made him. It was one of a dozen changes he'd been experiencing since the attack on Torridon over a month ago.

Everyone was awake when William made the turn onto St. Katherine-Nuweibaa Road. From here it was another sixty miles up a winding mountain road to the town of Saint Catherine and its centuries-old monastery.

And the Staff of God, Joseph thought. After two millennia of speculating, he was about to finally see it with his own eyes. His nervousness must've been pretty apparent.

"You okay?" Naomi asked, reaching forward and across the aisle and grabbing his shoulder.

He faced her and smiled softly. "It's been two thousand years. I honestly never thought I'd live to see this." He faced forward. "I thought that I would somehow die before seeing it with my own eyes."

"And at Saint Catherine's of all places," William added, voice low.

"What does that mean?" Jacob asked.

Joseph had to twist around fully to see Jacob. Gabriel was also sitting, waiting for an answer. "We looked here."

"Several times," William added.

"Yes, several times, over hundreds of years. As new regimes rose in respective areas, William and I, along with a few devout followers, would travel in search of information. We hoped that, as the years waned, that the Staff's protectors would loosen their tongues a little." He sat forward and sighed. "How wrong we were. Clearly, the Children of Moses are as faithful to their cause as we are. Even more so."

If I had been as faithful as the Children of Moses—the Medjay—would I have already completed this quest?

He looked back at the Fehrs again, garnering a reaction out of Naomi.

"What?" she asked.

He smiled. "Nothing. It's just uncanny how much you remind me of your mother."

Naomi smiled back.

Joseph returned his attention to the land outside the windshield. He decided that this was the way it was meant to be. He was meant to be here now, with these particular people. Even Gabriel and his *humor* were part of God's plan. It was why he had failed so many times before. It's not that *he* wasn't ready—though that was also probably true—it's that the *world* wasn't ready.

Times were rough globally. Only a privileged few could tell you that their lives had been unaffected by war, both military and political, or had no mental or physical illnesses due to unwavering stress. Drug and alcohol addictions were running rampant too. Sometimes, a person needed to experience hardship in order to see the light shining bright, right in front of his or her face. It was a tough pill to swallow, but if you looked throughout history, there were plenty of examples to use.

A more recent instance had been in the United States, post-September 11th. Even though Joseph had witnessed the atrocity from across the Atlantic, he had never seen the U.S. so unified. Political parties had blurred for a time. Nationalism was king. Every single American waved their banner proudly, shouting from the rooftops for al-Qaeda to piss off!

What if the world could do that as a whole? he asked himself. *What if we could all raise our fists against the evil plaguing our spirits. What if we could tell evil to go piss off?*

The only way for that to happen was for the Acolyte to be completely destroyed. Not a single high-ranking member could be left alive. The group needed to be burned to the ground, and Joseph knew of a way to do it.

And this part had nothing to do with Michael Mizrahi's current mission.

Without turning around, he mentally took in his people. They could never know his plan, for he knew that they'd do everything in their power to stop him.

It would be like killing two birds with one stone.

The Acolyte *and* himself, the cause of so much pain. Like his ancient enemy, Joseph of Arimathea needed to finally die so the world could heal. The past needed to finally be laid to rest. Mosiah was right. This shadow war had been responsible for so much death over the centuries. It needed to stop.

Mankind's future depended on it.

37

Cairo, Egypt

Liam Bailey landed at Sphinx International Airport to bad news. Both the Army of God and the Children of Moses had escaped the Egyptian military's attempts. And worse, both parties had suffered zero casualties.

He had underestimated his enemy again, while also overestimating the ability of the military to do what was necessary. In hindsight, Liam should've seen it coming. The soldiers were not Acolyte loyalists. They did their jobs as if the operation had been a normal one. But their targets had been anything but normal.

He stood in front of a group of casually dressed men and women, and did so without his face covered. This was the first time Liam had ever "publicly" announced his identity as Beta to anyone, including those within the Acolyte. As far as he knew, it was also the first time any of the other Hexad members had done it, past or present. The looks he had received had been amusing to him. They had been of equal shock and confusion. Really, these people should've known. It was already widely known throughout the ranks that PGN and Delphi were Acolyte owned and operated. Who else could the American Hexad boss be other than Liam Bailey?

The answer: no one.

One man stood closer than the rest. He was the agent Liam had contacted before leaving for Egypt. Aten Al-Khafaji was much shorter and slighter than Liam thought he'd be. To him, he resembled a crime boss' hands-off informant, not an ultra-successful assassin. But, in this business, looks could be deceiving.

Liam met Al-Khafaji's cold eyes. "Search Fayek's entire property. I want us to confirm their escape. If any survivors turn up, other than Laird, kill them."

"What about law enforcement?" Al-Khafaji asked.

"They are standing down, for now," Liam replied. "Keep monitoring their channels throughout Alexandria and here. I'll have my people filter through social media posts and news feeds."

"I'll check in with our agents at the train station and at both airports too," Al Khafaji offered.

Liam nodded. "Good. I don't want another fiasco like we had in Kirkwall."

Hart had paid for his failure with his life, thanks to an onboard explosion.

"What of the Staff?" Al-Khafaji asked. "If it is not hidden in Fayek's property, where is it?"

In truth, Liam had no idea, nor did any of the Acolyte's top researchers. The last evidence had said that the Staff had been moved to Egypt following the destruction of the Second Temple in Jerusalem in 70 AD. Then there was the incident involving Sultan Selim I in the 1500s. But everything between it crossing into Egypt and the sultan discovering it had turned up nothing. Same for the timeframe after the sultan until now. The Children of Moses had done a commendable job keeping the Staff's location concealed all this time. Their ability to keep a secret was something the Acolyte—and every other secret organization—could learn from. Intel leaks were a death sentence.

Just ask Gideon's victims...

Alpha's carelessness had been the cause of the man's warpath against the Hexad. If Liam had been in charge, he would've had every family member involved in the leak terminated, including Michael Mizrahi, the Mossad operative who would eventually rise to become the Acolyte's "Judge of Man." No individual was more important than the cause. Alpha had seen an opportunity overflowing with risk and had decided to act on it with little regard for what might happen.

In this case, he had created a vengeance-fueled killing machine.

Fool.

"Anything else, sir?"

Al-Khafaji's question stirred Liam. He blinked and nodded. "Yes, cast as wide a net as possible. Post an agent at Egypt's most important Jewish and Christian sites. There's no way they are hiding it in the middle of nowhere. I'd wager it's being concealed by something acting as its shield."

The other man's eyes narrowed. "We need to narrow it down more. There are too many sites."

Liam understood his concern. "Crosscheck the sites and find a commonality between ourselves, the Staff, the Children of Moses, and the Army of God. We must prevail, Mr. Al-Khafaji."

"I agree."

Liam turned, then stopped. "I'll give you the number for my people back at Delphi. Use whatever resources they can offer you. They will be at your disposal."

Al-Khafaji's eyes opened wide. Then, he nodded, spun while shouting orders to the men and women waiting.

Liam felt a tightness in his chest. Things were progressing faster than he could keep up with. The Army of God teaming up with the Children of Moses was the worst thing that could happen in his efforts to recover the Staff of God. Combined, their resources were infinite. If he were a religious man, Liam would've prayed for guidance. He believed in God and everything surrounding him, but not in a religious way. Liam had always seen this war as historical, not spiritual.

He believed in the supernatural power of what he sought, not what it represented.

Some said, it would be his downfall as a Hexad member. But Liam had always seen his divine disconnection as a positive. It allowed him to see things clearly, without the blindness that true belief could hold on someone.

And because of it, I will succeed.

He smiled, knowing there was nothing to be happy about. The Acolyte had failed time and time again since this battle had begun. So why was he smiling now? Liam knew why. He was enjoying being in the thick of it. He enjoyed leading his people, on the ground, with no restrictions. He was their general now, and this was where he'd stay until he possessed that which he desired.

You will be mine, he thought, calling out to the Staff. *We will change the world.*

38

Saint Catherine, South Sinai, Egypt

The sixty-mile drive into the mountains had been blissfully uneventful. The road gently swayed back and forth in some parts, while also, on occasion, aggressively switchbacked as they climbed higher and higher.

The town of Saint Catherine sat at nearly a mile above sea level. The impressive elevation kept the daily high at a manageable temperature in the summer months. Although not the city it was today, the land that Saint Catherine presently sat on had been part of the Egyptian Empire, dating back as far as the 16th century BC. To say the area was old would be an understatement.

Jacob would've loved to have seen what a snowy Saint Catherine looked like in person, but they weren't that fortunate. Desert mountains covered in a layer of snow were something that hit differently, especially in areas of the world that could routinely surpass triple-digit temperatures. To some people, snow in Egypt just didn't make sense.

They passed a restaurant on their right called VIP, then made the next left onto a well-traveled, compacted dirt road. They followed the slight incline, passing vehicles and camels alike. Jacob assumed the animals were used for guided tours rather than normal travel. Still, they were plentiful the closer they drew to the monastery.

A mile later, they arrived.

Saint Catherine's Monastery, as Naomi had revealed earlier, was the oldest continually inhabited Christian monastery in the world. It also contained the oldest continually operating library on Earth. Within its sacred walls stood what was claimed to be the burning bush from Scripture. Jacob found it interesting that the site of the bush had changed several times since the event had occurred, due to poor record keeping. Really, no one knew where Mount Sinai's factual, concrete location was.

The Bible describes the area as Mount Horeb, but it's commonly believed that Horeb and Sinai were the same place, only with a different name. The other geologic locations were Mount Serbal, Mount Saint Catherine, and finally Jebel Musa, Mount Moses, the current site. Saint Catherine's Monastery sat in a valley, at the foot of both Mount Saint Catherine and the neighboring Mount Moses, Mount *Sinai*. Jacob wondered if the current location was even correct. At this point, Mount Sinai could've truly been anywhere.

But if one man in the world knew where it was it was Mosiah Fayek.

Jacob watched Mosiah exit the lead vehicle, look around, then eye Jacob's vehicle and nod. William swiftly turned into a nearby parking spot and killed the engine. The only weapons anyone had on them were pistols. As long as the firearm was concealed, Mosiah had assured them his man could get them inside with it safely. Jacob didn't know what kind of security the holy site possessed, but he hoped it was lax.

"Who is Mosiah's contact here, did he say?" Naomi asked.

"He did not," Joseph replied from the front passenger seat. "Even though he is currently our ally, I would still be cautious, agreed?"

Everyone nodded. Jacob felt the same way. The only people he trusted with his life were currently in the same car as him. The list was as small as it usually was, but far more interesting now. In another life, Gabriel was the only one Jacob could see being here with him. Their past relationship leant to that. Jacob still couldn't fully process that his twin sister, Joseph of Arimathea, and King Arthur were also key pieces to this outlandish puzzle.

The Holy Grail, the Staff of God, the Ark of the Covenant, and the Garden of Eden, he thought, letting out a long breath.

"You okay?" Naomi asked, placing a hand on his forearm.

He nodded. "Yeah, I'm fine."

"At least one of us is," Gabriel said, patting his shoulder and unbuckling. "Now, could you please move? I'd like to get out."

Jacob popped the mini-van's side door and slid it open, instantly struck by the abusive heat. The day was warm, though, in retrospect, still somewhat comfortable. Like Naomi, he had become content with the chilling temperature of Northern Scotland. He didn't miss the wet air, however. The air of Stromness had been constantly moist due to its seaside locale. The dryness of the desert had been a welcome change for him, but he wasn't sure he wanted it full-time again.

Mosiah and the two men who had accompanied him here, Azmi and Fikri, met Jacob and the others halfway. The monastery was another 200 yards to the east.

"Let me call my contact and tell him we're here," Mosiah said.

"He's somewhat high-profile and talking to him in person could arouse suspicion."

"High-profile?" Jacob asked. "Who is he?"

Mosiah looked around and in a low tone said, "The archbishop."

Naomi's eyes went wide. "The Archbishop of Saint Catherine's Monastery is your contact?"

Mosiah shushed her and glanced around. "Yes, he is. Every archbishop has been a key member of my order for centuries. Andreas is no exception. This has always been part of their responsibilities, since the monastery was first erected. They have all been members of the Children of Moses."

Jacob gave Joseph a look. The ancient man shrugged. He had no idea.

"Impressive," Gabriel said. "Damn impressive."

Mosiah took him in. "We don't do this to wow others."

"Too late. I'm already wowed. Can't take it back."

Jacob was also wowed. "Make the call while we walk. We'll hang back a little."

The other man nodded, produced his phone, turned, and began the trek to the monastery. As Jacob had said, the others gave Mosiah some privacy while he phoned his prominent associate. The secrets of the Children of Moses were deep and spectacular. Naomi must've been going nuts with every new thing she learned. Jacob figured that was why he was still struggling to process everything. It was all very exciting, while simultaneously being unbelievably dangerous.

He looked at his sister as they walked. He watched her eyes. They darted around, taking in everything they saw and analyzing it to the tenth degree.

"You're really enjoying yourself, aren't you?" he asked.

Her eyes snapped over to him, and her mouth opened. When nothing came out, he knew she had been trying to come up with a lie. She looked away with shame. "I really am."

Jacob smiled. "I am too."

"You are?" she asked, eyebrow raised. "'Cause I got the impression you weren't."

"After all these years, you still expect me to be outwardly excited about anything?"

She softly laughed. "Yeah, I always forget that you're eternally a stick in the mud."

His face fell. "Not on the inside..."

Naomi let out a full-blown guffaw. It was nice to hear and see. Jacob hadn't seen her laugh this hard in some time.

"She alright?" Gabriel asked from behind.

Naomi replied with a wave of her hand as she got herself under control. William and Joseph had smartly distanced themselves from them. Jacob had quickly realized that he and Naomi had been the loudest ones in the area by a mile. Even the camels were staring at them. Jacob gave the closest group of pilgrims and tourists an apologetic wave, then shifted his eyes to the ground and kept them there until Joseph broke the silence that followed.

"Did you get through to your friend?" Joseph asked as Mosiah returned to them.

"Yes, Andreas will grant us all entry through a VIP entrance, but he cannot meet with us until nightfall."

"Why not?" Naomi asked.

Mosiah shrugged. "I did not ask. He wears many hats here. If he's busy, he's busy." He looked behind him before continuing. Satisfied that they weren't being listened in on, he returned his attention to the group. "A member of his staff will bring us to his office where we will wait."

Gabriel looked up and groaned. "We're going to wait in his office until sundown?" He checked his watch. "You do realize that's over two hours from now."

William grumbled under his breath, matching everyone else's tones. This wasn't what Jacob had hoped to hear. He was happy to know they'd be let in right away—armed too—but waiting two-plus hours felt like a colossal waste of time.

"What choice do we have?" Jacob said, looking at the group. "If this archbishop asks us to wait, we wait." He met Mosiah's intense eyes. "This VIP entrance, where is it?"

Mosiah tipped his head back toward the monastery. "Come, I'll show you."

He led the way, but slowly, not wanting to seem too eager.

"Question," Gabriel said, hustling up to Mosiah's side. "How did your ancestors build this secret temple without anyone knowing?"

"In the dead of night, every day until it was ready," he replied.

"How long did that take?" Joseph asked.

Mosiah gave him a quick look. "Nine years."

Everyone slowed but didn't stop.

"Nine years?" Naomi asked.

Mosiah nodded. "Yes. They worked tirelessly until it was ready."

They came upon another group of tourists, slowing even further.

"But where's the entrance into the mountain?" Jacob asked.

The Children of Moses' chief looked back at him. "When you see where the entrance is, you'll understand everything. You'll also understand why some secrets need to have their own secrets."

Jacob eyed the monastery. *Oh, believe me, I know all about that.*

39

To Naomi, the Saint Catherine's Monastery resembled a defensive fort more than anything else. Its high walls looked wholly impenetrable to anything except a powerful explosive. She thought back, picturing it during the time it was built. The only thing capable of breaking through it, in her opinion, would've been a heavy projectile flung from a catapult, or its larger, more devastating relative, the trebuchet. Even then, the defensive barrier probably would've held.

The vast majority of people entering, leaving, or simply hanging around outside, were doing so further ahead. Mosiah stopped sooner than that, at a simple chain-link gate. It was currently locked by a worn padlock and contained no guard. Once the entire team was on site, they waited for whoever it was that was going to lead them in to reveal his or herself.

Suddenly, a man appeared out of nowhere. He wore a simple black tunic and had an elegant crucifix hanging around his neck, signifying his position within the clergy. He was hunched, bent harshly at the waist, as if he could no longer stand erect. Naomi figured that was the case since the man had to have been close to ninety. The elder's features screamed of those of a person from the Mediterranean; olive skin, dark eyes, prominent nose, sharp jawline. *Greece*, she decided. Naomi couldn't get over how penetrating the man's gaze was. He uncomfortably studied everyone, never once opening his mouth.

Mosiah broke the unnerving silence. "Ah, Mr. Katsaros, it's a pleasure to see you again!" His greeting was boisterous, impossibly loud.

Katsaros? Naomi thought. *Definitely Greek.*

"Is he deaf?" Gabriel asked slyly, leaning away.

Katsaros' glare shifted to Gabriel. "I am not." His words hissed like a viper's. His head cocked ever-so-slightly to the right. "I choose not to speak, because there are already plenty of people in this world that speak too much."

Naomi tried to hold in her laugh, but failed, and it came out as a snort instead. She gave William a quick look. The corner of his mouth turned upward. He had thoroughly enjoyed the jab too.

Gabriel sheepishly looked around, then cleared his throat. "Yes, well, I'll let you know when one of those people make their presence known."

The old Greek grumbled, then unfolded his hands from around his back. He held an overstuffed keyring in one hand. After blindly selecting a key from the dozens present, he moved to insert it into the padlock. After a handful of shaky, failed attempts, he finally slipped it in, unlocking it with a snap of his wrist.

"Geez, finally," Gabriel muttered.

Katsaros must've had bionic hearing, because even Naomi had barely heard what Gabriel had said.

His hard eyes found Gabriel again. "Shall I leave you

outside?"

Now everyone glared at Gabriel, silently telling him to *shut up*. He shrank away. "No, sir. Apologies."

"Mmhmm," he said, opening the gate and stepping aside.

Mosiah ushered everyone through. "Even though he is the eldest member of the monastery's staff, I have found it wise to stay on his good side, eh, Mr. Katsaros?"

The Greek gazed at everyone else, not once looking at Mosiah. "That would be wise."

Only once the gate was locked did their journey into Saint Catherine's Monastery begin. It was a place Naomi had never been, even though she had once visited the summit of Mount Sinai. Never in a million years would she have thought that the legendary Staff of God was being housed within the same mountain. That fact had almost angered her—that she'd been so near it without knowing. Naomi gazed up at the surrounding mountains, wondering what other treasures were hidden directly beneath her nose.

On the other side of the complex's outer walls, and the gate they had just entered through, was a sparse courtyard lined with olive trees. They were planted six feet from one another, giving the red earthy tones of the monastery some much needed color. Naomi also spotted a cluster of cypress trees and a smattering of fig trees. The types of trees were not random, either. They each held religious and historical significance.

Olives, of course, symbolized peace in many religions, particularly in the three Abrahamic faiths: Judaism, Christianity, and Islam.

"This way," Katsaros announced. "Please, keep up."

Then they were off, zooming onward. Even though he hobbled along, the old man was spry. They were led through the courtyard and to an already open set of wooden doors. Naomi looked up and sneered as they passed beneath what she knew was an ancient, and hopefully retired, *garderobe.* The small rooms were easy to spot, looking like warts growing along a castle's façade. Saint Catherine's Monastery possessed them too, which made sense. The complex had been built at the beginning of the Middle Ages.

Gabriel stopped and looked up. "Are those toilets?"

Naomi smiled and looked up. "Yes, they are."

He comically took a large step to the left, then the pair continued under the medieval commodes. They rejoined the group. They'd fell behind a little, but quickly caught up in time to be led past a small alcove sporting a sealed well made of stone and a wheeled pulley system used to draw up water from the well. Naomi didn't need a professionally guided tour to know what they were standing next to.

"The Well of Moses," she said, wide-eyed, stopping and stepping beneath the archway of the eight-by-eight space. She gazed over at Joseph. "Jethro's Well."

He gave her a smile. "Where he would meet his future wife, Zipporah."

"Jethro?" Gabriel asked, finally recognizing the name. "Oh, right, Moses' father-in-law, where he claimed the—" He zipped his lips before he could shove his foot in his mouth further.

"The *what*?" Katsaros curiously inquired.

"Nothing," Mosiah quickly replied. "Just an interesting story. Nothing more."

The clergyman squinted his eyes at Mosiah. "Hmmm, yes. *Just* a story indeed…"

Jacob met eyes with Naomi. He must've been wondering the same thing. What did the Greek know? Did he officially know anything, or was he just deeply suspicious? Depending on how long he'd been here, he might know a lot. Naomi had visited several places like this before. Many of them possessed staff members that had been there for decades at a time. It wouldn't have shocked her to find out that Katsaros had been here for more than fifty years based on his age.

If he's close to ninety years old, it could be pushing seventy years of stewardship, she thought further, following the group deeper into the compound.

The temperature dropped drastically as they entered the shadows between buildings. The late-afternoon sun couldn't reach them here. The briskness of the shaded breeze relaxed Naomi some, but not enough to remove all of her worry.

They skirted around the hustle and bustle surrounding the chapel, though Naomi hoped she'd be able to see it before leaving. Monasteries weren't typically just houses of worship. Most of them also featured domestic quarters for the monks, nuns, or in some cases, solitary hermits. There were also sometimes infirmaries and libraries present. And depending on what part of the world you were in, there could be barns, forges, and even breweries.

Naomi had been tickled to learn some years back that the oldest operational brewery in the world had been founded in 1040 AD in Bavaria, Germany. There was some argument over the validity of the date, but nevertheless, the brewery was incredibly old. The *Bayerische Staatsbrauerei Weihenstephan* (Bavarian State Brewery of Weihenstephan) was located on the former site of a monastery, Weihenstephan Abbey.

As far as she knew, the monks of Saint Catherine's Monastery did not make beer...

Katsaros led them past the marvel of the monastery, the

burning bush. This singular bramble had been the reason Justinian I ordered the monastery's construction. Centuries later, the alleged body of Saint Catherine of Alexandria had been unearthed nearby. She was quickly taken to the monastery to be re-interred where it would eventually be renamed after her.

Naomi and her group passed directly beneath the bush. She did everything she could not to reach up and touch the low-hanging branches. She didn't care if it was the original bush or not. What it represented—where it grew—meant so much.

They snaked past the gathered crowd of patrons and continued down a tight alleyway, slowing as they did. It was only once Naomi leaned around the group that she understood why they had slowed. Katsaros had led them to a weathered staircase. At the top of four-stepped staircase was a wooden gate. It too was locked by a simple padlock. Beyond was an arched corridor that disappeared around a corner and into darkness.

Katsaros struggled up the steps but ultimately prevailed. He produced his keys and unlocked the gate, stepping aside to hold it open.

"Quickly," he barked.

Everyone moved as if they feared the old-timer. Naomi kind of did. This guy had probably seen everything, which meant he feared nothing. She instantly knew that wasn't true, though. She had seen plenty that Katsaros had not.

That would assume he isn't involved in the archbishop's secret dealings, she thought, swiftly dismissing the idea. If the Greek had known about the Staff, Mosiah would've known he knew. She needed to remember, even though the archbishop was involved in all this, Mosiah Fayek was still the *tribe's* leader. Nothing happened here that Mosiah didn't know about.

Once everyone was through, Katsaros relocked the gate

and scurried to the front of the line. "It's just up ahead," he announced to no one in particular. They passed an intersection of corridors, then made their next left...up more stairs.

Naomi heard Gabriel sigh behind her. She snapped her head around and gave him a death glare.

"I know, I know," he replied, tossing his hands up in defeat.

But Naomi felt the same way because, this time, there were three times as many steps to climb. She blew out a long breath and waited for her turn at inching forward and up.

40

After finally reaching the top of the worn stone steps, Katsaros paused outside a heavy wooden door. He, once again, produced his keyring and selected the largest key on it. It was iron and looked like it belonged to a medieval prison cell more than the office of a religious leader. The door unlocked with a loud clunk. The old Greek swung it open and stepped aside, waving everyone inside faster than they could move.

"Come now. Faster."

Last to enter, Jacob stepped past their guide, giving the corridor one last look before entering.

"Something the matter?" asked the clergyman.

"No," Jacob replied, eyeing him. "Should there be?"

Katsaros tilted his head right, urging Jacob to move. "If it's trouble you're looking for, the only thing you'll find here is what you bring with you."

Jacob nodded. *Noted*. He was rapidly beginning to understand why Katsaros was in the position he was in. He had a keen mind and seemed to be able to read everyone he saw. That, or he knew that whenever Mosiah came calling, it was because of something less friendly than friendly.

He checked his watch, then met eyes with his sister. The look on her face matched how he felt. It pained Jacob to think they'd now have to wait here for two hours until the archbishop could see them. But what could they do? Katsaros swung the door shut with a resounding boom. The concussion made Gabriel flinch. He'd been facing the other direction, taking in the décor of the room.

"Jumpy, are we?" Naomi asked him.

Gabriel looked around. "I don't like being stuck here."

"Same," William said, huffing out a long breath. "We should be doing more."

"Shhh," Mosiah hissed, quieting the group.

Katsaros was staring at them, standing hunched—or perhaps to him he was at attention—studying each and every one of them in silence. He re-wrapped his hands around his back and stayed put, keeping himself between the group and their only exit until the master of the monastery arrived.

Gabriel shrugged. "Might as well get comfortable." He crossed the sizeable space, stepping around an ancient globe of the Earth, and dramatically fell into one of two guest chairs positioned in front of the archbishop's desk.

The act got a low grumble out of Katsaros. But Naomi didn't seem to notice Gabriel, or care. Neither did Joseph. They were both transfixed on the globe positioned in the middle of the office. Now that Jacob had taken his attention off Katsaros' unnerving behavior, he realized that the office had been decorated *around* the globe. It was the room's centerpiece.

"Is this a di Rossi?" Joseph asked, speaking to himself more than anyone else.

"A who?" Gabriel asked, eyes closed, face in his hands.

"Giuseppe di Rossi was a famous Italian craftsman. Made some impressive globes in his time," Joseph explained, studying the piece further. "Early 1600s, perhaps?"

Katsaros cleared his throat. "Late 1500s, actually."

"This thing is five-*hundred*-years old?" Jacob asked, pointing at the globe.

Katsaros nodded. "And, as you can clearly see, it's in near-mint condition. If you were allowed to touch it, you would notice that it is in perfect working order."

Right, Jacob thought. *Don't touch it.*

Gabriel turned around in his chair to look at it. "How much is it worth?"

"That, I do not know," Katsaros replied.

Joseph leaned in close, bending at the hips until his face was barely a foot from it. He examined it closely, biting at his lower lip as he did. "If I had to guess, I'd say somewhere north of one-hundred-thousand dollars."

Gabriel choked on his own air. "That thing is worth a hundred grand?"

Joseph waggled his hand. "Give or take. Could be more. I almost won one in an auction some years ago."

"When was that?" Naomi asked.

Joseph glanced at her and flicked his eyebrows.

Jacob read him loud and clear. *A very long time ago.*

"It's beautiful," Joseph continued. "The archbishop is very fortunate to have one in such good condition."

"Yes," Katsaros agreed. "It is the favorite of his collection."

For some reason, that actually made Jacob smile. He liked the idea of someone cherishing a vintage globe of the Earth. There was something pleasing about it, but he couldn't put his finger on why. It could've been a piece of sports memorabilia, or a classic car, or an expensive painting. But it wasn't. It was a globe. The archbishop appreciated the world as a whole. That was confirmed by other decorative pieces present.

Behind the archbishop's desk was a map of the world. It was massive and seemed to be hand drawn. *No, not drawn,* Jacob thought. The map was actually individual sections of wood that had been connected like a jigsaw puzzle.

Positioned on the corner of the desk was a mounted Crucifix. It was fairly ordinary and worn. Jacob wondered how old it was and who had originally owned it.

Mosiah must've seen Jacob staring at the cross, because he stepped up close to Jacob and whispered, "That's been here for three hundred years."

Jacob's eyes opened wide. "Amazing." He looked around some more. "Simply amazing…"

To Jacob's left was a large bookcase filled with heavily weathered editions. Standing where he was, he could see that the vast majority of them were different translations of the Bible. Some looked downright ancient. This also made Jacob smile.

A man who appreciates history.

The archbishop showed up exactly two hours later. Jacob watched as Katsaros unfolded his hands, unlocked the door, and stepped aside to allow entry to the man in charge. The archbishop didn't even have to knock or use a key. Katsaros had known the man would be here precisely on time. Jacob decided that it'd be another *check* in favor of trusting him.

Before Katsaros could relock the door, the archbishop ordered him to leave. "Thank you, Mr. Katsaros." He turned and looked at the elder. "I will handle it from here."

Katsaros' perma-frown deepened, but he obeyed. "Very well.

I'll be close by if you need me."

The archbishop smiled. "I know you will."

The newcomer was bigger than Jacob had expected. The archbishop was thickly built, in his early fifties, and his voice was jovial—energetic. And like Katsaros, he was unquestionably Greek. His facial features and accent were unmistakable.

He faced the group, shaking his head softly and chuckling. "I'm sorry, you will have to forgive my uncle. He is very suspicious of everyone nowadays, especially since the attack a few years ago."

Jacob recalled the event. The Mossad had briefly taken a look at it when it had happened. ISIS attacked a nearby checkpoint, killing one police officer and injuring a handful more. But something else caught Jacob's ear too.

"Mr. Katsaros is your uncle?" he asked.

"He is," the archbishop replied, "though no one outside of this room knows. It's for his own safety. We," his eyes darted toward Mosiah, "have made quite a few enemies over the years."

Naomi stepped forward. "Does he know what you're involved with?"

"Goodness, no. He suspects something, but he trusts that I know what I'm doing. He knows there's a secret chamber built beneath the mountain, but he does not know what it holds." He smiled again. "Again, for his safety."

Joseph stepped around William, eyeing the archbishop. In turn, the Greek locked eyes with Joseph. "So, this is the man of the hour, yes?" Mosiah nodded, silently answering him. The archbishop crossed his office, stopping when he was within arm's reach of Joseph. But there were no hostilities. He offered Joseph his hand. "Despite what Mosiah has told me about you, it's a pleasure to finally meet you, Joseph of Arimathea." When

Joseph took his hand, the archbishop bowed to him. "Truly an honor. Any companion of Jesus Christ's is welcome here."

Joseph looked incredibly uncomfortable. He unconsciously adjusted the collar of his shirt and said, "Uh, thanks. It's nice to meet you too."

Gabriel stood from his chair. "Your, um, Holiness? Mosiah told us we'd get the full story of this place once we met you..."

The archbishop placed his hands on his hips and sighed. "Where are my manners? My name is Andreas Drakos, Archbishop of Saint Catherine's Monastery." His smile faded, morphing into a man that was tired. "But please, in private, you may all me Andreas." He continued around to the opposite side of his desk, but did not sit. "As I'm sure you can believe, I get enough formalities in my day-to-day life." Jacob looked at Gabriel and shrugged.

Joseph took this opportunity to introduce his people. Andreas gave each member of the Army of God his undivided attention when their names were spoken.

When the pleasantries were over, his eyes shifted to Mosiah. "Shall I begin?"

Mosiah gave the man another curt nod.

Jacob, Naomi, and Gabriel all looked at one another, each with a look of confusion. *Andreas* recognized it and explained.

"Even though I am in charge of this hallowed place, Mosiah is the leader of our people."

"You report to him?" William asked as rigid as ever.

Andreas faced him. "Without question. It's the same reason that you proudly serve Joseph, William Arthur Strom. Why does one of history's greatest champions serve another rather than only himself?"

"Because he believes in Joseph," Naomi replied, nodding her

understanding, "as well as what he embodies."

"Correct," Andreas said. He ran his hands through his salt-and-pepper hair. "Now, the Temple of the Staff of God…"

"That's a mouthful," Gabriel commented, earning a grin from the archbishop.

"It is, but it is also accurate. In house, we simply call it "The Temple," since it is our people's most sacred place." He smiled wide. "Would you like to see it?"

"Just like that?" Jacob asked, surprised.

Andreas shrugged. "If Mosiah has brought you here, then you are to be trusted."

Mosiah took a deep breath. "Go ahead, Andreas. Show them what we've built."

41

Naomi knew that when Mosiah had said *we* he meant the Children of Moses as a whole. She also understood that this had been done over the centuries. It had been a collected effort on the part of hundreds, possibly thousands, of people.

Andreas turned his back to them and bowed his head in prayer. Mosiah, Azmi, and Fikri did the same. Naomi had no idea what prayer they were silently reciting, but she watched the latter three men's lips. They were moving in unison with one another.

A ritual prayer, maybe? Or perhaps they are asking for the blessing to enter sacred ground?

Andreas lifted his head, then shrugged out of his robes. He hung his position's garment on the back of his chair, showing off a powerful, well-maintained physique.

He reached out to the oversized map on the back wall, touched the segment depicting Egypt, and pushed. The country sank away from the rest—like a button! Once it sank an inch, there was a clunk and a low rumble. Andreas released the button and watched with the others as a six-by-eight-foot section of wall sank into the floor to reveal the top of a stone-cut staircase.

No one said a word.

Andreas turned to face them. His face was serious. "The reason these grounds were chosen as the site for this monastery was because of this cave system beneath it. Our people have long been using it as both a Holy site and a confidential meeting place. We've strategized how to act in times of crisis, while also choosing to stand back and allow conflict to pass us by."

He faced the opening and continued.

"As the world has progressed, so have we. We couldn't allow this chamber to be found, so we've had to come up with ways to hide the entrance."

"Hence the false wall," Jacob said.

Andreas glanced at him and nodded. "This is the most recent addition. It was devised almost a century ago, following the fall of Hitler's reign."

"The Nazis almost found this?" Naomi asked.

"They were close," Mosiah replied, "but we had seen their infection spreading before they could. Were we lucky? Perhaps. Either way, our predecessors decided to strengthen this entry point with what you see now."

Joseph stepped up next to Andreas. "Why haven't you continued to upgrade? This is one hundred years old, correct?"

Andreas sighed. "The answer is quite simple. Tourism."

"Excuse me?" Gabriel asked.

"Saint Catherine's Monastery is visited by nearly one hundred *thousand* people every year. To reinforce this entrance further would take a serious amount of manpower and time. Both would be noticed by staff and visitors alike." He looked at Joseph. "We don't have the luxuriousness of privacy."

The last comment hadn't meant to be a jab. The point had

gotten across, regardless. Joseph had become a hermit. In doing so, he'd been able to secretly work on many projects without prying eyes. The Children of Moses did not have that ability and it had seriously hindered their advancement here.

"You seem to have done just fine," Jacob said. "Even if your efforts have been slowed," he motioned to the opening, "this place has yet to be discovered."

"Because of secrets," Andreas said softly. His bold tone waned. "So many secrets…"

Joseph placed a reassuring hand on the archbishop's shoulder. "If there's anyone who understands, it's me. Believe me, what you've accomplished is amazing." He glanced back at Mosiah. "Even I had no idea this existed."

A small smile formed on Andreas's face as he fully turned and faced Joseph. "Yes, that must count for something." The archbishop returned his attention to the rest of the group. "The way is mostly natural at the bottom of the stairs. It is smooth and even. The way is lit by motion activated lights as well."

"Question…" William drew everyone's attention with just the one word spoken. "You said that the monastery was built to hide your Temple. I thought the Staff only arrived here in the 1500s, yet the monastery was built 1,000 years before that."

"I understand your question," Andreas said. "But I would politely ask you to wait until you see the Temple before you are given an answer. Words cannot properly describe it."

Oookay? Naomi thought. She didn't know what to make of that counter offer. *What could be down here that preceded the Staff's arrival by a millennium, and be important enough for it to be included in the Temple of the Staff of God?*

"What about that?" Gabriel asked, noticing something.

A steel pipe ran down the right-hand wall and descended out

of sight, following the stairs' path.

"Communications," Andreas replied. He pointed at his desk phone. "Only Mosiah, my uncle, and I know the code to call. If I am needed in an emergency, my uncle can phone me using an intercom buzzer system."

"You have a working phone inside the mountain?" Gabriel asked.

"Not a phone," Mosiah corrected. "A buzzer system, like you'd find outside an apartment building."

"Or in an office setting," Jacob added.

Gabriel softly bobbed his head. "Oh, gotcha. Press a button and hear that ear-grating *buzz* noise."

Andreas turned. "Shall we?" Then, he started their descent into the mountain.

A couple months ago, Naomi would've been stunned by all this. She still felt the rush of it—of being on the edge of discovery, even if she was the only one who was discovering anything new. All of this was old hat to Andreas and Mosiah. Azmi and Fikri too. They kept close to their boss, staying silent the entire time. Come to think of it, Naomi wasn't sure if they had ever seen the inside of the Temple. So, she asked.

"Have you seen this?" she asked Fikri.

"Once before, during a welcoming ritual," he replied. "As much as I have dreamed of returning here, it is not necessary. I believe. I can close my eyes and see it whenever I need to."

'Need' to, not 'want' to.

To her, it was the same for a Christian when it came to going to church. There was a sense of need, not want. Something inside needed to be there—a longing for community—even if we don't necessarily want to go sometimes. That was Naomi growing up. She didn't always like the church atmosphere, but she did appreciate the feeling—the vibe—of being around so many others, like her parents, who had been diehard congregants. Fanatics, but not in a scary way.

Naomi noticed a hum of an air conditioner overhead as she stepped through. She looked up, to see a grated hole in the ceiling.

"It's not much," Mosiah explained, "but it helps keep the air fresh and the moisture low."

"Where does it connect?" Gabriel asked, next to travel beneath it.

Naomi gave it another glance before beginning her descent.

"It's connected to a unit that we service ourselves."

Mosiah, Azmi, and Fikri brought up the back of the pack. Mosiah entered last, then pulled on a nondescript lever. The reaction was instantaneous. The wall lifted from the floor and resealed itself. They would've been cast into an inky darkness had it not been for, aforementioned, motion-sensor lights. They'd been installed into the ceiling of the arched tunnel.

"Apologies, William!" Andreas called out from the front. "The original builders were not as tall as you."

Naomi spotted William walking with a slight stoop in his posture. He was a few inches taller than everyone here, and the only one that couldn't make the trip standing fully erect.

"A month ago, this would've been pretty spooky," Gabriel said from behind her. She looked back at him as she walked.

"I was just thinking the same," Naomi muttered.

"You've seen something similar?" Mosiah asked from further back.

Naomi wasn't sure what the man knew about the Army of God's more *private* undertakings. Did he know about Joseph's basement or the castle within the mountain? Did he know that the real-life Camelot had been there; that the Holy Grail, Spear of Destiny, and Excalibur had been stored there? Naomi looked forward, frowning when she didn't see the sword sheathed on William's back. They had been forced to leave it behind in the van. She couldn't comprehend the anxiety William must've been feeling knowing that it wasn't locked away in a vault, or on his body.

Only concealable weapons are permitted, Mosiah had said. Concealing a 2,000-year-old Roman gladius wasn't exactly easy.

The thin metal pipe housing the buzzer cable ran along the wall to Naomi's right. Like the lights, it had been attached directly to the rock by thick screws. Besides the minimal existence of modern ingenuity, the tunnel passage was entirely natural, dug directly from the earth.

"You said this was a cave system at one point in the past?" Naomi asked to no one in particular.

Andreas replied from ahead. "Yes, though as you can see, much of it was cut and transformed into something much more manageable. The grade dips and rises further ahead, then snakes left and right. But, for the most part, it continues due south into Mount Moses."

"Mount Sinai, huh?" Jacob asked from directly in front of Naomi.

"It is."

"Where did the confusion with Mount Catherine originate?" Joseph asked.

Andreas looked over his shoulder. "Us, actually. We fed that deception into the surrounding community so we would not be bothered here. Lying isn't something we enjoy doing, but it was necessary while our ancestors worked to create all this."

"That sounds familiar," Naomi heard herself say.

"You mean with Joseph and the whole Fisher King thing?" Gabriel asked.

Joseph glared back at him. "I created *him* to protect my true identity better."

"Exactly," Gabriel said. "It was smart to do so." He held up his hands. "I have nothing against it, or for fabricating the Arthur legend."

"It worked too," Andreas added. "Even our historians weren't sure what to believe for a long time. We knew Joseph was a real person, and that he was alive, but we also knew the Fisher King protected the Grail after it was given to him to watch over. Then, the darkness of the Middle Ages came, clouding reality even further."

Joseph actually sighed. "Ah, the Middle Ages…" William looked back at him. "A wonderful time for us." He quickly continued. "It was so easy to confuse people back then. Staying off the Acolyte's radar was child's play. We barely ever had to hide our faces. We could go wherever we pleased."

"Yeah, we all know about the wild, medieval bender you went on, *Daniel*," Gabriel jabbed. "Got a little too comfortable, if you'd ask me."

Joseph chuckled, ran his hand through his hair, then sighed. "Also, true."

Naomi smiled in response to Joseph's laugh. She enjoyed his stories, no matter how dreary and heartbreaking some of them were. Some were actually quite entertaining, albeit embarrassing, for Joseph to repeat. He'd been through a lot—William too. It was always nice to hear that they had enjoyed themselves from time to time. Just listening to them retell what it was like to live through that period of history took Naomi's breath away every time.

As Joseph's laugh faded, the stone passage transformed into quiet. The only noise you could hear was the group's footfalls and their labored breathing. The grade steepened, beckoning them deeper into the rock. It also took some of the effort out of the hike. They pushed deeper beneath one of the holiest sites on the planet. The fact that Mosiah and Andreas had confirmed that Mount Moses was, in fact, Mount Sinai, where Moses came upon a burning bush imbued with the consciousness of God and received the Ten Commandments, was beyond astonishing.

Naomi opened and closed her hands, then wiggled her fingers. Her nerves were firing on all cylinders.

"Relax," Gabriel said, speaking softly.

"I'm trying," she said, glancing back with a smile. He was watching out for her as he'd done since they had first met. "This place... Everything we've seen... My life's work..." She let out a long, shaky breath, attempting to keep her emotions in check. "This is everything to me, Gabriel."

"I'm happy to hear that, Naomi," Andreas said. He turned just enough for her to see his smiling face from the front of the pack. "And I can't wait for you to see the Temple." He faced forward. "I have a feeling it will also please you immensely."

Naomi looked past him, deeper into the darkness of the passage ahead that had yet to come to life with lights. She tried to picture what was there besides the Staff of God. Based on what the archbishop had said, the *Temple* was more than just a cave with a crude speaking platform and altar. And it contained something else they found important enough to include alongside the Staff.

A void in the eastern wall of the tunnel caught her eye. As she drew nearer, she spotted a second iron gate. Beyond it was cast in unwavering darkness, making her want to know, even more, where it led.

"We're here," Andreas announced, slowing.

Naomi blinked out of her thoughts and looked at her watch. It had only been fifteen minutes, a distance of around half a mile, depending on how fast they had been walking. She was both relieved and shocked that the Temple was so close to the monastery. Naomi was anxious to see what lay ahead.

Everyone packed into the tunnel's exit. The space was vast, though it didn't feel as large as the cave that had held the Citadel—Camelot. Andreas reached to his right. Naomi now saw that a metal box had been mounted to the wall. The archbishop opened its lid and depressed a bulbous red button. There was a loud snap, followed by ceiling mounted lights. One after the other, they came to life inside the cavern. The group shuffled in and beheld it.

Andreas faced them, holding out his hands wide. "Welcome to the *Temple of the Staff of God*, the Children of Moses' most sacred place."

42

Gabriel took in the temple. He was last to enter besides Mosiah and his two men. The ceiling wasn't all that high, maybe twenty feet above his head. The lights that the archbishop had just ignited ran down the center of it. These weren't motion activated. When they all came to life, they stayed on. The footpath stayed true, pointing directly south. And it was the only thing here at "ground level."

To his west was a six-step staircase leading down into the rock. The stepped entrance ran along the entire length of the 200-foot-long path, a path that had been designed to perfectly divide the Temple in half. The eastern section of the Temple was built to mirror the west. It also sported a duplicate six-step entrance down into the earth. Each side reminded Gabriel of a Greek or Roman amphitheater, ones that were commonly constructed in the ground by digging out the earth instead of building atop it.

Makes sense, he thought. He didn't need to be a scholar to know that the Children of Moses had been exiled from Israel during the Roman Empire's reign. The group's builders had designed it off what they knew best.

As he stepped further into the Temple, his eyes lingered on the eastern half of it. Everyone else was currently enthralled with the western half, since it was the half that housed the Staff of God. But the western side contained a sarcophagus.

"Interesting," he mumbled, turning to see what all the hubbub was about behind him. "Oh..."

The Staff was exactly as Joseph had described it. It really was made of part sapphire and part stone. Gabriel used his higher vantage to study the artifact, understanding what it truly was. The Staff swirled with sapphire of the most gorgeous blue, gleaming in the artificial light. It grew within its darker counterpart like the roots of a tree.

Or a lightning strike, he decided. It was gorgeous.

The other material within the Staff was black, igneous, fire-born rock. It usually accompanied lava flows and could be as dark as the dead of night. That's what the Staff contained; half-sapphire, polished to perfection, half-volcanic rock. The contrast in materials and their finishes made the sapphire stand out unbelievably well. Gabriel was interested in how the two materials had fused together.

Duh, God.

Gabriel had decided to stop trying to quantify things. He didn't understand half of it and he probably never would. Beating himself up over it wasn't a healthy way to go about his day. As he listened to the others converse about the Staff in hushed, respective tones, Gabriel, once more, turned to face the eastern half of the Temple. Something about the sarcophagus interested him more than the Staff, which was odd, considering it's what they'd been searching for since they had left Scotland.

He descended the eastern steps, alone with his thoughts, and the mystery of who'd been interred here. If this was Mosiah's tribe's most sacred site, who would be worthy of such reverence? He passed through one of two aisles separating three rows of crude, stone benches. Each bench, upon closer inspection, was just a solid rectangle of stone. Nothing more. Comfort of the worshipers, obviously, wasn't a priority to the builders. No matter. Gabriel didn't plan on sitting any time soon.

He slowed as he approached the grand burial. The lid was ornately carved, and like everything else, made entirely of stone. It featured a man lying on his back, pretty standard for a sarcophagus. The figure was plainly clothed in robes and held his clutched hands to his chest. Within his hands was the Staff.

"Who are you?" he softly asked. The first thing that popped into his head was that it was the first Chief of the Children of Moses. He would definitely be worth burying here.

His eyes lowered to an engraving that had been carved into the sarcophagus' wide base. It was in Hebrew and it only contained two lines of text. Gabriel quickly translated the text in his head, reading it three times before processing what it meant.

He squinted. "Can't be..." He turned his face and called out over his shoulder, never taking his eyes off the inscription. "Hey, guys?"

"*Yeah?*" Naomi asked. "*Gabriel, where are you?*"

He fumbled his response. "You... You need to see this!"

"*No,*" she replied, "*you need to see this!*"

Gabriel blinked, then snarled. He wasn't in the mood to play telephone. He faced the steps and shouted, "*Dammit, get your asses over here—now!*"

43

Mosiah and Andreas stood at the center of the group, happily answering any questions they could with respect to the Staff. Jacob and Naomi were to Andreas' left. Joseph and William stood next to Mosiah, on his right. Azmi and Fikri hung back, whispering to one another.

The Staff stood upright. A portion of its handle was inserted into a hole dug into the rock. It only slightly resembled that of a shepherd's crook. The top was, indeed, curved, but not as much as a traditional crook. To Jacob it looked like it had formed that way naturally. It had been bent by the force behind its creation.

Jacob squinted, estimating its length. *Six feet, maybe?*

"How did it happen?" he asked.

"What, the Staff?" Andreas replied. Jacob nodded. "Some have called it magic. Others have described it as simply being the power of God."

"But where did the power originate?" Joseph asked.

Andreas shifted his stance, then explained. "It began at the Dawn of Creation—the beginning of time itself."

"The Big Bang?" Naomi asked.

The archbishop shrugged. "Call it what you will, and you're more than welcome to argue over how long it took. Time is something that we humans created for our own use. Time had always meant very little to God. Did he create the universe in six days? To him, sure. But what is the length of a 'day' to God? Regardless of how it happened and how long it took, the energy that was given to the universe was said to imbue itself into certain unique items. One of them is the Staff before you. It is eons old."

"The Grail..." Joseph mumbled.

"What about it?" William asked.

He gazed up at William. "It was all his plan, wasn't it? Stonebreaker too. The power within them was planted long ago for us to find in the future, because *he* knew we'd find it."

"*Nothing in all creation is hidden from God's sight. Everything is uncovered and laid bare before the eyes of him to whom we must give account.*" Andreas recited. "Hebrews 4:13."

Joseph leaned around Mosiah and Andreas and looked at Jacob and Naomi. "Just as I said. You two are meant to be here, right now, in this very moment." His eyes turned back to the Staff. "There is no denying it."

"Is it dangerous?" Jacob asked.

"To those unworthy of wielding it, yes," Andreas replied. "Only those with the Holy bloodline can hold it without...complications."

"Is that what happened to Sultan Selim I?" Naomi asked.

Mosiah nodded. "It is. His kingdom overpowered our people and entered its original holding place. Believing it was his divine right to possess the scepter of God, he grasped the Staff but instantly fell ill. His people left the Staff and deliberately disremembered its location, seeing it as a curse or a weapon of evil."

"Shouldn't this be recorded somewhere in the monastery's records?" Jacob asked.

Andreas gazed at him. "We didn't allow that to happen."

Mosiah held out his hand to the Staff, but didn't dare touch it. "Our people foretell of the coming Messiah. He is prophesied, in our Scriptures, to wield it as his scepter, proof of his divine right to rule."

Jacob swallowed, then glanced over at Joseph. The other man was staring at him intently. Then he nodded at Jacob.

He thinks I'm the 'coming Messiah?' Even after everything Jacob had experienced, he thought that was utterly ridiculous. Then he thought about it some more. *Is that how I'm supposed to help open the gates to Eden?*

Gabriel's voice picked up from somewhere behind them. "*Hey, guys?*"

"Yeah?" Naomi asked back. She turned and looked around. "Gabriel, where are you?"

"*You... You need to see this!*" he shouted, his voice bouncing around them.

"No," she replied, looking back at the Staff, "you need to see this!"

There was a pause. Then Gabriel unleashed with, "*Dammit, get your asses over here—now!*"

Everyone looked at Mosiah and Andreas. The archbishop tried to hide his grin. "You should probably listen to him..."

And with that cryptic explanation, Jacob and Naomi headed back to the western side's steps. Joseph and William fell in line behind them with the four Children of Moses members bringing up the rear. The Fehrs climbed the six steps quickly, continued over the central pathway, spotting Gabriel standing in front of what was obviously a sarcophagus. Jacob had been so preoccupied with the Staff that he hadn't noticed this half of the Temple.

Besides the fact that there was a stone coffin here, it was an exact duplicate to the half holding the Staff. Naomi began her descent first. There was no doubt that the archaeologist in her was in Heaven right now. All of this must've been like Christmas morning to her. Jacob was halfway down the steps when his sister finished. She hurried to Gabriel's side and before Jacob could reach her, Naomi's hands went to her mouth, and she took a step back.

"What is it?" Jacob asked intrigued *and* concerned.

"I read it too," Gabriel said. "Does it say what I think it does?"

Naomi nodded, staring at the sarcophagus. Then she did something that struck Jacob as odd. She knelt before it.

"Naomi?" Jacob asked. As he stepped up next to her, he placed a hand on her shoulder and read aloud an inscription that had been carved into the base. "*Here lies the True Prophet. May his wisdom live on.*"

"Is she okay?" Joseph asked, kneeling next to her.

Naomi nodded. She sucked in a deep breath and calmed herself. "When your people were exiled out of Israel in 70 AD," she looked back at Mosiah and Andreas, "the Staff wasn't the only thing they brought to Egypt, is it?"

The archbishop joined the others at the foot of the sarcophagus. "No, it is not. Our ancestors stopped in Jordan first."

"Jordan?" William asked.

"Because," Jacob replied, staring at the sarcophagus, "that's where Moses was supposedly buried." Even Jacob had become overwhelmed with emotion. His eyes watered and he dipped his head in respect and admiration.

Unbelievable.

"On Mount Nebo," Joseph added, softly. "It's said that he was there, within sight of the Promised Land, when he passed away at 120 years old."

William looked at the Fehrs, then Joseph and Gabriel, finally turning and facing Andreas. "Wait, are you telling me that in this sarcophagus are the remains of Moses—*the* Moses?"

All four of the Children of Moses members stood at attention, facing the burial. Then, as one, they bowed. When Mosiah, their chief, opened his eyes, he looked at William.

"Yes," he replied, "that is exactly what we are telling you."

Naomi stood with the help of Jacob. He didn't let her go right away. He held her beneath her arm and around the small of her back.

"How did you get him here in secret?" Jacob asked.

"It wasn't easy for our ancestors to do so, but we always knew where he was buried," Mosiah replied. "Even before our people's exile, we had contemplated moving him."

"To Jerusalem?" Joseph asked.

Mosiah nodded. "Yes, to the First Temple, then the Second Temple. Thankfully, we did not. It would've been impossible once they were destroyed."

"Under the cover of night," Andreas continued, "the highest-ranking members of our order carefully exhumed Moses and spirited him away to Egypt, never once stopping. They took shifts and kept moving until they reached their destination."

"What about the centuries between then and when the monastery was built?" Jacob asked.

Mosiah winked. "I thought you would've figured that out by now…"

Jacob's eyes opened wide. "His body was here the entire

time."

"Correct," Andreas said. "The monastery became a clever way to hide the Temple's entrance as the world grew more curious."

"You coerced the Byzantines into building the monastery here, didn't you?" Joseph asked.

Andreas glanced away, as if it were him that had done it. "Our people may have played a role in helping Justinian I decide, yes. As I have shown you, the Children of Moses have had people in powerful positions for centuries."

"Including influential advisors within the Roman Empire," Mosiah added.

"This is what you've had here—long before the Staff," Naomi said. "When Sultan Selim I discovered it, you decided to reunite it with its master."

Andreas nodded once. Then he looked at William. "I told you that seeing it would be so much more impactful than me simply telling you who rested here."

William nodded back. The archbishop had been correct.

So far, Jacob had thought of Joseph as the master of shadow influence. But it was clear that the Children of Moses, a group much older than even Joseph of Arimathea, were the true masters of purposeful deception. And like Joseph, they didn't do what they did for financial benefit, but to protect something mankind should never have in their possession. Not yet.

The Holy Grail and the Staff of God were not meant to be wielded by warring tyrants, nor was the Ark of the Covenant, for that matter. Jacob could only see one result if the Relics of God *did* fall into the hands of evil.

War and death.

44

Cairo, Egypt

Liam had called in as many favors as he could. He had his men on location, scouring records for anything pertaining to—and connecting with—the Staff of God, the Children of Moses, the Army of God, and the Acolyte. He had loyalists within the Vatican sifting through their archives, as well as the Acolyte's remaining agents in the Mossad. He even messaged someone he knew in the FBI, just in case.

So far, the only factoid they'd come up with that moved the needle was a vague account involving men inside the Eastern Roman Empire, the Byzantines. Liam wasn't exactly sure of the correlation since, by then, many of Rome's leaders were practicing Christians, following in Constantine's footsteps.

The Army of God was also a Christian cabal, but they wouldn't have been involved in any of this. This was the Children of Moses' turf. Egypt belonged to them.

There must be something else here, he thought, trying to force more information out of his messages. *Why were you so involved in Roman affairs?*

"Sir," Aten Al-Khafaji said, startling Liam. "I may have something."

Liam whirled around. "What is it?"

Al-Khafaji handed him a handful of printouts. Among them was a blueprint of a monastery of all things. Saint Catherine's Monastery was one Liam knew well enough to know that a cult of Jewish warriors would have nothing to do with it. It had been in use since its construction by…

"Hmmm," Liam uttered, looking over the blueprint. "Interesting…"

"But, sir," Al-Khafaji said, "I haven't even told you what we found."

He looked up at his operative. "I think I already know."

"You do?"

Liam nodded. "Yes, you see, I received reports of the Children of Moses' involvement in the Byzantine Empire. Until now, I wasn't sure why it mattered to us." He held up the blueprint. "This monastery was commissioned by Justinian I, a Christian Roman emperor."

"Yes, we know that," Al-Khafaji said. "He also commissioned a nearby dam and allowed water to be collected from the mountains."

Liam smiled. "Do you know where the monastery is built?"

"In Saint Catherine, Egypt, sir."

Liam's smile grew bigger. "At the foot of what many believe to be Mount Sinai."

Al-Khafaji's eyes opened wide in response. "I see. So, you think the Children of Moses somehow had the emperor build the monastery there for a specific reason?"

"I do, now, yes."

"Are we to move out?" Al-Khafaji asked.

Liam bit his lip, deep in thought. "I'm still waiting to hear back from another contact. In the meantime, prepare a small team. I want two helicopters available to us too."

"Us?" Al-Khafaji asked. "You will be joining us?"

Liam stood tall. "I didn't become who I am by sitting around and allowing others to fail over and over again. I am not Alpha, and I am done relying on men who can't follow through."

He didn't care how Al-Khafaji responded to the dig. It was the truth. His people continued to fail, even with everything the Acolyte was supplying in the way of finances and intelligence. At every turn, they had failed and the Army of God had slipped away, or flat-out beaten them. A small band of rebels against a modern-day empire.

It honestly embarrassed him.

But no more. This was where the Acolyte would finally prevail.

45

Saint Catherine, South Sinai, Egypt

Georgios Katsaros liked to think of himself as the keeper of the monastery. No one knew it better than him. He had closely inspected every stone—every crack—within its outer walls. But at the end of the day, he was still a servant of God. He also served under his own flesh and blood. Andreas was an impressive man. His faith was deep and his appreciation for life even deeper. That's where he and his nephew differed in the way they approached service.

Andreas Drakos focused on the people. Georgios focused on the reason the people came to visit. He was Saint Catherine's Monastery, and the monastery was him. It was stout and firm, withstanding the test of time with powerful grace. Georgios may have thought highly of himself at times, but he never let it get in the way of his duties—both to the Greek Orthodox Church and his nephew.

He knew Andreas was up to something. He had been for as long as Georgios could remember. Once, he had confronted his nephew about it.

"Are you sure you know what you are doing, Andreas?" he had asked, never once accusing him or anything directly. Luckily, their relationship was strong, and Andreas knew exactly what he had been talking about.

"Uncle," Andreas had replied, "first, yes, I do know what I'm doing. Second, there are things in this world worth fighting to protect. I am doing that as we speak. It is a calling from God, even greater than the one that called me to the church." He lowered his voice. "But it is dangerous. Enemies that seek power would benefit from what I know. They are the reason I cannot reveal more to you."

That opened Georgios' mind. Andreas was devout. If he meant what he had just said, then there was no reason to think otherwise.

"Very well. I will do what I can to be your second set of eyes." He gave his nephew, the archbishop, a curt bow. "I have faith in you, Andreas."

Now, Georgios stood before a third-floor balcony that overlooked the quaint courtyard housing the burning bush. He studied everyone meandering about below him. He even kept an eye on those who were giving the tours. Had Georgios become exceedingly paranoid and untrusting of others over the latter years of his life?

I have, and for good reason, he thought.

Georgios had decided that until someone proved their trust to him, he would keep an eye on them. Evil was everywhere, more so now than ever. Good was losing its grip on the world around him. Georgios could feel it. All you had to do was turn on the television to prove it.

It had been some time since his nephew had led Mosiah Fayek

and company, men who were not part of the Greek church, into the bowels of the mountain. A part of Georgios was envious. After years of servitude, he one day hoped that he too would be permitted entrance. Georgios had never seen some of them before. Who were these strangers, and why were they given access so easily?

He closed his eyes and calmed. *That is not your decision, Georgios. It is God's.* He truly believed that too. His ninetieth birthday was swiftly approaching, and he had experienced very little in his life when it came to hardship. Even now, after decades of working on his feet, Georgios was in excellent health. What he was most proud of was the sharpness of his mind. God had allowed him to lead an exceedingly healthy existence. *And I thank you.*

His mind quieted as his ears picked up on something strange in the air. He closed his eyes and quieted his thoughts, focusing instead on the world around him.

He opened his eyes and looked up just as two black, unmarked helicopters came roaring in from the west—from behind him. They were 300 feet overhead, now idling directly above his position on the balcony. Georgios instantly knew what was happening.

There had been many terror attacks on the monastery over its long history, but none such as this. He spun in time to see one of his fellow clergymen, a young man named Sebastian, come stomping up the stairs.

"Mr. Katsaros!"

"Here," Georgios called.

The other man wheeled around and fast-walked to him. "Something is happening."

"I know," he said.

"Is it local police or the military?" Sebastian asked, fear in his eyes.

Georgios shook his head. "No, it is something else."

"What do we do? Do *we* call the police?"

Somehow, Georgios didn't think it would matter. If these two aircraft arrived here as effortlessly as they had, he doubted there would be anything in the outside world to stop them. *This* was what Andreas had warned him about all those years ago. This was the evil he had feared.

"Evacuate the monastery," Georgios said softly.

"What?"

Sebastian wasn't questioning what Georgios had said, he was merely reacting to it.

"We are called to help others, yes?" the fearful young clergyman nodded. "To do that, we must also protect them, correct?" Sebastian nodded again. "That means we must get as many people outside of the walls as possible."

Sebastian looked out over the monastery. Something in him must've clicked, because some of his resolve came rushing back into him. He closed his open, fishlike mouth and met Georgios' hardened stare.

"Tell the others," Georgios said.

Sebastian nodded. "I will, but what about the archbishop, I can't find him anywhere?"

Georgios' mind returned to the office, to the secret entrance that was concealed within it.

"I will find him," he replied. "Now, go—quickly! We must hurry."

Georgios followed the young man down to ground level, but instead of helping with the evacuation, he returned to Andreas' office. He moved as fast as he could, making it there in record time. Georgios unlocked the door, threw it open, not bothering to close it behind him. He continued inside, heading right for his nephew's desktop phone.

The stoic clergyman's heart pounded in his chest. He got his breathing under control before he picked it up. When he did, he dialed an extension that only one other member of the monastery's staff knew.

71113, which stood for P1113, or Proverbs 11:13.

As he waited for the call to connect, Georgios recited the verse aloud to himself. "*A gossip betrays a confidence, but a trustworthy person keeps a secret.*"

Shouted voices picked up somewhere nearby. And, of course, for the first time ever, he hadn't bothered to shut the door. Georgios made the decision to drop the receiver and hurry back to the heavy door. He swung it shut, quickly throwing the deadbolt. Then he, once again, made his way to his nephew's desk and returned the phone to his ear. It still had yet to connect.

"Come on," he pleaded, tapping his fingertip on the desk.

The voices were closer now.

"Come on…"

46

They'd been beneath the mountain for over two hours now. The tranquility of the subterranean atmosphere had lulled Jacob into a much-needed state of calm. So had the discoveries. He was still processing everything he'd been told. He sat atop the steps, facing east toward the tomb of Moses the prophet. He had a lot going through his head at the moment, and it must've been easy to see.

Joseph sat next to him with a groan. "I'll never get used to it."

"To what?" Jacob asked, staring at the sarcophagus.

"Getting old." He caught Joseph grinning in the corner of his eye.

Jacob clasped his hands to together and looked at his feet. "You really think I'm the one meant to wield the Staff?"

"I do."

Jacob looked over at him. "Are you sure?"

Joseph blew out a long breath, then sat back with his hands on the cool stone pathway. "As sure as I am that Jesus Christ was who he said he was."

So, yes, pretty sure.

"Even two millennia ago, I knew it was you. Our life forces—our spirits—each have a unique signature, if you will. Just as God has willed all of this to happen, I understood who was meant to wield his staff."

"But you've only just met us. How could you know?"

He shrugged. "Because I do." That wasn't what Jacob wanted to hear. "Have faith, Jacob. You'll see, very soon, what I'm talking about."

"But how do *you* know?"

Joseph sat forward and turned to face him. "Because of where we're sitting and who I'm with. I've tried several times to gain entry to this place and failed. Then, the first attempt with you and your sister by my side—*BOOM*—it happens." He gazed back at the Staff to the west. "And once she came into possession of the Holy Blood, well, that was all the convincing I needed."

Jacob still wasn't so sure.

"You know, your father was adamant that you two would change the world someday?"

Jacob smiled softly. "Yeah, he used to say that to us all the time when we were growing up. Then again, I wasn't sure how a paleontologist could change the world."

"Paleontologist?"

Jacob shrugged. "I was seven at the time. You know, boys and dinosaurs and all that."

Joseph smiled and patted his shoulder. "When all this is over, you'll have plenty of time to go dig up some bones."

Jacob rolled his eyes, then he twisted his upper body around to look at the Staff for the first time since sitting with his back to it.

"*If* I am some great leader, the, uh, coming Messiah... What can I expect when I touch the Staff?"

Instead of an answer, he was given another question.

"Do you know what the word Messiah means?" Joseph asked.

"Well, yeah. The Messiah is the next king of the Davidic line. He or she is foretold to deliver Israel from bondage."

"In Judaism, yes. But the generic meaning of the word is simply 'one that is a savior—a liberator—of a group of people.'" He squeezed Jacob's shoulder. "When I think of you as the Messiah, I think of you as the world's savior, not just that of a specific sect of people. There's always been more to this fight than what religion you follow, you know that."

"And the other keys? What about Naomi and whoever is meant to embody the Ark?"

"They are equals to you. That's what you need to understand, Jacob. Yes, this is, and will be, a heavy burden—the heaviest you've ever experienced. But know this... You are not alone. Some of us will be beside you, leading this charge against evil."

"And others will have your back." Both men spun to find William standing there. "Believe in yourself as others believe in you."

"Thanks," Jacob said. "That's really not helping."

William sat on the other side of Jacob. "It's what Joseph said to me when I became the legend."

"Arthur?"

He nodded. "I had a devout fellowship, but I did not see what they did. I only saw the blood on my hands—hands that were unfit to lead, let alone rule."

"Just like Saint Longinus, huh?" Jacob asked.

"To a degree, yes," William replied. "I had done some terrible things in my life before meeting Joseph for the first time, but he told me the same thing he's telling you. You have allies and friends that believe in you. Forget your past, what might disqualify you from being what we know you are, and believe."

"You know, this is the most you've ever said to me at one time?" He quickly followed with. "But, thank you."

William's eyes narrowed. "I'm worried that Gabriel's *humor* is rubbing off on you."

"*Someone say my name?*" Gabriel asked from somewhere behind the trio.

"No!" William shouted back.

"*Okay, geez. Sorry I asked.*"

Jacob shook his head and sighed. He had nothing to add to the exchange. Just being present during William and Gabriel's back-and-forths was enough.

"Jacob," Joseph said, "all I can tell you is to trust us. We've seen a lot, and we've experienced just as much. I can read people better than anyone alive because I've experienced mankind long enough to encounter every type of person." He looked at the Staff again. "It is meant to be in your hands, and soon, it will be. What happens when you wield it will be up to you."

"The power it holds, what is it really? You say it isn't mind control, that it is nothing but a tool to use to gain an audience." He stood, descended the steps until he was eye level with the sitting men, and turned. "That doesn't sound *all-powerful* to me. Why would anyone care about a man holding a stick?"

Neither Joseph nor William replied.

"Why?" Jacob repeated.

Finally, Joseph looked up at him. "I don't know. The Staff is ancient compared to even me. Its power is still very much a mystery to us. Scripture says that Moses and Aaron did remarkable things with their staffs." He also stood and descended the steps. "Do we need you to perform a miracle? Possibly... Honestly, that's probably a yes." He looked away.

"What it is, I have no idea. But I doubt it involves splitting a rock to find water."

Jacob's right eyebrow rose, and he playfully asked, "Did you just mock Moses?"

Joseph's posture straightened. "Heavens, no." He glanced at the sarcophagus. "I'd never."

A piercing, buzzing sound broke the stillness of the cavern air. Both Mosiah and Andreas reacted immediately, sprinting back to the Temple entrance. When they arrived, Mosiah nearly ripped off the lid to the control box. Andreas reached in and picked up a corded telephone receiver. He rambled on in Greek. Jacob figured it was Katsaros, his uncle, on the other end.

Now everyone was making their way to the entrance. Once Jacob arrived with the others, Andreas hung up, looking grim.

"What's wrong?" Mosiah asked, apparently not understanding the exchange either.

Andreas looked down the tunnel. "They're here."

"Who, the Acolyte?" Gabriel asked.

"Yes," the archbishop replied, "they have landed a helicopter nearby and have begun to move armed men inside."

"How did your uncle see this from your office?" Joseph asked.

Still turned toward the tunnel, Andreas pulled out his cell phone. "We have several cameras positioned around the monastery. A handful of staff members have access to them on their phones."

Jacob stepped closer. "What's next?"

"We can't go back," William replied. "Returning to your office will be like walking into a prison cell."

Andreas faced them. "He's right. We have to trust that they won't discover the entrance."

Gabriel looked around. "Don't suppose you have a back door

out of here?"

"Of course, we do," Andreas replied with a look of disapproval. "Our engineers were some of the finest in the world at the time."

"Easy, tiger. I didn't mean anything by it." He glanced around. "I don't see one is all."

"The other iron gate," Naomi said. "I saw it on our way here."

Andreas faced her. "Yes, it leads to a secondary exit."

"Can you get inside through there?" Jacob asked, weighing their options.

"No, not without knowing where it is, and not without a lot of explosives."

Joseph scratched his head. "Thank God they don't know where it is, because they'll definitely have explosives."

"What about Georgios?" Mosiah asked.

"Who?" William asked.

Andreas looked over his shoulder. "My uncle, Georgios Katsaros." He turned to Mosiah. "He knows what to do. I trust that he'll get everyone to safety, including himself."

"And if he doesn't?" Jacob asked.

The archbishop's eyes darted away from the group. "Then he has served the Lord proudly all these years."

"Sorry if this is a bad time to ask this," Gabriel said, "but there's one thing I don't get."

"And what's that?" Mosiah replied, snapping the words off.

He pointed at the archbishop. "You. You belong to the Christian church, yet you protect a Jewish relic and protect Moses' remains, who was also a Jew."

"And you are part of an ancient society whose leadership is Jewish," William added.

"Are we really getting into this now?" Naomi hissed. "We

need to leave."

Gabriel looked around. "We can do both at the same time, yes?"

And, they did.

Mosiah descended the steps, pounding toward the Staff. "Azmi, Fikri, with me."

Jacob had no idea what was happening, but he wanted to help. He followed Mosiah, along with William. The others stayed up top with Andreas, while he explained his *unusual* involvement with the Children of Moses.

"It's actually quite simple," Andreas replied. "We protect two pieces of the greatest story ever told. It is both history and belief. I don't have to be Jewish to think that Moses was an extraordinary person, someone that God chose to use to advance his will. I was born into this tribe. My personal religion has little to do with it."

Jacob agreed, then shut out the rest of the conversation as he focused on what was happening in front of him.

Mosiah and Azmi continued to the front of the Staff altar while Fikri headed around to the back of it. Jacob hadn't gotten close enough to see what was behind the narrow space between it and the western wall of the Temple. A moment later, he found out.

"A steel case?" William asked, immediately understanding its presence as soon as he asked. "For the Staff."

"Precisely," Mosiah said, accepting it from Fikri.

He knelt, set it down, and opened it. Inside was nothing except dense foam and a pair of white cotton gloves, the kind someone would use to handle priceless artwork. The case reminded Jacob of a rifle case, or the case William had used to transport Excalibur into Denmark. Mosiah quickly slipped into the gloves, then stood and took in the Staff.

"When's the last time it was removed?" Jacob asked.

"Not as long as you would expect," Mosiah replied, still staring at the Staff as he stepped closer to it. "We clean it regularly—three times a year."

"You clean it?" William asked.

He nodded. "I have, but no, Andreas does it most of the time." Mosiah breathed in deep then muttered, "Here we go…"

He gently wrapped both gloved hands around the Staff of God, of the prophet Moses, and plucked it from its place of honor. Based on the way the Egyptian handled it, the Staff had some weight to it.

"How heavy is it?" Jacob asked.

"Just over ten pounds," he replied, kneeling again. "Though there are many rumors floating around. One of them states it weighs forty *seah*!"

"How heavy is a *seah*?" William asked.

"Equal to about seventeen pounds of water!"

Jacob was confused. "People think this thing weighs…" he did the math in his head, "680 pounds?"

Mosiah set the Staff inside the case, then removed his gloves and set them inside. He shut it, flipped close the latches, then stood. He faced Jacob and William. "My understanding is that it is merely a mistranslation."

William glanced down at the case gripped tightly in the man's hand.

"We've prepared for every eventuality," Mosiah explained, proudly holding it up for him to see.

"I'd hope so, all things considered."

"Are we ready?" Andreas called out from above.

Mosiah headed for the steps. "We are. Let's move."

"Where's the exit?" Gabriel asked.

Andreas pointed into the tunnel. "Through the second gate. It will lead us to the surface."

"Where precisely?" Joseph asked.

"The Byzantine Dam. It was also commission by Justinian I."

Jacob understood. "Who was advised by your ancestors."

"Correct," Andreas said. He waved them forward. "Come, you will see it soon."

"Uh…" Gabriel said, stopping in place.

"What is it?" Naomi asked.

He looked at her. "Am I the only one that's a bit nervous about both places being tied so closely together?"

"He's right," William said. "It could be a trap if Bailey was smart enough to figure out the connection."

"Doesn't matter," Joseph said. "We *cannot* return to the monastery. The dam might be our only means of escape."

"Can't we just wait it out down here?" Naomi asked.

"Negative," Gabriel said. "What if they find the entrance and force their way in?" He looked up at the ceiling. "Or worse… What if they seal us in and wait for us to starve?"

She visibly shivered. "Okay, yeah, the dam it is."

47

They traveled east, then followed the route as it wrapped around the Temple, going in the direction of the original tunnel: south. They did so by flashlight. There was no motion-activated lighting here. By Naomi's calculation, they were nearing the peak of Mount Sinai, though far below it. They came to a sharp incline, but it wasn't a footpath worn by time or by those traversing it.

There were steps here. They were narrow and rose dramatically to their exit, the Byzantine Dam.

Please be safe, she thought, trying to force it to happen with only her will.

As he'd done since entering through his office, the archbishop led them, mounting the steps without breaking stride. Naomi could feel the man's anxiousness from here. It radiated outward like the heat of a hot summer day.

"I'm sure your uncle is fine," Naomi said, unsure if she should have said anything at all.

"If there is one person who can take care of himself, it's my uncle, that's for sure. He's proven his mettle time and time again." Naomi followed Andreas, Joseph, and Jacob up the steps. The stairwell was much too tight for the archbishop to look back at her while he spoke. "He's faced down rebellious teens, protestors, even Islamic extremists. My uncle answers to only one."

"His nephew too," Gabriel snorted. "That must burn his butt sometimes."

"That is not what I meant..."

Naomi understood. *God.*

"So," she said, "I guess that's two people he answers to."

Andreas let out a tired laugh. "Make it one and a half. I barely have any say in what he does, mostly because, quite frankly, that man makes me nervous."

"Same," Gabriel added. "His eyes. They saw my soul, I think."

Everyone let out a hearty laugh, but it faded soon.

"The exit is just up here," Andreas explained.

"Where is it exactly?" Joseph asked.

The archbishop slowed and lowered his voice. "There is a small shack, near the southern edge of the dam. It is locked from the inside and checked over regularly."

"That's it?" Jacob asked. "A shack?"

"It's all we need."

Mosiah spoke next, bringing up the rear. "What Andreas has failed to explain is that the Saint Catherine's Monastery is in charge of maintaining all surrounding historic sites in the area, including the dam."

"Oh," Naomi said, getting it, "so you control who has access to what?"

"Precisely," Andreas replied. "Apologies, I do not usually speak of this subject aloud. I sometimes forget what is and isn't public knowledge."

They stopped when they came to a small landing at the top of the steps. Built into it was, yet another, iron gate. Andreas swiftly unlocked it and stepped through to a tight space that was only six-feet-wide and four feet in depth. As Naomi finished her ascent, she saw that the room beyond ended at a wall, one with a robust railing, like a handicap railing made of steel piping.

Or is it a handle?

"Help me with this," Andreas said, motioning to Jacob.

The two men grasped the handle and pulled—not pushed. The wall slid backward without trouble. Andreas and Jacob slipped around it, allowing the others to do the same. Naomi and Joseph were next, filling the available space.

"When you said a 'small shack,' you weren't kidding," she said.

"I do my best to not exaggerate," Andreas said. "Now, be prepared for anything. We don't know what awaits us on the other side of this door."

Naomi reached beneath her shirt and rested her hand on her holstered pistol. Andreas inserted a key into the lock, causing Naomi to squeeze the weapon's grip. The door unbolted with a *snap*, making her heart skip a beat. She let out a breath and eyed the grounds beyond the door as it was slowly pushed open.

It only made it halfway before Andreas stood bolt upright, slammed the door, and shouted, "No!"

Naomi had seen it. A lone man was standing in front of a landed chopper, and he held a gun to Katsaros' head. But there was also a dozen or so civilians of all ages, kneeling before a firing squad further back. What put the icing on the cake for Naomi was that the lone man was white, one she recognized from the news and social media.

"He's here," she said under her breath. Jacob looked at her, pistol already drawn. "Bailey is here, and he has a gun to Mr. Katsaros' head." She then relayed everything else that she had seen.

Murmurs erupted throughout the group. The new head of the Acolyte was on location—here and now. Mosiah whispered something about taking him out. William agreed, offering to use himself as a shield. But Joseph had another idea.

"Let me talk to him." Everyone shut up and stared at him. "It's me he wants."

"And the Staff," Mosiah said, from further behind. Naomi looked over her shoulder. He was gripping the case tightly to his chest.

"Yes, and the Staff," Joseph agreed. "Perhaps there's a deal that can be made?"

Jacob glanced at Naomi. "What kind of deal? You can die now."

"Yeah," Naomi added. "What can you offer him? You're vulnerable now, and he holds all the cards."

A small smirk formed on Joseph's face. "Not all of them. Plus, he doesn't know who I really am, and that I can die."

"What are you doing?" William asked, squeezing closer. He was now right behind Naomi, though still beyond the false shack wall.

"I have an idea…" It was clear that they weren't going to get a better explanation than that. So, he faced the archbishop. "Let me try and help those people, Andreas. Your uncle too."

Naomi had no idea what Joseph was going to try to do. Saving the people outside was the right thing to do. She just didn't know how he was going to do it.

"I'm coming with you," William said.

"No, you aren't."

Naomi let out a long breath. "So am I." Both Joseph and Jacob stared at her. "We're a team. We do this together or not at all."

Joseph's eyes didn't waver, but neither did Naomi's. She was serious. They'd been through hell together. This wasn't the time to split up, she could feel it. Something in her was saying that they needed to stay together.

Finally, he relented. "Okay. You win. Together." He held up a finger. "Except for Mosiah and the Staff."

Naomi opened her mouth, but didn't argue. "Alright, yeah. That makes sense."

Joseph stepped up to the door and shoved it open. He exited the shack with his hands raised. Bailey's eyes locked in on him, narrowing with what looked like unbridled rage. Jacob and Naomi were next, followed by Andreas, William, and Gabriel. Both Azmi and Fikri stayed behind with Mosiah. Naomi hadn't even seen them pass through the false wall.

Naomi was shocked that Bailey wasn't wearing a mask of some kind. Alpha had worn a futuristic helmet when he had been on location in Torridon. But not Beta.

He's either incredibly stupid, or very confident.

"Daniel Laird..." Bailey said, his piercing blue eyes staring daggers into Joseph.

Joseph glanced back at his people, flicking his eyebrows. As he had just said, Bailey did not know his true identity. No one in the Acolyte did. That secret had died long ago.

"Liam Bailey. I'm pleased to say that this is not that much of a surprise. Ever since your news group released that smear campaign against us, we pretty much knew it was you behind it."

He shrugged. "Yes, well, that cat was eventually going to be let out of the bag. Why wait, you know?" His nostrils flared and his voice dropped an octave. "Now, give me the Staff." He withdrew the muzzle of his gun from Katsaros' temple only to jam it between the man's ribs. "Or you, your people, and these innocent tourists, die."

Andreas stepped forward. "I'm sorry, Uncle."

Katsaros said nothing. He just gave his nephew a nod.

"This is your uncle, huh?" Bailey said, eyes as wide as saucers. He had the look of a madman now. Naomi wondered how long ago he had been slipping down this particular path. "Well, allow me then." He stepped away and leveled the gun at Katsaros' head.

"Enough!" Joseph said, holding his hands high. "Stop this madness, Bailey! We'll give you what you want, alright? Give me a moment to talk to my people, okay?"

Bailey gave him a condescending bow. "Take all the time you need, but be warned, my men have itchy trigger fingers." He grinned. "As do I."

Andreas' eyes darted to Joseph. "We can't do this."

Joseph put a hand on his shoulder. "We must." He lowered his voice to a whisper. Naomi could barely make out what was said. "We'll get it back, I promise."

"How do you know?" Andreas asked.

Joseph smiled. "By having faith in the people around you."

Jacob stepped closer to them. "How do we know he won't just kill us after we hand it over?"

Naomi glanced back toward the shack. She spotted a reflection. *What is that?* she thought. *The case!* Mosiah was near, and he was listening.

"Because, Jacob," Joseph replied, "we're going to offer him

something else to sweeten the deal..." His eyes finished on William before he turned to face Bailey again.

William's face fell. "No..."

"What's wrong?" Naomi asked.

William was defeated. "He's going to hand himself over too."

"What, no!"

Joseph held up a hand. "Listen to me carefully. This is what's going to buy us some time."

Naomi thought back to something from earlier. "This was your plan all along, wasn't it? When you said you had an idea, this was it. You're abandoning us!" She didn't really mean that. She understood what he was doing and how it was meant to save them.

"What happens when they find out that you're mortal?" Gabriel asked softly.

"I'll worry about that when the time comes," Joseph replied. "Besides, I have another idea..."

Gabriel grinned. "You're going to lead them on a bit first, aren't you?"

Joseph didn't verbally reply. He just smiled.

"Daniel, I'm waiting!" Bailey called out.

Joseph spun on him. "Be patient. I'm doing everything I can to spare you and your men their lives." He turned and faced his people again, leaving Bailey shocked and a little confused. "Also, no one except for William and I know where the entrance to Eden is."

"Come to think of it," Jacob said, "you never told us."

"For good reason," he said. "This reason, actually. If they believe I'm immortal, they know they can't do anything to hurt me. They'll have to agree to my terms and let you go."

"He's right," Mosiah said, stepping out of hiding. The

line of gunmen shifted their weapons away from the kneeling innocents, bringing them up to him instead. He slowly made his way to the front of the group.

"Why is he right?" Naomi asked.

"Because killing solves little," Mosiah replied.

Andreas wasn't so sure. "It would remove a thorn from their paw."

"Yes, but I think they'll want to get moving as soon as they can once they have me and the Staff," Joseph countered. "And, if I'm correct, they'll take me to where the Ark is being held."

William's fearful eyes morphed into those of a man who understood the bigger picture. "That's brilliant. You can get a look at their operation from the inside."

Bailey stepped away from Katsaros, shoving him into the arms of a waiting henchman. "Enough of this. Hand over the Staff, or I'll kill you all myself!"

Joseph glared at him. "You can try. William and I will just take the Staff back into the mountain and barricade ourselves inside. I don't know if you know how long 'forever' is, but that's how long we can wait." He cocked his head to the side. "Can you wait that long?"

Bailey growled, stomped his foot, and turned away.

Joseph relaxed and stepped up to Jacob. "Whatever happens, I need you to be patient and wait for the perfect opportunity. Do *not* come for me in some rash rescue operation." He stared into Jacob's eyes. "Lead with precision."

Naomi was proud to watch her brother nod.

Joseph turned to her. "Be their heart, Naomi. Be their shining star."

"How will we find you?" she asked, voice catching and eyes welling with tears.

He tipped his chin toward William, Jacob, and Gabriel. "I trust these three can figure that out." He took in the former Mossad men. "I assume you both still have dependable connections?"

Gabriel shrugged. "Dependable-*ish*."

"I may know a few people that can help too," Andreas offered.

Joseph gripped the man's shoulder. "Thank you."

Andreas leaned in close. "There's no way I'm abandoning Joseph of Arimathea. Just because I am a man of the church does not mean I won't put up a fight."

Mosiah handed Joseph the case. "May God protect you."

Joseph took it and looked over his group.

"We *will* find you," William said. His voice exuded confidence.

Joseph smiled one last time. "Take care of each other." Then, he turned and crossed the space between good and evil.

48

He paused when he was five feet in front of Bailey. "Our deal: The lives of everyone here, for this...and me." He held up the case, but then cut Bailey off from responding. "And before you say anything stupid, remember, William can easily make it over here and kill you with his bare hands. The only reason he hasn't is because there's a chance that he can't save the hostages too. So, if you value your own life, I'd choose wisely." His eyes flicked over to Katsaros. "Let them go."

Bailey sneered but shouted, "Release them!"

The firing squad lowered their weapons and stepped back. As soon as they did, the hostages got up and fled as fast as their feet could take them. Two of them helped Katsaros along, pulling him away from the tense situation.

"So, why did I just agree to this?" Bailey asked.

Joseph lowered the case. It looked as if he would be carrying it, acting as Bailey's luggage valet. That was fine by him. He would much rather have it in his possession anyway.

"The promise of my cooperation." He glanced back and watched as his people retreated into the shack. Jacob was the last to enter. He gave Joseph a single nod, then shut the door. Joseph waited to hear it lock. When it did, he continued and faced Bailey. "There's still a lot you don't know."

"We know enough," Bailey said, turning and holding out his hand.

Both men casually headed for the awaiting aircraft.

"I remember being as arrogant as you," Joseph said. "It's a lonely way to live. And no, I guarantee that you don't know half of what I do."

"That may be, but I have everything I could ever want in life."

Joseph slowed as he neared the helicopter. When he did, the rotors fired up and began spinning. He faced Bailey. "And, after centuries, I have more. I could've bought your company ten times over by now and shut it down, but what good would that do the world? I'd be just like you."

One of Bailey's agents then stepped up to Joseph and relieved him of the case. *Well, that's that.* At least he got to hold it for a few seconds more. They started toward the aircraft again, not that Joseph rushed himself. He stayed in control and moved to his own drum.

"In," Bailey said, waiting for Joseph to climb inside first. He did. At this point, there was no more delaying the inevitable.

They sat and placed earphones over their heads. With them, they would be able to talk to one another without issue.

"Okay, I'll bite," Bailey said. "How would you be like me?"

"That's easy. I'd willingly suppress the truth to meet my own goals."

Bailey snorted. "Your version of it maybe."

"That's you and the Acolyte's biggest downfall. There are no *versions* of the truth. It's all the same story, just told from two different perspectives. You could learn a thing or two about that."

"Spare me."

Joseph shrugged. "I will. I always will." He leaned forward, strictly for effect. "But what about Michael Mizrahi? Last I checked, he's been very successful with his mission to hunt the Hexad into extinction."

Joseph was happy to see the man's posture turn rigid, and it did just as they lifted off. For a moment, Bailey was startled. Joseph sat back and smiled wide.

"That was you!"

Sadly, Joseph was forced to shake his head. There was no reason to lie to him. "No, that was Hirsch's doing. He created a monster that he, in the end, couldn't control. All we did was set Mizrahi free of the lies surrounding his life. And thanks to Hirsch, Mizrahi blames all of the Hexad, not just your former Alpha."

Bailey didn't have anything else to say about Mizrahi, so he shifted gears instead. "The Grail, tell me where is it?"

Joseph knew this was coming. "You don't need it to open the gates to Eden. You only need me. Also, you are not of Jesus' bloodline and are, therefore, unable to use it."

"Tell me where it is," Bailey repeated, persisting.

Joseph crossed his arms. "No. I said you won't need it. It has no power other than to amplify my own. To you, it would only be a trophy."

"Exactly," Bailey said. "A trophy declaring Acolyte victory over the Army of God. And I will be the only Hexad member to ever have done it."

Joseph's eyebrow raised. "That's awfully juvenile. You want one of the most revered artifacts in history as a victory banner?"

"I do."

Joseph stared into his eyes. "No."

Bailey slammed his fist into the back of the neighboring seat. "Curse Joseph of Arimathea for ever entrusting you with it!"

Now *that* made Joseph smile.

It also got the reaction Joseph had been hoping for. Bailey yanked off his headset and hurled it across the inside of the aircraft. For now, he would pause his attempts to drive the man crazier than he already was. He didn't need Bailey to test his immortality, not yet. Instead, he sat back and looked out his window, just barely being able to see the shack below. Knowing his team, they were already forging a plan to get him back.

Be patient, Joseph thought.

There was still a very valuable wild card out there, one who, if he ever decided to join the Army of God in their fight against Bailey, could tip the war in their favor.

49

Jacob, Mosiah, and Andreas stayed above once they relocked the shack door. Everybody else slipped around the false wall and descended the steps beyond the iron gate. Once they heard the helicopter take off—with Joseph in it—Jacob and the others, likewise, retreated inside. Mosiah and Andreas pushed on the thick steel handle. The wall slid back into place, sealing them in. From the outside, there would be no handle, no way to gain entry without blasting through.

They continued their trek back down to the Temple in silence. The only sound Naomi heard, other than their footfalls, was the closing and locking of two iron gates, this one and the one at the offshoot's starting point. Defeated, the group reentered the sacred temple with one less member and one less supernatural relic.

The only place Naomi could think to sit was in the front row of the eastern half of the Temple. This was where Moses lay. The *bench* was flat and hard, she barely noticed its presence beneath her. Naomi was too lost in thought, contemplating the most recent events. She didn't know how long Joseph had been planning to turn himself over, but he did. She understood why too.

Mosiah sat next to her.

"He isn't afraid of them," she said, staring at the sarcophagus lid.

"Who, Joseph?"

She nodded. "He isn't afraid of the Acolyte having the Relics of God in their possession." She looked at Mosiah, watching his eyes dart around. He was contemplating what to say.

"Nor do I."

That, honestly, surprised her. "You aren't?"

He leaned forward, placing his elbows on his knees, and stared at Moses' crypt. "Do I want them to possess them? Of course not. Do I fear they have the ability to actually use them? No, I do not." He readjusted and faced her. "What do we know about the Ark of the Covenant?"

"Very little other than it kills anyone who tries to open it," she replied.

"Precisely. Think about it like this… Do you believe the Acolyte have anyone in their ranks that God would allow to open the Ark?"

She snorted. "Not a damn chance."

"I couldn't have said it better myself." Mosiah grinned. "Believe it or not, the Ark is safe where it is. It's in limbo, which is exactly where it needs to be for now."

She let out a long breath. "It'd be better if it were on our side of limbo."

"No argument here," he said. "As far as the Staff is concerned, I have a feeling that it'll be much of the same for the Acolyte. Yes, many in my order believe that if evil should ever wield it, they will be able to rule the world with an iron fist."

She stared at him. "What do *you* believe, Mosiah?"

His eyes found Moses' sarcophagus again. "I personally believe that the Staff is waiting for the right person to come along, someone the world will not expect. Bailey may be a descendent of Moses, but that does not make him worthy of possessing such favor with God." He looked at her. "As I'm sure you can understand, blood is not everything." He gently tapped her chest. "What's in here matters too."

Mosiah stood. "Excuse me, I must see to something."

She nodded her goodbye and stared at the sarcophagus, once more. Then, she recalled what Joseph had said to her before giving himself over to the Acolyte.

Be their heart. Be their shining star.

She didn't quite know what to make of that, but she was pretty sure she was slowly figuring it out. Naomi needed to be the heart of this side of the war. She needed to be steadfast in her beliefs—in God's plan here and in the ability of the people around her. She could never show her inner conflict.

Naomi needed to radiate confidence and care.

She looked over her shoulder and found her brother talking quietly to Gabriel and William. Then she thought back to what Joseph had said to Jacob.

Lead with precision.

Jacob was the other half of their call to leadership. Joseph wanted them to team-up and take over the Army of God.

She would be its heart—its emotion, as well as its defense against moments like this.

Jacob would be its mind—its decisiveness, as well as its offense in the imminent climax.

Naomi also recalled something else Joseph had told them several times now.

You are meant to be here.

Something in her clicked. Naomi felt an upwelling deep inside of her. She was still afraid, but she no longer feared it. She allowed it to guide her. She would use her fear to guide her and everyone else. She stood and turned, seeing every member of their team. All of them—every single one—was a warrior in some way. Even Andreas, the archbishop.

But Naomi wasn't. She was *just* a history nerd. But that didn't mean she still couldn't do her part.

She'd keep them grounded and focused on the bigger picture.

She'd cheer them on and be their biggest fan.

She'd believe in them just as Joseph did.

She would be their heart.

Naomi would be their shining star.

50

This was the first time, in their long time together, that William and Joseph had been separated because of defeat. Each had gone their own way from time to time, but never like this. They'd been joined at the hip for centuries. It didn't take William long to start seeing Joseph as something more than a friend and mentor. Joseph had become a father to William.

His heart had been hardened by war and loss long ago. Nowadays, it took everything in William to see life as something other than the next conflict. It's why he was always so prepared. He devoted every minute of every day to the next conflict.

But this hadn't been in his calculations. William was at a loss.

A warm hand found the back of his arm. He looked down at the shorter, brown-eyed woman. Naomi simply looked at him and smiled. It was all he needed. Her presence, as Joseph believed, was more than just being one of three keys.

She is our heart.

"I think I know where they will take him," he said, sifting through years of memories and millions of hours of research and preparation.

"Where?" Jacob asked.

"The Watchtower," William replied. "It is the codename for a castle somewhere along the Austrian-German border."

"*Somewhere?*" Gabriel asked. "You don't know?"

He shook his head. "No. We've narrowed it down to a handful, but have never been able to zero in on one. It's why we've always believed that it operates autonomously from Hexad rule."

Mosiah joined them. "I can see that. The Acolyte are like a leaky faucet, constantly dripping intel for all to see…if one knows what to look for, of course."

"We don't know where it is, either," Andreas added. "Whoever runs the Watchtower has done a commendable job with their secret keeping."

Naomi glanced at her brother.

"Which means their people are a special kind of extreme," Jacob said.

"That's what we've come to think as well," Mosiah said. "The only thing we really know is that there has never been a member defection."

"They're that loyal?" Gabriel asked.

William wasn't so sure. "Or, they silence anyone they suspect of going AWOL before it happens."

Mosiah nodded. "That too."

During the conversation, William noticed something in Naomi that was different. Her posture was of someone in control, not someone who happily shrank into the shadows. She had been asked, by Joseph, to lead these people, along with her brother.

She faced Andreas and Mosiah. "Think you can get copies of everything your order has on the Watchtower *and* the Ark of the

Covenant—maybe even Liam Bailey's family history?"

Both men shrugged.

"Sure," Mosiah replied. "Shouldn't take more than a couple of days."

"I will do the same," William said, giving her a nod of respect. "We have everything in print and digital backups in Torridon."

"It wasn't destroyed in the attack?" Andreas asked.

Gabriel smiled. "You gotta see the basement for yourself."

"We need to split up," Jacob said, quickly holding up a hand to prevent any outrage, "for now. Gather whatever intel we have and regroup in Torridon." He faced William. "Think you can give Isla and Ian a heads up? We don't need a repeat of Gabriel's introduction."

Naomi smiled. So did William. The sight of what had happened still amused him greatly, though he had recently warmed up to the man. Gabriel was unashamedly himself, and William could respect that.

"Har, har," Gabriel said, rolling his eyes. Mosiah, Andreas, Azmi, and Fikri all looked around, confused. They hadn't been there when Gabriel had been knocked out, tied up, and presented to the Army of God as a captive. "I'll, uh, tell you later."

"One thing," Andreas said. "I would like to bring my uncle into the loop, please. After all this, he deserves to know what is going on."

He faced Mosiah, looking for permission. But the Children of Moses leader did something William did not expect, he deferred the decision to Jacob and Naomi.

"What say you?" he asked.

The Fehrs glanced at one another. Jacob nodded at Naomi, giving her the green light to answer.

"Do it," she replied. "Quite frankly, I'd be too nervous not to at this point."

Gabriel didn't share in the jovial comment.

"Something bothering you?" William asked.

"Yeah, I feel like we still need more people."

Mosiah stepped forward. "I can fix that. Until the Staff is safely back in our possession, you have the entire Children of Moses at your disposal."

William recalled that there had been over a dozen or so men back at the construction company property, plus however many people Mosiah had throughout Cairo, Alexandria, and the other cities of Egypt.

In the matter of a few weeks, the Army of God had transformed from a unit of a few to an army of many.

"Alright," Jacob said, "let's retrieve Mr. Katsaros and get moving. We have a lot of work to do."

51

Füssen, Bavaria, Germany

Time had become something of a blur for Joseph. To the best of his knowledge, it had been three days since he had boarded Bailey's helicopter in Egypt. They had flown straight to the Abu Rudeis Airport. It sat along the western coast of the South Sinai Governate. The last time he had seen the outdoors until now, was when he had ascended the folding stairs of Bailey's private jet. It was there he had stayed aboard, with the window shades closed, for what he guessed was three days.

Bailey had happily disembarked, leaving Joseph with a trio of armed guards for hours on end. All he could do was sit in a seat he'd been cuffed to and wait. The chair was the only positive thing, it was plush, leather, and ultra comfortable. Other than getting up to use the onboard toilet, Joseph was always made to sit and wait.

He had been forced to practice what he had preached to Jacob.

Patience, he thought, needing to practice it himself.

Joseph wasn't stupid. He knew what Bailey was doing to him. He was delaying their arrival to confuse him and his people as to his whereabouts. The Acolyte was under no illusion. They knew the Army of God would eventually come to Joseph's rescue.

But where?

Joseph found out midday on the third day of his capture.

He was just outside Füssen, Bavaria, in the south of Germany. There were three castles he could name off the top of his head: *Hohenschwangau*, *Schwarzburg*, and the most famous of them, *Neuschwanstein*, the castle that had inspired Disney's Sleeping Beauty's castle. But of the three, only one possessed a deeply disturbing past…or so the legends say.

Joseph's suspicions were confirmed fifteen minutes later. His driver parked outside of the least impressive of the three castles, Schwarzburg, the "Black Castle." In all of his years of research, the only mention of there being "royal blood" being involved here, had nothing to do with Jesus or Moses, but had everything to do with the Nazi's master race, the Aryan race.

The stories surrounding the Black Castle were grim to say the least. The family that had built the high-walled, fortress-of-a-home had owned deep ties to several ancient Hermetic orders, including the Order of the Golden Dawn, and later, the Thule Society, though most scholars didn't present the latter as a Hermetic organization. Nevertheless, both had been seriously into the occult and other mystic practices. To Joseph's knowledge, this was where the idea of the master race had been born, down in a secret chamber, far beneath the castle grounds.

But again, there had never been concrete evidence, just local legends, most originating hundreds of years ago when the castle had first been built. Joseph knew from personal experience that the Middle Ages had been ripe with paranoia, where fictional stories thrived, believed by the ignorant masses. If this was truly where the Acolyte stronghold, the Watchtower, was, then he had to give it to them for keeping it a secret for as long as they had.

These guys are good. These guys are 'very' good...

He wouldn't give the Acolyte a share of the credit, though. Like William, he knew the stories surrounding the people running the Watchtower. They didn't answer to anyone, even the Hexad. They'd been given the freedom to operate on their own, only sharing in information, not their physical location.

Bailey sat across from Joseph, facing him in the back of the six-passenger limo. With them were three guards. Two sat on either side of Joseph, while one sat up front with the driver.

"We're here," Bailey said, nodding to one guard. The man produced a key and quickly unlocked Joseph's handcuffs.

"You're giving me a sizeable leash," Joseph said, resisting the urge to rub his wrists.

Bailey sighed. "Unfortunately, we are in a very populated area. Optics are everything. My involvement in the monastery incident has not yet gone global. I must still use caution." He stroked the case sitting next to him. "For now..."

"You're really going to go public with the Staff of God and show the world how great you think you are?"

Bailey stared down at the case. "And why shouldn't I?"

Joseph shook his head. "I don't know about you, but I don't like looking like a fool."

"Let's go," Bailey ordered.

His man complied and opened the rear door. The goon to Joseph's right stepped out first. Then it was Joseph's turn. The guard from the front seat met them and waited. Bailey exited next and was immediately followed by the third, and final, guard. The five men stood at the bottom of the steps of Schwarzburg.

Bailey gripped the case's handle in his right hand, looking very proud of himself. He eyed each of his men, as if giving them a silent message. The feeling between them was charged with nervous energy. Joseph was curious whether they'd be welcomed or not. If Bailey held no power here, would he be seen as friend or foe?

Bailey must've caught Joseph gawking at the elaborate front façade. "Remarkable, isn't it? Sure, I mean, it's no Neuschwanstein or Hohenschwangau, but I still find it impressive that a place that receives over one hundred thousand visitors a year is also the site of the Acolyte's most secure location."

"You're enjoying this, aren't you?"

Bailey couldn't hide his smile. "Considering you're the one who's usually in the position to gloat, yes, I am enjoying myself. Very much."

I'll let you have it, Joseph decided. *But only for now.*

"Why not keep me close to you?" Joseph asked. "Why hand me over to this place?"

Bailey looked around. "Because I know your people are out there. And I also know that it will be impossible to break you out. This is the safest place for someone like you right now."

Joseph slowed as he neared the top step. When he arrived, he stopped and looked straight up. "The home of the Ark, huh?"

"And yours for the foreseeable future…until your usefulness runs out."

Joseph knew this was the best plan, but he was also extremely nervous about entering the unknown—the *real* unknown. No one outside a privileged few knew what lay beneath the Black Castle.

No one.

Home to the Ark of the Covenant for the last century, he thought, not fully believing himself. *This is it.*

Joseph followed Bailey to the front door. He didn't open it, though. Someone from the inside did. They greeted them in German then quickly followed with the English translation.

"Good afternoon and welcome to Schwarzburg!"

Bailey blew straight past the young blonde woman. Joseph gave her a curt nod and a smile, then entered. The foyer's ceiling was tall but not cavernous. The tapestries on display were beautiful. They were well-preserved and vibrant. In Joseph's experience, that either meant they were worth a fortune or were a fake. There was nothing wrong with an immaculate replica, in Joseph's opinion, just as long as it wasn't being pawned off as the real thing.

Tourists meandered about. To Joseph's right was a group of people being led by another young woman. She spoke in clipped English, which was common since most people coming to a place like this wouldn't be local. Bailey marched onward, heading directly for the front desk.

No way, Joseph thought. *It can't be this easy?*

"*Hallo,*" greeted a youthful man, "and welcome to Schwarzburg!" He looked up from his computer screen. "How many is it?"

"None, actually," Bailey replied. "I have a gift for the Administrator."

The German man titled his head to the side. "The who?"

His phone rang instantly. The local picked it up. Joseph couldn't hear the other end of the conversation, but it looked as if he was getting his ass chewed out by someone.

The young man swallowed, then spoke. "And what is this gift, may I ask?"

"Tell him it's Daniel Laird," Bailey replied, smiling proudly.

Him... Well, that's one domino.

The local did, then hung up. He stood and took in Joseph and the others. "Please, follow me."

And just like that, they were off. The local left his post, despite the line that had formed, and continued to his left until he had exited the long counter. Bailey rounded the workstation first with Joseph hot on his heels. They followed the rigid employee through the central corridor of the castle's first floor, passing through several roped off sections and four separate staircases leading up. They made a left then stopped at the second door on the first right. It was a keycarded door that read "Official Use Only" in English and German. Joseph spoke and read a bit of German but would keep that to himself. The local didn't unlock the door himself. It buzzed as soon as they stepped in front of it. He didn't enter, nor did he even open the door.

"Inside, please," he said, turning away.

Geez, Joseph thought. *Even their own people don't know what's really here.*

Bailey quickly pushed through, entering without the escort. Joseph found all this very odd, and before he could question the young German man, he shut the door, leaving them to themselves. Another buzz followed, locking the door.

"*Continue forward,*" a German-accented, mechanical voice said.

Joseph searched for the speaker from which the voice had been projected but couldn't find anything. All that was here was a mirrored corridor. The floor and ceiling were bleach white, but the entire stretch of the room featured nothing but mirrored walls on both sides. Joseph was ushered forward by the muzzle of a pistol. One guard had drawn a firearm in the time between the local leaving and the mysterious voice's order.

Joseph glanced at the mirrored wall to his left, deciding that the mirror was actually of the two-way variety. There were probably security personnel on the other side performing a bevy of scans on them as they walked. Thirty feet later, they reached another, identical door. It too buzzed, allowing them entry without asking for it.

"*Inside,*" the same voice called out. Joseph was having trouble deciding whether it was male or female. There was also a possibility that the voice was entirely false, artificially producing the tone and accent to hide the real speaker.

Or it's just a German man with a trebly voice speaking into a cheapo, drive-through speaker system.

That, he highly doubted. Nothing about this screamed "cheap."

The corridor on the other side was identical to the last one, sporting mirrored walls on both sides. The biggest difference was that it didn't end at another *door*. It actually ended at an elevator.

"Going up?" he asked.

Bailey looked back at him as he moved. "Quite the opposite, actually."

Once they were halfway to the elevator doors, they opened, and out stepped two, heavily armed solider-types. Their uniforms were solid black and contained no insignia. They were outfitted from head to toe in rugged armor, including a hardy helmet with a face shield. They carried German-made Heckler & Koch UMP submachine guns. The compact, select-fire weapon was perfect for the narrow hallway Joseph currently found himself in.

"Stop," one guard said. His English was also accented in German.

They did. The second one stomped toward Joseph and removed a pair of handcuffs from a pocket on his kitted chest rig. Joseph knew the game, so he didn't fight them. He just held up his hands and allowed the soldier to cuff him. Then, he was led into the elevator and spun around so he was looking back out the open doors.

Bailey did not follow.

"You aren't coming?" Joseph asked.

He smiled. "In due time, but I have something very important to take care of first." Joseph looked down at the case. "The world is about to get its first look at its new king."

Joseph closed his eyes, and his chin dropped to his chest. "I've told you several times, the Staff does not work that way. It can't control people's minds. They will never be your slaves, Liam."

"And I've told you that I have very little reason to believe you." Bailey held up the case. "My blood will give me what I want. This has always been my destiny."

"I'm sorry to say that you've been misled and are mistaken. You are not meant to wield it."

"Oh, come now, *great* Fisher King, you've been living a lie for centuries. Why should I believe you now? When I need a lecture about the Grail, I'll come to you. Until then, sit tight. Oh, and I can't promise that you'll have a comfortable stay." He looked at the right-hand soldier and tipped his chin. "Do what you must to get him to talk, but under no circumstances is he to die." He eyed Joseph. "Not yet." His smile grew. "Have a pleasant stay at the Black Castle."

Joseph could only think of one reply. He just held up his cuffed hands and extended his right middle finger.

The soldier on his left inserted a keycard into a slot in the elevator panel, one that displayed a panel with no buttons of any kind. Jacob, Naomi, and the others were going to have to be smart to gain access to the lower levels of Schwarzburg. The doors shut as soon as the card was removed. Apparently, this elevator only traveled to one floor. There were no other choices.

At least there's that… There'd be no confusion once they made it this far. They would go as far as the elevator took them.

Then they descended.

And kept going and going and going.

Joseph looked at both soldiers, one at a time. "Huh, I had no idea the entrance to Hell was in Southern Germany?" He faced the doors and eyed his reflection and sighed. "You learn something new every day."

52

Silicon Valley, California, USA

The press conference was scheduled for noon. To the vast majority of the world, this was out of the blue. But not everyone was surprised when the CEO of Prophecy Global Inc. announced that he'd be taking the stage outside of his corporate headquarters to go over a "life-changing discovery," one that would change the world forever.

It had been seven days since Joseph of Arimathea was taken from them. Jacob, Naomi, and Mosiah, chief of the Children of Moses, were on hand for the presser. Everyone else had gone about their duties of gathering up as much intel as they could. Then, they all hopped on various planes to Scotland to meet up with Isla and Ian MacDonald at Joseph's Torridon estate.

Jacob had just gotten off a group call with them all, even Archbishop Andreas Drakos and his uncle, Georgios Katsaros, though the two clergymen had done so via a video call from Andreas' office. The effort everyone had been putting in to locate Joseph was inspiring. They had a couple of good leads too.

Mosiah sent the brothers, Azmi and Fikri, on ahead to Southern Germany to scout a handful of locations. They were also hoping that their visit to the region would be flagged by Acolyte scouts.

"Hopefully we can force them out of their hole," William had said.

Gabriel and William were leading the intelligence gathering operation while Mosiah and the Fehrs were in the United States. If this went the way Jacob thought it would, they might be able to retrieve the Staff quicker than originally thought. Either way, they'd need to act fast. Bailey had people everywhere, especially in California.

But will they come to his aid while he's on stage and in public? Jacob wasn't sure. Alpha would've never done anything this foolish. Bailey was changing things rapidly and within an organization that had been doing things a certain way for a long time.

The three Army of God operatives hid in plain sight while they waited for the public press conference to begin. An estimated three thousand people had shown up for the event. Several people were already live streaming it on their social media platform of choice. Influencers were everywhere. Yet, each one had very little to offer the world except for a vapid opinion. They weren't *reporting*. They were just *yapping* and doing so loudly.

Jacob, like Naomi and Mosiah, had arrived alone and at different times. The presser was taking place at the center of Bailey's massive headquarters. Eight buildings were laid out in a circle, with a vast common area, complete with sidewalks and park benches, between them all. Jacob did have to give it to the people of Prophecy Global Inc. They really did have everything here—so much so that he wondered if anyone ever left.

To him, it looked like a tech nerd's Woodstock. The grassy

area was covered with people, as if Jimi Hendrix were about to play the national anthem from his grave. There were vendors everywhere too, each one hocking their wares. The food trucks had caught Mosiah's attention first, but he quickly countered the smells with the pat of his stomach.

"I've decided that I need to drop a few pounds." He looked longingly at a nearby taco truck. "I have a feeling there will be a lot of running in our future."

Gone was Mosiah Fayek's thick beard. He was almost unrecognizable. His head was still bald, but now, his face was clean shaven, minus a stylized goatee. Jacob was still beardless, though he had begun to grow a mustache much to the chagrin of his sister. Naomi had made the biggest change of them all. She had cut her hair even shorter. It now framed her face beautifully, stopping at her jawline. She still wore her faux glasses, as well.

"*Any time now,*" Mosiah said, his voice coming through in their hidden comms system. "*He's running fifteen minutes late as it is.*"

The three operatives wore earbuds similar to the ones Apple made. It was easy to get away with because hundreds of others wore something similar. They were currently in a group call together, coordinating their movements as they each snaked closer to the stage.

"*Bailey seems like someone who enjoys the drama of it all,*" Naomi added.

Jacob agreed. "*Yeah, this is definitely his thing.*"

"*I personally can't wait to watch him squirm when it fails,*" Mosiah said. Then he added, "*Oh, and I'm fifty feet from the west side of the stage.*"

"Copy that," Jacob said, lining up with the center of the stage, heading north.

"*What if it doesn't fail?*" Naomi asked. "*I think it will, but we've never really discussed what happens if the Staff works.*"

Her question was valid. They were all staunch believers that this circus was going to flop and do so hard. But there was still a possibility, even a small one, that the Staff would do exactly what Bailey wanted it to do.

"*It will not work,*" Mosiah insisted, voice rising. He calmed. "*I bet my life on it.*"

"Same," Jacob said. "It's not going to work."

Naomi also agreed. "*Ditto. I just want to make sure we've at least talked about it. Okay, I'm thirty feet from the eastside of the stage. Mosiah, do you have anyone blocking your stairs?*"

"*Yes, one unintimidating kid.*" Jacob could see everything from where he was. The *kid* Mosiah was talking about was a fresh face, for sure. "*I swear, they get younger and younger the older I get.*"

But Jacob didn't advance the banter. Liam Bailey had arrived.

"I've got him," Jacob announced. "He's backstage and about to come out." His heart skipped. "And he has your case, Mosiah."

Mosiah cursed in Arabic. Jacob could see him from here as he stepped toward the stage.

"Stand down, Mosiah. This doesn't work unless he acts first."

The other man grumbled. "*I know, I know...*"

Then, Liam Bailey proudly, gleefully took the stage. The entire place erupted. If Jacob hadn't known better, he'd have said that these people were already his mindless slaves. He wondered if anyone here cared that Bailey himself didn't design anything he sold. Like a lot of tech giants, the companies' faces were purely there for PR, nothing more. Bailey was the boss, that's where his involvement in "life-changing discoveries" stopped.

"Thank you! Thank you!" Bailey said, shouting into a microphone that was already much too loud. He held the case by his side as he welcomed the audience. "What a fabulous showing! This is incredible! Give yourselves a round of applause for being here—and on such short notice!"

Like the trained monkeys they were, his *adoring* fans clapped when told too.

"*Ugh, please,*" Naomi said. "*Can I punch him now?*"

Jacob grinned. "Later." He looked toward Naomi's position and spotted her standing nearly ten feet from the stairs on her side. "Are you going to be able to get past your guy?"

"*Shouldn't be a problem,*" she replied. "*I think he's even smaller than Mosiah's.*"

Still, Jacob didn't like them being split up any longer. When they retrieved the Staff, they'd need to move quickly.

"Change of plans. Naomi, head over to Mosiah's side. We'll push up his stairs together."

"*You sure?*" she asked.

He spotted her again and nodded. She was looking right at him. "Yes. I want us together, especially if things degrade."

"*Copy that. Moving now.*"

Jacob didn't, though. He stayed put, hat low over his eyes, with only three rows of people between himself and the stage. He wanted to see what was going to happen from here.

"Now," Bailey continued, "I've called this press conference to announce something amazing." A handful of cheers picked up around Jacob. "I've recently come into something that is going to revolutionize the way we do things." He held up the case. "Even the way we think."

That got everyone's attention.

"*At least he's a quality showman,*" Mosiah said, his words

oozing with disdain.

"*Yeah,*" Naomi said, almost directly behind Jacob now, "*a regular politician.*"

Jacob wasn't listening. He was too busy watching Bailey as the man set down the case.

"Double-time it, Naomi. The show is about to start."

"*Or not,*" Mosiah added, slyly.

Jacob agreed, but they needed to be ready to move.

Naomi slipped past Jacob, running her hand along his back as she did. He didn't physically acknowledge her. "*Either way, we'll be getting a show to remember.*"

Jacob sighed. The hairs on his arms were standing on end.

Bailey dramatically looked up at the crowd from a kneeling position. Gone was his practiced showmanship. The crazed Acolyte fanatic had returned in a matter of seconds. Bailey's eyes were wide now, and the muscles in his face twitched. Jacob knew the man had been dreaming of this day his entire life. It was why he didn't take Joseph's warning seriously. There was nothing on this earth that was going to stop this from happening. Jacob didn't want it to stop, either. He wanted Bailey to follow through.

Bailey flipped open the lid. His lips nearly peeled back as he let forth the toothiest smile Jacob had ever seen. Bailey was near combustion level now. He pulled a single glove out of his jacket pocket and put it on.

"Looks like he wants the world to see him touch it for the first time," Jacob said, voicing his thoughts.

"*Probably not the smartest idea,*" Naomi said. "*This feels like something you should test first.*"

Jacob spied Mosiah ten feet from the stairs. "*At least he's confident in himself...*"

Bailey stood with the Staff of God in his hand. Jacob took in the people around him. Every person in attendance was utterly confused. This wasn't at all what they had expected. To the public, Bailey was a media mogul, not a religious zealot. What he did now would've been better suited in the Dark Ages, back when William was wiping out his enemies as Arthur.

Bailey set his microphone on a nearby stand, gazing awkwardly at the Staff. Jacob did have to admit that it looked downright radiant out in the open, in the bright afternoon sun. The only time he had seen it, until now, was underground with nothing but artificial light to see by. The sun's rays made the sapphire glow.

"*Magnificent*," Mosiah muttered.

Naomi swooped in. "*Focus, Mosiah. You with us?*"

Mosiah cleared his throat. "*I...never left.*"

Jacob rolled his eyes and nearly cringed when Bailey held the Staff above his head.

"This is the instrument of ages. This is what will change the world." He looked up. "And I will be its shepherd. I will lead humanity into a new era!"

Bailey's amplified voice bounced off the surrounding buildings. Not a single attendee clapped. Everyone just stared at him, mouths agape. Even Jacob couldn't take his eyes off the train wreck.

"Come on," he mumbled, "do it."

Bailey did look a little nervous. Even he wasn't sure what would happen. He believed he knew, just like Jacob and the others did.

Jacob held his breath as Bailey reached his ungloved, open hand up, hovering it around the middle of the Staff. Jacob expected there to be a light show, but when Bailey closed his fingers around it...nothing happened.

The entire audience held their breaths. Then, one by one, they began to chuckle. The live streamers never stopped recording. Jacob flashed his eyes over to Naomi and Mosiah. They were together now. Jacob needed to be there soon too.

He began his journey through the throng of rising laughter, then he leaned into one man and said, "Friggin guy thinks he's Moses, am I right?"

The random person busted out laughing, gaining the attention of someone else. The laughing man repeated what Jacob had just told him. Then, the jab spread like wildfire, igniting into a sea of cackling and pointing fingers.

Bailey was horrified.

He jammed the Staff into his armpit and ripped away the one glove with his opposite hand. Then he gripped it with both hands, squeezing the artifact as hard as he could. He looked up at the crowd of onlookers and took a step back. Jacob hurried. They needed to move. Now.

"Get ready," he said, shoving people aside.

"*Ready when you are,*" Naomi replied. "*Mosiah is already sizing up the security guard.*"

Jacob glanced at Bailey, then picked up his speed. "Not yet... Not yet..."

Bailey flinched when a random audience member shouted at him. He took another step back, stumbled, then fell on his ass, dropping the Staff with a clatter.

"Now, Mosiah. Go!"

Mosiah stomped up the side stairs. He was instantly met by the scrawny guard. Mosiah towered over him, even though he himself wasn't all that tall. Jacob arrived, following Mosiah up. Naomi closed in behind her brother, sandwiching him between them.

"Move, or be moved," Mosiah growled.

Naomi leaned around both men. "I'd do what he says. He's wanted in a dozen countries, you know?"

The guard looked at Mosiah, then back to Naomi. Then he slowly stepped aside, raising his hands as he did. All three Army of God operatives arrived onstage with no other confrontation. Everyone, even Bailey's own people, Acolyte and not, didn't know what to make of all this. They had all frozen in place. Their boss was now cowering, sitting onstage with his knees in his chest, sobbing uncontrollably. Jacob could see the fake headlines tomorrow. They'd talk about Liam Bailey having a mental crisis because of the stress of running such a successful company and that people should lay off him.

But that wasn't it. Bailey had broken. His eyes stared through whatever they were pointed at.

Mosiah continued across the stage, taking up position to the east to repel anyone who tried to stop them. Naomi did the same on the side they entered on. Jacob didn't see them do either. His attention was on the Staff of God. He stared at it, focusing his mind. He silently asked it permission to pick it up, though he had no idea why. Maybe it was just out of respect. It was the Prophet's Staff, after all.

He knelt and hovered his hand over it. He looked up at Mosiah who nodded. Then Jacob looked at his sister.

"Do it," she said, cheering him on. "Do it for us all."

Jacob didn't respond. He just closed his eyes, took a deep breath, and said, "I believe."

When he closed his hand around the Staff, the sapphire instantly came to life, quieting the crowd. Now, no one laughed or jeered. They just stared in awe. The light that came from within the Staff undulated like the waves of the ocean. It was gentle too. It didn't violently strobe. It just pulsed brighter, then softer. Brighter, then softer. Jacob realized something. The pulsation matched his heartbeat.

"I am the second key," he said, feeling a calming sensation flow into his body.

He stood and faced the crowd. His eyes were still closed from when he first gripped the Staff. When he opened them, Naomi and Mosiah, and the rest of the audience all took a step back.

They pulsed with the same blue energy as the Staff of God. He couldn't see it, but he knew that's what was happening. Jacob turned his head and looked at Naomi. Tears fell freely from her eyes.

Then Naomi took a knee, bowing to him in reverence.

Jacob looked at Mosiah next. The man was already getting down on one knee.

Hundreds of people out in the crowd also began to bow. Jacob didn't have to say a word. The message was clear, though he still felt like he should say something. So, he stepped up to the microphone and held the Staff over his head, nearly mimicking Bailey.

"We are not your enemy," he said, hearing another voice speak within his. It was as if there were two separate people talking now. "The Army of God is not a terrorist organization, which is what is being reported in the news. That is false." Jacob half-turned so he could see Bailey. The man had come out of his stupor long enough to witness Jacob wield the Staff. Bailey was staring into Jacob's pulsating eyes.

Jacob pointed at the Hexad member. "Liam Bailey is false. Prophecy Global News is false. Delphi is false. Like their CEO, they are nothing but lies." Jacob faced the crowd again. "I cannot make you see the light, but I have faith that you will. Lift your darkened veils and see the truth."

Upon the word "truth," a blue energy surge advanced outward, charging through everyone in attendance. Some of the people, blinked, shrugged, and went about their business. This "clown show" wasn't for them. But most people stayed. They weren't shouting obscenities or texting their friends about the events happening here. They just stood and watched. They were just being present.

Jacob realized something then. He felt it more than anything.

He could've told these people what to believe. They weren't just standing there and watching.

They were waiting for Jacob to say something else.

Everyone who had told him that the Staff of God wasn't a mind control devise had been wrong. It *could* be one if something wanted it to be. But that would defeat the purpose of one of God's most sacred promises.

Humanity had been given the gift of free will, something that could've just as easily been withheld if God hadn't been so benevolent. Yes, bad things happened all the time, but those bad things happened because people were given that right. Jacob's father, Joshua Fehr, had put it like this when trying to explain why terrible things happened to good people.

His explanation had planted a seed in Jacob, one that, twenty-five years later, made his decision on Bailey's stage even easier.

"No one likes to see good people suffer, Jacob. No one," Joshua had said. "Try thinking of it like this... Like many things in our world, there's balance, right?" Young Jacob nodded, following along so far. "Nature keeps everything in check with the predator-prey relationship. There's the rising and setting of the sun too. Even the planets maintain their structure due to perfect gravitational balance. Without that, we'd have no Earth."

Jacob opened his mouth to ask something, but was stopped.

"I'm getting there. Hang in there, okay?" Jacob nodded. "The point is, you can't have one without the other. That is the rule of the universe, including good versus evil. The bad has to exist for there to also be good in the world."

"Like the Serpent being allowed to exist in Eden?" Jacob asked.

Joshua smiled. "Exactly like that. God could've destroyed the Serpent with the snap of his fingers and allowed Adam and Eve to live peacefully in their perfect sanctuary."

Jacob nodded, getting it. "But that would mean God would be in control of Adam and Eve's lives, not them."

His father beamed with pride. "A-plus, son. Yes, if God intervened and destroyed the Serpent, he would've chosen for them, and we, humanity, would've never been given the right to choose for ourselves. It's why he allowed Eve to pick the apple. He could've stopped that too." He gripped both of Jacob's shoulders and stared deep into his son's eyes. "Free will was his greatest gift to us. Whatever it is that you do later in life, please, don't forget that."

Young Jacob nodded. "I won't. I promise."

Epilogue

Huangpu, Shanghai, China

Yao Xiaowen was on edge. So far, Gideon had already killed Alpha, Delta, and Zeta. It was no secret that his mission was to wipe out the Hexad completely. As the Epsilon of the group, Yao was now the second highest ranking head, with only Beta ahead of him. The current Gamma was the newest addition, having taken over the role from his father after American forces had infiltrated his facility four years ago. But the Americans had missed the former Gamma's main facility and had only shut down a smaller, less significant operation.

But they had successfully killed that Gamma too.

Yao had been relieved to hear that the main facility had been spared when it had happened. It meant that his chemicals would still be shipped to Colombia to be produced into his company's lifeblood, fentanyl. And no, he didn't care how many people it killed every year. Business was business, and Yao had become incredibly wealthy because of it. Addiction was the driving force behind such industries as drugs and alcohol, though nobody liked to admit it. But Yao also believed that addiction would exist regardless of what they were addicted to. The compulsive obsessions would simply shift to something else. Then something else again.

But he wasn't concerned with any of that now. Yao just needed to make it into the safety of his home before Gideon could approach him on the streets. His driver pulled up to his modest seven-bedroom mansion. It wasn't the biggest or most luxurious in the area, but it suited Yao's needs just fine.

Unlike his *former* Russian contemporary, Zeta, Yao didn't throw his wealth around, hosting lavish parties or spending every waking hour surrounded by intoxicated young women. He was a man who enjoyed his privacy, someone that was wholly engrossed in his work. His facility brought in enough money to finance the Acolyte by itself. He had to include Gamma's operation in that too, though Yao knew several other processing plants that would do the same work—better and for much, much cheaper. Unfortunately, he was linked to Gamma for the foreseeable future. He didn't like it, but it was just the way things were.

Unless I can convince Beta otherwise, he thought, picturing Gamma's facility suddenly bursting into flames.

There were rumors swirling about that Beta wanted to shift the Acolyte into more of a monarch-style leadership. As long as Yao had a say in some things, like who he could partner with, he didn't care. But the murders of Alpha, Delta, and Zeta had also put something else into perspective.

Perhaps it was Epsilon that could be king of the Acolyte and not Beta. What if Gideon went for Beta next and not him or Gamma?

Yao opened the back door of his driver's car, climbed out,

and rushed to his home's gate. He punched in his nine-digit combination and shoved it open when it clicked. Yao slammed it and all but ran for the front door. It was just starting to rain and he preferred to not get drenched. By the time he reached the door, the heavens unloaded on Huangpu. Luckily, Yao's home sported a large overhang and the Acolyte boss was spared of the deluge.

He unlocked the door, slipped inside, and immediately threw the deadbolt. Yao disarmed his security system, then decided to go ahead and rearm it now, not taking any chances of their being a break-in before he could do it later.

"Yong, Zhi?" he asked, calling out the names of his two, live-in bodyguards.

Once Alpha had died, he moved the pair into his home. Then Delta and Zeta were killed, Yao had chosen to do so at the correct time. Yong and Zhi were two of his more cunning and ruthless agents. Like Yao, they had connections throughout Southern China, over to Japan, and down into Korea, Thailand, and India. Epsilon had an army at his disposal.

So did the others, he thought. *And look what happened to them!*

"Yong, Zhi, answer me!"

But his home was silent. It *was* possible that the men were out back. Yao's residence featured a sizeable outdoor bar, complete with a multi-level patio, a basketball court, and his personal favorite, a pool that led into a concealed grotto, where there was another, smaller bar. The men seemed to prefer the game of basketball to anything else.

Are they playing one-on-one again?

Yao crossed the high-ceilinged foyer, continued through an arched hallway, then popped out inside his home's massive great room. The living room-kitchen combo was enormous and the northern end of it was lined with impact-resistant sliding glass doors. The curtains were still drawn back, which was odd considering the hour. Usually, they'd be shut by sunset.

Yao stepped up to the doors, but didn't open them, mostly out of fear, but also because he remembered he had just re-armed his security system. He took in the tree-lined grounds but saw no movement. Even the basketball court was vacant.

"Where are they?" he asked himself.

He was about to turn away and continue his search, but his eyes caught an anomaly along the pool's unlit, shadowy surface. Yao reached for the panel controlling the backyard lights. His hand shook as he did. He swallowed down his fear and activated them.

There wasn't just one body floating face down in the pool.

There were two.

Yong and Zhi were dead, killed brutally based on the amount of blood in the water.

Yao scurried away from the grizzly scene, backpedaling then turning and running back the way he'd come. But instead of rushing through the front door and flagging his driver, he turned and headed up the banking staircase. It led up to five of the seven rooms. Naturally, the grandest of them was his own.

But he also had a gun safe in his closest. People of his stature were afforded luxuries that others in China were not, like free press and firearms. The Chinese government was the global king when it came to information control. They suppressed everything damning about their country on a national level. But people of Yao's ilk weren't stifled like the other commoners, not that it meant he could openly say or write whatever he wanted. Yao was powerful, but the president could still make him disappear quite easily.

Yao stumbled when he hit the top step, falling and sliding on his belly. He crawled like a dog for a moment, then regained his footing, knocking a very valuable painting off the wall as he did. Yao didn't care what damage he'd caused. He could buy another one.

If I survive the night.

The realization that Gideon was already here sent a shiver through his body. It also released his bladder. Yao piddled down his legs as he retreated, uncaring that it was happening—uncaring that it was destroying his one-of-a-kind upstairs carpeting. The door to his personal quarters was at the end of the hallway. He could see it now. And as usual, the door was shut. Once he was inside, he would call the only man that could help him.

"I must...call...Beta." Yao said, gasping for air.

He slid into his bedroom door with gusto, nearly causing himself to fall. But he righted himself, grabbed the door handle, and opened it. Yao leapt inside, slammed the door, and locked it. He backed away from it and dug into his pocket. He dialed the number for Beta and waited for it to connect.

It didn't.

"No!" he shouted, trying again.

Still no answer.

Yao fumbled with the devise and searched the web for anything. No other prominent public figure had been killed in the recent days, though Liam Bailey was in the news for something rather embarrassing.

"The Staff of God?" Yao asked, seeing Beta hefting the Staff high over his head. "He found it?"

The article had been written this morning. It went into

heavy detail, describing Bailey's meltdown and subsequent disappearance from the spotlight. He wasn't available for questioning and Prophecy Global Inc.'s stock price had already begun to plummet.

Yao spun and ran into a brick wall. Gone was his phone, and his glasses. He fell back, then rolled onto his stomach and froze. The barrier he had hit wasn't completely solid. It had given a little. He shook and searched for his glasses, frantic. Yao's eyesight was abysmal without his glasses. He turned but only found his phone.

"You dropped these," a voice said, causing Yao to whimper.

He crawled forward, discovering two blurs that looked like booted feet. He traced them up a pair of polls—legs—and found his glasses being graciously presented to him. Slowly, Yao accepted them, but nearly refused to put them on. He didn't want to see the man standing before him.

"Th...thank you," he said. Finally, he put them on. Maybe he could talk his way out of this. "I—"

When he looked up at the intruder, the only thing he saw was the tip of the suppressor aimed at his face. It was so close that he could smell the gunpowder residue originating from the shots that had killed his men outside.

Without another word, Gideon pulled the trigger.

About the Author

MATT JAMES is the international bestselling author of over thirty-five action-packed titles, including the fan-favorite Jack Reilly series, *The Cursed Thief*, and *The Blood King*. He specializes in globetrotting thrillers that fans of James Rollins, Steve Berry, and Ernest Dempsey will devour!

He lives twenty minutes from the beach in sunny South Florida with his wife, three children, a lovable pitty, and an overly dramatic black cat.

Go to **MattJamesAuthor.com** and subscribe to his newsletter for early and exclusive news and updates! You will NOT be mercilessly spammed with junk mail. And don't forget to click the **FOLLOW** button on his Amazon page to receive new release alerts!

YOU CAN VISIT MATT AT:

Website: **MattJamesAuthor.com**
Newsletter: **MattJamesAuthor.com/Newsletter**
Facebook: **Facebook.com/MattJamesAuthor**
Facebook: **Facebook.com/groups/MattJamesReaderGroup**

Made in the USA
Las Vegas, NV
25 February 2025